Hell for the Holidays

Hell for the Holidays

K. Simpson

Fortitude Press, Inc.
Austin, Texas

Published by Fortitude Press, Inc., Austin, Texas. For further information about this or other titles, please contact Fortitude Press, Inc., P.O. Box 41, Melbourne, FL 32902, or visit our website at www.fortitudepress.com.

ISBN: 0-9718150-9-7

First Edition, December 2002
Printed in the United States of America

Edited by Cindy Cresap
Cover and book design by Ryan Daly

Acknowledgments

As always, I owe a debt of thanks to Shaun Day, Maureen Sak, Ian Rowan, Elles Munstra and Veronica Holmes, who are world-class beta readers, which is to say hard markers. I like them anyway.

The same goes for Fortitude Press. Cindy Cresap edited this book with great tact and skill; for the tact alone, she deserves the Nobel Peace Prize. I'm also grateful to get to work with Brenda Barton, Mary K. Priddy, Shari Lowes and Rachel Dickinson. Particular thanks to Francine Love for being that rarest of combinations: a publisher *and* a genuinely good person.

To Mom and Dad, who are *not* in this book

Introduction

You are holding a twofer. That's Midwestern for "two for the price of one"—which it isn't really, but that's not the point. This book contains what used to be two stories, *The Very Devil* and *Now Playing on the Jukebox in Hell*, which were written for the Web as the third and fourth installments in a series. Fortitude Press thought they'd work as a single book, so here you go.

You should know a few things about what you're about to read. The series centers on Devlin Kerry and Cassandra Wolfe, who lead very complicated lives. That's only to be expected: They're in advertising, they're a couple, and they both have demons. The first two books—*Several Devils* and *The Average of Deviance*—explain how Dev, Cassie, and the demons Monica and Vanessa got together. (Technically, Dev got together with Monica first, as in slept with her. Cassie hates that.)

At the end of *Average*, things had gotten into a bit of a state. There was trouble with a fundamentalist group called the Family Foundation, run by a terrible man with the terrible name of Howard Abner. There was trouble with TV stations. There was trouble with people turning into possums. There was trouble with just about everything, really. The owner of J/J/G Advertising was home in bed under round-the-clock medical supervision; the creative director and a senior copywriter were locked up in a psychiatric hospital; and Dev and Cassie were taking a badly needed vacation at the beach. Their demons were taking the vacation, too, and one of them had just turned the other into a seagull. It all makes a little more sense in context.

Which brings you to this point. *Hell for the Holidays* picks up right after *Average* and takes you on two more vacations with Dev and Cassie: Thanksgiving with the Wolfes and Christmas with the Kerrys. Demons being what they are, Monica and Vanessa weren't about to be left out—hence, the *Hell* part of the title.

Some of what follows is true. The Thanksgiving chapters are set in Kansas City, where I lived for a while in the '80's. I still have great affection for both KCMO and Johnson County, Kansas, and any inaccuracies are due to faulty memory. Some of the Christmas chapters take place in the fictional town of Hawthorne, which is loosely based on my real hometown but not to be confused with it. Finally, the Kerry and Wolfe families are imaginary. (Mostly.)

Thanks for taking this long, strange trip with these characters and me.

Thanksgiving

The First Word

Somewhere Over the Midwest

This is Cassie speaking, and the first thing you need to understand is that Devvy exaggerates a little. I'm not saying she made up everything so far, but she does make up things for a living. So you should get one fact straight right off: Monica is *not* all that gorgeous.

I mean, *Monica.* Honestly. What was Devvy thinking? I asked her once whatever possessed her, and she gave me one of those looks and said, "Exactly."

I'm working on her attitude.

Anyway, she wanted to write everything down, in case anything happened to her, so someone would know. I think that's ridiculous, because nothing's going to happen to her. Unless *I* do something.

That's looking like a real possibility right now. We've been on an airplane for a while, and Devvy's getting restless. She got mad when I took the PowerBook away—I *told* her not to bring it; I *told* her we were on vacation—and then she made a great big production out of reading a magazine. Except that she wasn't really reading it, just rewriting all the ads. So I had to take the magazine away, too. Now she's sulking and listening to one of those in-flight music channels. They were playing that "La Vida Loca" song a few minutes ago; I could tell just by her expression. She said the most awful things about Ricky Martin all summer after *I* said I thought he was cute.

That was before, though. Now that we're together, she just laughs and trashes my taste in men.

Like she should talk about taste. She slept with the witch for *months.*

Monica, I mean. What a bitch. Devvy's not crazy about *my* demon either, but Vanessa isn't half that bad. Also, Devvy never slept with her, which is all good if you ask me.

Besides, Vanessa does me favors. For one, she keeps an eye on Monica. For another, she helps me keep an eye on Devvy. (I don't think Devvy knows that, exactly.) She even does things for both of us. It's not like J/J/G isn't a loony bin already, but she just helped put two of our biggest problems—Jack and Kurt—in a *real* loony bin. And thanks to her, Jenner (he's generally harmless, but he owns the agency) is home in bed. We think they'll all be out of commission for a while, so it was finally safe for us to take this vacation.

This isn't to say we might not be playing with fire by having demons around. They have a really bad way of showing up whenever they feel like it and doing whatever they want, and Devvy doesn't trust either of them. I know *I* don't trust Monica.

But I'm not going to think about that right now. We had a great time at the beach, I got Devvy to relax a fraction of an inch, and now we're on our way to spend Thanksgiving with my family. I think that's what she's *really* sulking about. She and Daddy had a fight the last time they saw each other, and she thinks he wants to kill her now.

He doesn't want to kill her. Not really. At least, Mom says he doesn't. But I think just to be on the safe side, I'll make sure they're never alone together. Daddy has a temper, and Devvy...

Well, I'm working on that, too.

I have to go; she just found the phone in the seat back. She's been wanting to call the office all week. I may have to hurt her, in front of all these people.

Just remember what I said about the making-things-up part. I don't think we're going to have a demon problem at Thanksgiving—Vanessa's still at the beach, and the witch is still a seagull, which is good enough for her—but you never know. I love her to death, but Devvy is trouble.

Chapter One

The first thing I wanted in Kansas City was lunch. We'd been trapped on a plane for hours, and I figured we'd earned a couple of sirloins or at least some barbecue.

"This is not a cow town anymore," Cassie said, annoyed.

"I never said it was. But they still have steak here, don't they?"

"You don't need steak. We're having lunch at Mom and Dad's."

I did so need steak. After a week of seafood, I would have killed for even a White Castle. Irritably, I watched her drive for a second. "I'm not going in there on an empty stomach."

"Whose fault is that? You could have had something on the plane."

"What? Those little pretzels?"

"They'd have brought you more if you'd asked."

"I don't like pretzels."

She adjusted her sunglasses with one hand, making her bracelets rattle. "Then look in my purse. I think I have some Altoids."

"You're missing the point here. I need actual food. I'm *starving.*"

"Mom said she's making quiche. You'll—" She glanced over at me, and the rental car swerved slightly. "What is that *look,* Devvy?"

"What look? Watch the road."

"Don't tell me you don't like quiche either. I've seen you eat it. Besides, you've never had my mother's. She makes the best shrimp quiche in—*what?!?*"

"Watch the *road,* Cass."

She informed me that she'd been driving since she was fifteen, thank you very much, and got all A's in driver's ed...and there was probably going to be more of that speech, except that she almost hit a Mitsubishi, which distracted her for a moment. What was up with her today, anyway?

To be fair, though, things were up with me, too. I'd had maybe two hours of sleep, followed by last-minute packing, taxis, air travel and close confinement with a woman who kept taking things away from me. Now I was sentenced to seafood again. And turkey tomorrow. It was enough to make me want to eat a whole cow.

"If you loved me," I complained, "you'd at least drive through a Burger King."

She only laughed.

"That line always works on *me,"* I said, injured.

"Yes, it does. Every time." Good humor apparently restored, she tried to pat my knee, but I blocked her. "Something wrong?"

"Nothing a burger wouldn't fix."

"We'll be there in fifteen or twenty minutes. Then you can have quiche."

Maybe it was time to try a different tack. Frowning in concentration, I felt along my wrist for a pulse. The silence made her look over again. "What are you doing, Devvy?"

"Checking for vital signs. I had some a few hours ago."

She blew me a very wet air kiss and kept driving.

"So you're saying you *don't* love me?"

"I adore you, and you know it. But Mom'll be insulted if you don't have seconds at lunch. You don't want to start off the weekend by insulting my mother, do you?"

No, but there was something to be said for getting it over with. Mrs. Wolfe would be insulted a dozen times over before sundown anyway; why put it off?

"I *said*, you don't want to insult my mother, do you?"

"Of course not, sweetheart," I lied. "I'll be on my very best behavior."

Cassie glanced over, instantly suspicious.

"You don't trust me?"

"I've seen your very best behavior," she said. "I still have nightmares about it."

"Monty Python's loss," I muttered. "You missed your calling. You should've been a comedian."

"There were no women in Monty Python, honey," she said serenely.

What *was* up with her? I couldn't even get a decent argument out of her today. Frustrated, I turned on the car radio and started punching buttons. Maybe I could find that Santana song. By good fortune, I found something Latin-sounding and turned it up.

Unfortunately, what I'd found was "Livin' La Vida Loca." With purpose, I changed the channel.

Cassie, never taking her eyes off the road, reached over and changed it back. So I changed it again. Then she changed it back.

That meant war. "Menudo," I said coldly. "That's where he came from, you know. *Menudo.*"

"That was a long time ago. And *you* have a George Michael CD. Does the name 'Wham!' mean anything to you?"

I narrowed my eyes at her. "Duran Duran."

"So what? The Bangles."

"I *like* the Bangles. Adam Ant."

"Ha! Paula Abdul."

"Bon Jovi."

The rental car swerved again. Touché. She hadn't known I knew she had that tape.

"Olivia Newton-John," she snapped.

I wasn't taking that bait, not for anything in the world. Leaning into her space, I crooned a few bars of "Livin' on a Prayer."

Cassie looked daggers at me. "Don't make me sing 'Physical.' Not if you ever want to get physical with me again."

"We've already had this conversation, Cass. Nothing happens this weekend."

"Not if you're going to be like *this* all weekend," she agreed.

Thinking quickly, I went a few moves ahead of her. I could either win this argument or get lunch. "Don't worry—I probably won't be. I probably won't even make it to your parents' house in the first place. Any second now, I'll fall over dead from starvation, and you'll have to call 911. If you can actually *make* calls on that little toy phone of yours."

She didn't say anything, but I could tell she was listening; her grip on the steering wheel tightened.

"Tell your mother I'm sorry about lunch. It'll probably get burned, what with her having to leave the house to go bail you out of jail for manslaughter, but—"

Without warning, Cassie whipped the car off on the exit ramp that we'd almost just passed. Then, tires still screeching, she made for the stoplight doing about 60.

"Are you trying to *kill* me?" I shouted, gripping the dashboard for balance.

She didn't answer; she was too busy ignoring the stoplight, which was just turning red. I couldn't look.

But nothing crashed into us, or vice versa, and when I thought it was safe to look again, I saw that we were pulling into a McDonald's.

"I love you," I said, meaning it.

"You're buying," she replied, meaning that too.

Fine. The last thing I wanted in Kansas City was trouble.

A Quarter Pounder and fries later, Cassie decided to forgive me. She'd been starving herself, as it turned out, and she didn't like quiche much either. We solemnly swore to keep the burgers a secret.

"As long as we clean our plates, Mom'll be fine," she said. "We'll just let the dog in the dining room. He eats everything. Here, sweetie—have another fry. Want some ketchup?"

"Thanks."

"The trouble will be keeping him out of the bedroom," Cassie continued, looking thoughtful. "If you feed him, he'll like you, and if he likes you, he won't let you out of his sight. The last guy I brought home—"

"The last *guy?*"

"You know what I mean. Buster followed him everywhere. Even the bathroom. Whenever we tried to have sex—"

People at other tables started looking very interested. I gave them the evil eye, to no avail. "I don't want to talk about this, Cass."

"Jealous?" she asked, sounding hopeful.

Hell, yes. "No."

"Good. If you *weren't* jealous, you'd be in big trouble." She dunked another fry in ketchup and offered it to me. "Anyway, Buster might be a pest. We'll have to put a chair under the doorknob in the bedroom so he can't get in."

"Do whatever you want. If he gets into my room, he gets—"

"There is no 'my room,' Devvy. We're sleeping together, and that's final. If you don't stop it, I'll make you sleep in my old room with me."

There were many implications in that, all of them horribly Freudian. But I figured she was bluffing. Surely not even Cassie would want to do those things in her childhood bedroom, with her parents down the hall—especially not with me. "How is that a threat?"

"Did I tell you the room is pink?"

"Yes, but—"

"Did I tell you it's Barbie pink?"

Involuntarily, I winced, thinking of the Barbie section at FAO Schwarz.

"With a canopy bed," she continued, watching me intently. "With heart-shaped throw pillows and a lace bedspread and a pink-and-white quilt. The blankets are pink, too."

"Charming," I said.

"Did I mention the vanity table?"

"No, but I get the pic—"

"It's white. But everything on it is pink. Pink combs, pink brushes, pink nail polish...ooooh, you'll hate this...pink plastic headbands. Remember those?"

Not amused, I shifted in my plastic chair. "All right, Cass."

"No, wait—I'm not done. I had pink barrettes, too. Sometimes I just tied my hair back with a pink ribbon. Except when I had on my cheerleader uniform, because pink clashed with it. But I always wore pink underpants, because boys liked them, and—"

"All *right,* already. Enough."

"I win?"

"Yes, goddammit. You win."

"You're sleeping with me?"

I could feel the heat of the open stares around us. "Try and stop me."

She didn't even bother to try not to look smug. "You're cute when you're embarrassed."

"I'm not embarrassed. And stop picking fights with me today. You're going to make me mad."

"You're even cuter when you're mad."

A teenager a few tables over snorted Coke all over himself. Served him right for listening. Lowering my voice, I gave Cassie a very hard stare. "I am *not* cute."

"Well, not cute like a little bunny. More like cute like a baby tarantula."

I hated this conversation. "Cut this out *now.* What's wrong with you, anyway? All this talk about 'pink' and 'cute' and little animals—"

"I don't know. Maybe I'm regressing. I *am* going home." She sucked on the end of her straw for a second. "I might be nervous."

"Nervous? You?"

"Maybe a little."

It wasn't a good explanation, in my opinion, but it *was* an explanation. It might even be the truth. She'd been really brave and feisty about our relationship from the start, but that was easy at J/J/G; everyone there was worse than we were. And she'd been outright brazen at the beach, but that was easy too, because nobody knew us. I had a feeling that Cassie's family was going to be a much harder sell. As far as I knew, girls didn't just take girls home to Kansas City and expect their relatives' heads not to explode.

"How far are we from your parents' house?" I asked.

"About fifteen minutes. Why?"

"How long if we take a scenic route?"

Her eyes lit up, but she tried to frown anyway. "We don't have time for that. I said we'd be there by 1."

"We'll call from the car. Tell them our flight was late. If we're lucky, maybe they'll start lunch without us."

"I really don't think we should, Devvy. I told them—"

"Well, this'll teach them to listen to *you*. So how about it? Do they have scenic routes in Kansas City? Or is this still just a cow town?"

She gave up with visible pleasure. "Just you wait, wise guy. Have I got a route for you."

"I'm not a g—"

"You *know* what I mean."

Chapter Two

The rental car clock read 2:00 when Cassie turned onto a quiet street. She didn't make any announcement about it, so I figured we were still on the scenic route. But the next thing I knew, we were going through a gated driveway, headed for a big, big house.

Disbelieving, I turned just in time to see WOLFE lettered on the gatepost.

"Home," she said.

"You're not serious."

"Really? I'm not? Why not?"

"I've seen pictures, Cass. This isn't your parents' house."

"You've seen *old* pictures. We moved here when I was ten."

Unconvinced, I took another look. "What happened when you were ten? Did God die and leave you his estate?"

"Close. It was a repossession."

A repossession. She didn't seem to notice the irony, so I decided not to point it out. Still and all, it gave me a strange feeling. "You said your dad's a banker. You didn't say he actually owns the bank."

"Very funny."

"I'm not trying to be. Why didn't you tell me?"

"Tell you what?"

"This is just going to make it worse, you know. It's bad enough that I'm me. But if he thinks I'm after your money—"

"It's not my money."

Well, it probably wasn't anymore. The SOB had probably already cut her out of the will on grounds of deviance.

With growing trepidation, I watched the house get larger in the windshield. God, it was big. There could be a whole soccer team living upstairs, or a boatload of Chinese assassins. What did Chinese assassins go for these days, anyway? Surely it took real money to import—

"Devvy?"

I jumped a little. "What?"

"We're here. What's the matter?"

"Nothing."

"Nothing." Shaking her head, she turned the engine off. "All right, let's have it. I am *not* taking you in there looking like that."

"Like what?"

"Like you think something terrible's going to happen."

"You don't?"

"It's just Thanksgiving. It's just my family."

"And the assassins on the second floor," I said darkly.

Cassie reached over to put a cool hand on my forehead. "You might be just the least bit paranoid, honey."

Irritably, I shook her off. She just smiled, though, and leaned in for a kiss...just as the front door opened. Figured. We hadn't been there a minute yet, and I was in trouble already.

But the trouble turned out to be four-footed: a golden retriever, bounding down the steps with an expression of welcome. Cassie gave me that kiss, very quickly, and jumped out of the car into an armful of dog. With its paws on her shoulders, it was almost as tall as her, but not half as beautiful.

I kept a suspicious eye on the house as I got out of the car. No Wolfes yet.

"This is Buster," she reported, dodging another sloppy kiss. "Buster, be nice. Go say hi to Devvy."

The dog licked her face one last time, let go and trotted over to check me out. Remembering something I'd read somewhere, I crouched down on the blacktop, careful of the tail of my new coat, and held out a hand for him to sniff.

"Should I pet him now? He looks—yow!"

"Buster," Cassie said severely, "be good."

Be good? Her dog had just stuck his nose *there,* and that was all she was going to say? With one hand, I tried to hold the animal off. "Nice doggie. Good b—*damn!*"

This time, the jolt knocked me right off my feet. Swearing with feeling, I shoved the dog away.

Only then did I notice Cassie's parents on the front porch. By the expression on Mrs. Wolfe's face, they were well within earshot.

Buster took advantage of my state of shock to do it again. This time, Cassie grabbed his collar, hard, and kept hold of it.

"Welcome to Kansas City, pookie," she said, doing her best not to laugh.

The next five minutes were the longest year of my life.

Cassie and her mother had gone off somewhere with Buster, theoretically to calm him down, which left me and her father. Alone. In the foyer. With motive.

"Nice day," I said, trying for détente.

Mr. Wolfe just stared at me. You'd have thought I was some horrible winged thing that had just swooped in from Hell with his daughter.

Very faintly, I smiled. His expression didn't change. In blatant silence, he scanned me up and down disapprovingly, taking extra time on the long black leather coat.

What did he think I was—an amateur? Drawing on years of experience in scaring clients, I scanned him back and raised an eyebrow.

No good. He just went back to staring, which was getting on my nerves. It was also starting to remind me of Cassie in a certain mood. Father and daughter had the same intense blue gaze, hard to hold up under, and though I could usually sweet-talk Cassie out of looking at me like that these days, that line of talk was not going to work on him.

The grandfather clock on the opposite wall ticked off the seconds as the silence went on. Where the devil was Cass?

I tried again. "Nice house."

"I got a favorable interest rate," Mr. Wolfe said.

More silence. The clock ticked louder and louder. Then, in a sort of slow motion,

I saw his right hand move to his pants pocket. There was only one thing to do: jump out of the line of fire.

A second too late, I saw what he was holding: a handkerchief.

"It's not loaded," he said dryly. "Take it."

"Sir?"

"Lipstick," he explained.

Lipstick. Wonderful. Absolutely swell. Exasperated, I took the handkerchief and wiped off.

"I suppose you have luggage," he said.

"We do. It's out in the car. I'll just—"

"I'll see to it."

"Not a problem. I can get it. But thanks for—"

"Of course it's not a problem. She's my daughter. I'll get it."

Cassie's father or not, I was starting to want to deck the man. "Don't trouble yourself, sir. It's not much. I can handle it."

"That may be. But in *my* house—"

"Is anything wrong?" Cassie asked, all innocence.

We both wheeled around, thwarted.

"I hate to interrupt," she told her father, "but Mom wants to see you in the kitchen."

"In a minute, Cassie. I'll just get your luggage first."

That did it. I took one step toward the front door, to intercept him—and felt her grab the belt of my coat in a death grip. Her expression, though, was perfectly calm. "She said *now*, Daddy."

Mr. Wolfe, who was already reaching for the doorknob, let his hand drop helplessly. "Now?"

"That's what she said."

He heaved a sigh of painful experience and headed off to find out what was wrong. Or, more likely, what was wrong *this* time. Watching him trudge down the hall, I felt an unexpected twinge of sympathy.

"Now," Cassie said, still gripping my belt, "I want to know what that was all about."

"Nothing. We were just discussing luggage."

"I *know* that. I want to know what you were just about to do."

"Bring it in?" I asked, hoping that was the right answer.

"Before or after you hit each other?"

"I wasn't going to hit him, for God's sake. He's your father. But he was getting all macho about the luggage, and I...well..." Suddenly, it all seemed indefensibly stupid. He was a middle-aged man with gray hair, whose daughter I loved, who felt threatened, and the least I could do was let him drive me crazy for a few days. After all, I'd have the rest of his life for payback. "Never mind. I'll go get it."

"*We'll* go get it." She gave my belt a sharp yank for emphasis. "Now come on. I'm going to let *you* get the heavy bags."

By mutual agreement, bedtime was early that night. Cassie told her parents we were tired, which was the truth, but not that we were miserable, which was also the truth. What with Buster being exiled to the back yard for his behavior, we'd had to eat all that quiche ourselves.

"Go on and get ready for bed," Cassie said as soon as we got to the guest room. "I'll go find us some Alka-Seltzer. How many do you want?"

"As many as you can find."

She nodded, understanding completely, and took off down the long dark hall while I searched the suitcases for nightclothes. What with one thing and another, we hadn't worn any at the beach, so we'd never thought to check whether Vanessa had packed any for us. Fortunately, she had: my favorite pajamas and a nightshirt of Cassie's.

The nightshirt, unfortunately, was pink. But I reasoned that Cass wouldn't mention the color tonight, in her condition, and I wouldn't even see it in the dark.

Wearily, I changed and went into the bath. When I came back out, Vanessa was standing by the bed, dressed up like a nurse, mixing something fizzy in a glass.

"You," I said with no particular emotion. It had been a long day.

"Your powers of recall are amazing. Here. Down the hatch."

"What is it?"

"You don't want to know."

"No, I don't. Go away, Vanessa. Cassie's got it covered. Besides, you don't even have the uniform right. Nurses don't dress like that anymore." Critically, I studied her from little white cap to sensible white shoes. "Where did you come up with this getup, anyway?"

"Haven't seen her old room yet, have you?" Vanessa pushed the glass into my hand and started turning back the bedcovers. "She's not kidding you about the Barbie stuff. Now drink that. You'll feel better."

"I'll feel better when she gets back. Would you mind telling me what you're doing here? Aren't you supposed to be at the beach keeping an eye on Monica?"

"Well. About that. I don't know how much you know about demons, Devlin—"

"More than a person should have to," I grumbled.

"—but these spells don't always stick. Who's the dog in the back yard?"

That scene in the driveway flashed through my mind—and without an instant's hesitation, I drained the glass.

At which point Cassie came back. "I hit the mother lode, honey. You wouldn't believe their medicine cabinet. Do you want Pepto-Bismol or—*you?*"

"Hello, Cassandra," Vanessa said. "Wait just a second. I'll mix you up another."

Cassie turned to me for an explanation and saw the empty glass in my hand. "Another what?"

I shrugged.

"What are you *doing* here, Vanessa?"

The demon didn't answer right away, being occupied with conjuring up another glass.

"What is she doing here?" Cassie demanded of me.

"I was just getting to that part," Vanessa said. "There was a little problem with Monica."

"Buster," I said grimly. "She's in the dog."

Cassie was dumbstruck, but Vanessa only laughed. "Oh, for Lucifer's sake, Devlin, we don't do dogs. That's only a myth. Jackals sometimes, sure, but—"

"You asked me who the dog is," I reminded her.

"I was just curious. It's talking to a seagull out back. This seems kind of far inland for gulls, so I wondered—"

"*No,*" Cassie insisted. "You said she'd leave us alone this weekend."

"I didn't say it *was* her. It might be anybody. But I think I'd better stick around just in case. She could make a lot of trouble for you, you know."

Cassie sat down hard on the bed, looking even greener around the gills than she had before. Concerned, I took the glass from Vanessa and offered it to her.

"What is it?"

"Alka-Seltzer," Vanessa said. "What did you think?"

Muttering something—all I could make out was "newt"—she drank it.

"Now into bed with you. Both of you. You've got a long day tomorrow."

"Don't even think about sleeping here," Cassie warned her.

"Don't be silly. I'm staying in the pink room. It is *so* cute, girlfriend. Do you mind if I put up your Rick Springfield poster?"

I raised an eyebrow. Cassie, muttering again, grabbed her nightshirt off the bed and disappeared into the bath.

"You'd better go," I told Vanessa.

"I'm going; I'm going." She paused on the threshold. "Her little sister's coming tomorrow, isn't she? Bringing the hubby and kiddies?"

"As far as I know. Her mom said nine for dinner."

"Ever met them before?"

"No. Why?"

"Tomorrow," Vanessa said, and then vanished into thin air.

Chapter Three

Cassie knew many inventive ways of waking me in the morning—not to mention in the middle of the night—so when she licked my face, I just smiled. Whatever Vanessa had given us, it must have worked; both of us seemed to be feeling a whole lot better.

Another lick, longer and wetter this time; also a little tickly. Cassie was good at that. Half-awake now, I pulled her closer, enjoying the warmth of her body under the half-open nightshirt, the silky feel of the blonde head on my shoulder, the heat of her breath in my ear...

Wait. How could a person's head be in two places at one time?

My eyes shot open. Cassie was still asleep, and there was a wide-awake golden retriever next to my side of the bed, peering at me with great interest.

Well, that explained the breath problem. "Go away, Buster."

The dog started wagging its tail.

"Hell," I muttered. Then I remembered and looked hard into his eyes. "Monica? Is that you?"

No answer—just a gaze of pure canine devotion. Meanwhile, Cassie was waking up.

"Everything's fine," I told her, stroking her hair. "Go back to sleep."

She mumbled something, then gripped my pajama shirt tighter and snuggled closer, just as Buster tried to climb up into the bed.

"Down, dammit!" Reluctantly taking one arm away from around Cassie, I tried to hold him at bay. But he was a big solid dog, and I didn't have much leverage lying down, so he won. Contented, he flopped down on top of us like a ton of furry bricks.

"Is that Buster?" Cassie asked, eyes still closed.

"Afraid so."

"Make him go away."

"I don't think I can."

Sighing, she disengaged a little and gave the dog an evil look. "Off the bed, Buster."

In reply, the dog licked her too.

"Yuck," she complained, wiping her face with my pajama sleeve. "His breath is awful. Buster, I said off."

"Maybe if we both push," I suggested.

We did. It worked, but only for a minute. No sooner had Buster landed than he was back on all fours, waiting for another chance to get up on the bed. Defeated, I lay back down.

"Daddy must have let him in before he went to bed," Cassie said. "I don't know what this is all about. He has a perfectly good dog bed downstairs. Did you shut the door all the way last night?"

"I thought Vanessa did."

"Oh. Right. Forgot about that part. Well, let's not think about it yet." She sat up, yawned and stretched, then rubbed her eyes. "What time is it, anyway?"

Turning my head on the pillow to check the travel alarm, I came nose to nose with Buster. He licked me again. "Yuck" was right. What had he been eating—raw squirrel? "A little before 8. Should we get up?"

"Might as well. Lucy'll be here early, and I want to get lots of caffeine in my system first." She reached down to brush the hair out of my eyes. "Yours too, sweetie. Why don't I go down and get us some coffee, and you warm up the shower?"

"I'll just go ahead and take one."

"Not without me. Not this morning."

"Cass, I really don't think—"

"It'll scare Buster off. He hates water."

Sold. I got out of bed and went in to turn the shower on. When I stuck my head back into the bedroom, all I saw of Buster was his hindquarters hurrying through the door.

Cassie gave me a triumphant smile and followed him out.

We reported to her parents in the front parlor about an hour later, freshly showered, nicely dressed and in very good spirits. Mr. Wolfe lowered his newspaper a bit to inspect me over the top of his reading glasses, and I tried very hard not to look like someone who might have had carnal knowledge of his daughter under his roof—or in his guest room shower.

His countenance darkened.

Oh, well, Mrs. Wolfe was only looking at me as though I'd picked up the wrong fork. Caught, she forced on a social smile. "Did you sleep well, Devlin?"

"Very. Thank you."

Cassie smiled knowingly—but only because her parents couldn't see from that angle.

"Looks like another nice day," I added.

Mrs. Wolfe agreed. Conversation stopped again.

"Have I mentioned how much I admire your house?"

Lowering his paper again, Cassie's father addressed her mother. "I explained about the interest rate."

"We got a very favorable one," Mrs. Wolfe told me. "Calvin's bank gave us attractive terms."

Silence brooded over the parlor. All right, damn it all, enough was enough. "I wonder if I might have a word with you both. About the elephant in the corner."

Mrs. Wolfe looked faintly alarmed. "Elephant?"

"An expression," I assured her. "It means ignoring something that's just too big to ignore. In this case—"

"Devvy, don't," Cassie said.

"—the fact that Cassie and I are together. I can understand that you're not comfortable with it. This can't be what you expected for your daughter. It's not what I expected either, to tell you the—"

"I don't care to discuss this," Mr. Wolfe snapped, slamming the paper down on the carpet next to his chair.

"—truth, but I want you both to know that—"

"My daughter could have had any man she wanted."

"—she means a lot to me, and—"

"Until *you* came along," he added, glowering. "Filling her head with strange ideas."

Cassie had heard enough. "Daddy, stop. You too, Devvy."

"—I swear to you that..." I paused, finally hearing what he'd just said. "Strange ideas?"

Mrs. Wolfe jumped out of her chair to busy herself with the coffee service on the sideboard. "Would anyone care for more coffee? I just made a fresh pot."

"She was a nice, sweet, normal girl," Mr. Wolfe said, getting up himself. "Popular with the boys. The best boys from the best families, and a date every night of the week if she wanted."

"How nice for you," I growled. "Good for business, was it?"

Cassie, exasperated, looked from one of us to the other but couldn't decide which one to yell at.

"She could have been married by now," he informed me. "Should have been married years ago. Her sister Lucy has three children already."

Here we go. "Your daughters aren't breeding stock for your grandchildren program. With all due respect. *Sir.* This is Cassie's decision to make, and if she doesn't want children—"

"Would anyone mind if I got a word in edgewise?" Cassie asked icily.

"—then she doesn't want children, and you don't have a thing to say about it. In fact—"

"She's my daughter. I think I have everything to say about it. If it weren't for you—"

"STOP IT!"

Interrupted, Mr. Wolfe and I both scowled at her. But we did stop it. After which it got very quiet in the parlor again.

"Coffee?" Mrs. Wolfe pleaded. "Anyone?"

No one answered. Somewhere outside, something started baying.

Then the doorbell rang. Cassie's mother practically dissolved in relief. "That must be Lucy. I'll go let her in."

Cassie, who was glaring at me, didn't break eye contact for a second. "That would be nice, Mother."

The woman all but ran out of the room. In her wake, Mr. Wolfe cleared his throat. "I think I should go, too."

"Perfect, Daddy," Cassie said, still glaring.

Now what? I waited till her father was safely gone to glare back. "What did I do?"

"I was saving this fight for Sunday morning. I was going to start it. Then I was going to let you finish it. And *then* we were going to have to leave to catch our plane."

"So what? We just got a head start."

"Oh, we got a head start, all right. Now my parents are both upset, and my sister's here, and they're probably telling her *all* about it right now, and we still have to be here for two more whole days. *That's* so what."

Well, yes, when she put it that way. Still, it wasn't the end of the world. "All right, it might be a little uncomfortable. But it already was. Your dad wants to kill me, Cass. I just—"

"I'll bet he wants to kill you *now*," she agreed.

I took a deep breath, to argue back, and then let it out again. She was right.

Shaking her head, Cassie closed the distance between us and gave me a hug. "You meant well, honey. You were trying to defend me. But you've got to take it easy here. They're my parents, and I love them. It's not like I have a choice."

"I know. That's the hell of it." Ruefully, I kissed the top of her head. "I'm sorry, Cass. If it's any consolation, mine are even worse."

She looked up, half-smiling. "Would it be tasteless of me to agree with you?"

"Easy for you to say. You only met them once." Footsteps and conversation floated through the door from the direction of the foyer; we were about to not be alone again. I let her go. "Remind me to kiss you later."

"Coward." But she backed off. "Listen, Devvy, about my sister—"

"Ix-nay," I said softly. The woman herself was just coming into the room, and by the look in her eye, she was going to be a problem.

It was interesting, in the bad way, to be surrounded by Wolfes. There was a certain anthropological value in it, though. Take the family resemblances. Cassie had her father's eyes, her mother's looks and a few traits from both, but she and her sister didn't even look related. Except for the dark hair, which was Mr. Wolfe's doing, Lucy might not have passed for a member of the family.

She might have been as pretty as the rest of them, though, if it weren't for the permanent scowl. As hard as I tried not to, I kept seeing the Red Queen whenever I looked at her. Maybe it was all that childbearing.

The produce in question were somewhere upstairs right now, playing with Buster. By the squeals, thuds, thumps and occasional woofs, everyone was having fun. Were children always this loud?

Mr. Wolfe, dug in at the head of the breakfast bar, lowered his paper to look at the ceiling doubtfully. Then he shrugged, apparently trusting insurance.

"They're all excited today," Lucy said, a bit defensively. "They couldn't wait to see Buster. *And* their Aunt Cassie, of course."

Like I believed that. They'd barely let her kiss them hello before they made tracks upstairs as fast as six feet could take them. It had hurt Cassie's feelings a little, I could tell, and all three of them were on my list now.

"I can send them outside to play if they're bothering you, Daddy."

He grunted something from behind the paper. Mrs. Wolfe and Lucy exchanged glances over the turkey they were basting; then Mrs. Wolfe shook her head. Apparently the Lord and Master was fine with the racket—for now.

"Michael always says he likes the pitter-patter of little feet," Lucy continued. "I honestly think he wants another baby. But we just got Jeremy potty trained, and I think three is enough, don't you, Cass?"

Cassie finished buttering her coffee cake before she answered. "That's between you and Michael, isn't it?"

"Oh, I don't know. It's nice to have your family's approval before you do important things. Don't you agree, Devlin?"

Under the table, Cassie locked her feet around one of mine; over it, she silently pleaded for peace. *Oh, all right.* "Very nice. But it *is* between the two of you."

Lucy didn't quite know what to say to that. But the pounding upstairs was starting to make speech difficult anyway. One particularly solid thump made us all look up; the chandelier was swaying slightly.

Mr. Wolfe put the paper down and gave his younger daughter a meaningful look that I recognized at once. So Cassie came by it honestly.

"I'll have Michael speak to them when he gets here," Lucy told him. "He said he'd be here by 11."

"The house may not still be standing by 11," Mr. Wolfe said.

She looked puzzled. Apparently she hadn't inherited many of the IQ points in the gene pool, either.

But I saw a chance in the situation. "Why don't I take them outside to play? It's a beautiful day. I could use some fresh air myself."

Cassie started to protest, but the relief on the others' faces was so clear that she reconsidered. "Be careful. You don't want to ruin your coat."

"I'm not planning to."

"What coat?" Lucy asked, as though it were any of her business.

Too casually, Cassie said, "Oh, a nice black leather duster. I made her buy it. It's *very* sexy."

I left the room on the double, to thunderous silence.

Finding Lucy's brood was no problem whatsoever. Talking them into going outside was a little more trouble—until I told them I'd seen the *South Park* movie. We'd have to discuss it outside, I said; parents got so weird.

Then Buster tried to say hello again in his own special way, but this time I was ready; I put a knee in his chest and sent him sprawling.

These two things combined impressed the children mightily. A grownup who knew bad words and could punch a dog out! They raced me to the stairs and were already waiting at the picnic table when I got there.

About fifteen minutes later, Cassie came out to find the children playing nicely on the swing set; Buster curled up on the ground nearby, keeping a watchful eye on them; and me leaning against a tree with my hands in my coat pockets, probably looking as satisfied as I felt.

"There you are," she said. "What happened?"

"Nothing much. I told them about the *South Park* movie—"

"Devvy, you *didn't.*"

"—and then I told them that Cartman was nothing compared with what I'd do to them if they dissed their Aunt Cassie again."

Several emotions fought for control of her face, but one of the softer ones won. Glancing at the swing set to make sure she hadn't been seen yet, she slipped her arms around me and kissed my cheek. "You didn't have to do that, honey. They're just little kids."

"No excuse. I meant it."

"I know you did. That's what worries me." She checked the swing set again; the coast was still clear. "You know they'll tell Lucy."

"No, they won't. I had a talk with them about *that*, too. If they tell, their mom and dad are going to think they really saw the movie themselves, and they'll be grounded till spring break."

"Thank God you're on my side," Cassie said, laughing.

"Always."

She gave me a real kiss, which I obligingly returned. We cut it short, though, just to be safe.

"Mom sent me out here to bring you all in," she said. "Michael just called from the car. He's on his way."

"This should be good. Do the kids look like him?"

"Unfortunately."

I shook my head. "Something wrong there. But I figured there was anyway. What kind of person insists on being called 'Michael'?"

"The kind of person he is. You won't like him. That's all right, though; I don't like him either."

"Can't wait," I lied.

She gave me a little squeeze and then let go. "Come on. Lucy'll be out here next if we don't bring the kids in." Turning back toward the swing set, she cupped her hands around her mouth. "Chad! Rachel! Jeremy! Time to go in now!"

Buster had to hustle to keep up with them as they raced over to Cassie—and then almost knocked her over in a group hug. I stepped back a few paces to memorize the scene and the look on her face.

That was more like it. Now I'd have to do something about the rest of the family. *South Park* probably wouldn't work on them. But demons might.

Chapter Four

And then there was Michael.

I didn't like him right from the start. It might have been the junior-executive nerd-boy coat with the fur collar; it might have been the mean piggy eyes; but I was having more trouble with the artificial hair. His teeth were all capped, too. He'd gone to a lot of trouble on himself, for some reason. But it was no use without working out, and he clearly didn't run except for jelly doughnuts. What did Cassie's sister see there? Maybe it was true what they said: Viagra puts flagpoles on condemned buildings.

"What's funny?" Cassie demanded in a whisper.

I drew her aside to tell her. She almost doubled over laughing, just managing to grab my arm for support.

Michael didn't seem to appreciate the wanton PDA. But he didn't make a point of it—simply peeled his coat and gloves off and handed the lot to his wife. Narrowly, I watched her bear them off to the coat closet. His arms didn't look broken; what was his damage that he couldn't hang up a coat?

"So how is business, Michael?" Mr. Wolfe asked, almost smiling for the first time that day. "Keeping busy at the office?"

"Twenty-four-hour job, Dad. Even this morning. Thank God for wireless." He patted his jacket pocket comfortably. The word *burgher* popped into my mind; bemused, I pictured him in lederhosen and one of those little hats with the feathers. "We've got a huge deal going down in Singapore right now. I'm leaving the beeper on just in case. Hope you don't mind if I have to leave again."

Mr. Wolfe assured him that business was business. There followed a several-minute discussion of same, during which Cassie got increasingly restless; finally, she simply pulled me out of the room.

"I hate when they do that," she said. "It's like being drafted into Rotary. I'd rather sit in the kitchen and listen to Mom and Lucy talk about childbirth."

Startled, I dropped a step back. *"Do* they do that?"

"Of course they do. When they're not talking about Martha Stewart or what's on sale at Saks or why I still haven't gotten married."

"They talk about that in front of you?"

"You may not have noticed, but we're not shy in this family."

"Neither am I. And if they're fool enough to bring it up today, in front of *me*—"

"You said you'd be on your best behavior. You promised me."

"This won't count. I get an exemption for people who ask for it."

She pulled me to a stop. "They're my family, remember? I don't always like them, but I love them. And if *you* love *me*—"

"This is so unfair," I grumbled.

"If you love me, you'll cut them some slack. They really do care about me. They just have a strange way of showing it sometimes." When I didn't argue the point, she loosened her grip, but only a little. "They just want the best for me. You don't get that this is a test, do you?"

"What are you talking about?"

"You really *don't,*" Cassie said, a note of wonder in her voice. "What do you think I brought you home for? Why do you think my father's been trying to start fights with you?"

My inner Cartman started jumping up and down, howling. "If you're trying to tell me we're doing that goddamn sex-roles thing—"

"You are *so* touchy about that. Want a pink barrette? I know where I can find some."

I didn't even smile.

"Relax, Devvy. It could be worse."

Of course it could be worse; no doubt it would get worse soon. But for the moment, nothing supernatural was happening, and I wasn't afraid of anyone or anything in this house. Except maybe Cassie if I let her down.

"All right, dammit. Let's go hang with the womenfolk. Help in the kitchen or bear some live young or something."

"You do your chromosomes proud, honey," she said, not even bothering not to sound sarcastic.

Dinner began precisely at noon. Mrs. Wolfe was very particular about that. She and Lucy had hovered over the turkey in the kitchen like midwives from 11:30 on, and only at the stroke of 12 would she serve.

We all reported to the main dining room, which was a paradise of Baccarat, Limoges and starched linen, bristling with intimidating silverware. There was also a huge fireplace, burning about a cord of wood. Fire struck me as being strangely appropriate.

While we found our seats, I tried to figure out what the tiny forks were for. We'd never gone beyond three forks in my family and went to three only on the grandest occasions.

"Oyster forks," Cassie whispered, slipping into the chair on my left.

"Thanks," I whispered back. Then I noticed the place card in front of her. "Wait a second. That says 'Michael.'"

She shrugged and tore it in half, under her brother-in-law's disapproving eye.

"Never mind, Michael," Lucy soothed him. "Devlin was supposed to sit next to me. You can sit here instead. Won't this be cozy?"

Considering that the new seating arrangement followed battle lines—Cassie and me on one side of the table, Lucy and Michael on the other, and her parents at either end—I wouldn't have called it "cozy," but at least it would be convenient. It was good, too, that children and dog were having their dinner in the other room. Things would get messy enough in here without them.

Mr. Wolfe tapped his wineglass for order. "We might give thanks."

Under the table, in private, Cassie took hold of my hand. I smiled back at her. Yes, there were things to be thankful for this year.

"Because you're our guest," he continued, "we'll allow you to do the honors, Devlin."

Cassie squeezed my hand harder than she probably intended and then let go. I suddenly felt sorry for every male who'd ever been dragged home to meet the girlfriend's family. I felt sorrier for myself, because I wasn't even a guy—and if they didn't believe me, they could ask Buster. Just because this ritual was the only one they knew didn't make it right.

"Whenever you're ready," Mr. Wolfe prompted.

Unwillingly, I rummaged around in memory for a Methodist grace from childhood. Too workaday for this room. Then I remembered Sunday dinners at my Catholic friend Mary Bernadette's house. "Bless us, O Lord, and these thy gifts, which we are about to receive—"

Mrs. Wolfe almost didn't gasp. "Why, Devlin, we didn't know you were Catholic."

"I'm not, Mrs. Wolfe."

"Oh." Uncertain, she glanced at her husband, who didn't look convinced. "You have a very Irish name. What are you, then?"

She's her mother. She's her mother. "Not all Irish are Catholic, Mrs. Wolfe. You may have heard about the Troubles. As for what I *am*, I was brought up Methodist."

While she located me on the social scale—Episcopalians at the top; Presbyterians next; Methodists second-to-last, ahead of Baptists—I tried to remember what denomination the Wolfes were. Mr. Wolfe, of course, worshipped at the Church of Mammon, which had temples everywhere.

Michael cleared his throat impatiently. "I think we might have a toast, Dad. May I?"

Mr. Wolfe said that he might. Looking dubious, Cassie moved her chair slightly closer to mine.

"To freedom of religion," Michael intoned, "the reason this great country was founded. And to all the immigrants who came here to make a decent life."

Well. By his tone, he'd just stopped short of calling me a bog-trotting infidel mick, but he was probably saving the personal stuff for dessert. Coolly, I lifted my wineglass. "To the never-ending health of the Aryan people."

Cassie kicked my foot, but not very hard.

"I wasn't quite done," he said. "To the family. Without family values, none of us would be here today."

"To reproduction, which crosses all political lines," I replied.

Cassie kicked a bit harder this time. "Well, that was fun," she told the table brightly. "Now let's—"

"Civilization is based on the family," Michael retorted, starting to breathe a little hard.

I gave him a thin, cold smile. "Nice try. I've met your children."

At the head of the table, Mr. Wolfe made a strange noise that sounded more like laughter than coughing, which got him lasered by both his wife and his younger daughter.

"At least I can *have* children," Michael snapped.

"We have oysters," Mrs. Wolfe interrupted. "Cal, would you like to start—"

"Sit down, Elizabeth," he told her, almost happily.

Cassie had been suspiciously quiet for a while; I glanced over to see what was wrong. She was staring somewhere over Lucy's head, toward the bay window, so I followed her sight line.

A large raven was perched on the window ledge, looking in. Bad. Then, as we watched, it simply vanished. Much, much worse. She was supposed to be a seagull right now, but when it came to Monica, "supposed to" never meant much. She was here, all right, and my guess was—

"I *said*, at least *I* can have children," Michael repeated.

"Not now, Nature Boy," I said, rather absently.

"I don't think I like her, Cassie," Lucy told her sister. "She's rude."

Cassie only half-heard that. "Later." She pushed her chair back and tugged on my jacket with both hands, still focused on the window. "You and I need to take a little walk."

"But we haven't started dinner yet," Mrs. Wolfe protested. "And it's starting to look like rain."

It was at that. The beautiful clear weather of an hour before was gone; now the sky was lead-gray, threatening lightning. In fact, in the brief silence that followed Mrs. Wolfe's weather report, we heard thunder.

"We're not going far," she said. "Start without us. Devvy hates oysters anyway."

Thanks a lot, Cass. "I don't hate them all, Mrs. Wolfe. I'm sure yours are—Hell!" Manners forgotten, I grabbed Cassie and shoved her behind me, keeping a sharp eye on the raven that had just shot down the fireplace. "Don't anyone move. Let me handle it."

No one said a word. Suspicious, I turned. They were all rooted to their chairs in silent shock—all except Michael, who was missing. I figured I knew where to look, though, and sure enough, that was where he was: under the table.

Making sure I knew where Monica was first—she was busy swooping around the room, trying to get her bearings—I checked Lucy. Our eyes met, and I saw embarrassment in hers. I filed that information for later, along with a note to try to feel sorry for her.

By now, Mr. Wolfe had recovered his senses; he was pushing his chair back, looking determined. "I'm going to sue hell out of that contractor. There's supposed to be a screen on the chimney. Why didn't that bird burn up in the fire?"

"This one doesn't burn," I informed him.

"Keep it away from the turkey, Cal," Mrs. Wolfe pleaded. "We spent all morning—"

"I'll handle it," he said, grabbing the carving knife. "Michael?"

Michael stayed right where he was. Looking very much like the deadlier of the species, Lucy reached for her oyster fork and stabbed him under the table with it.

Mr. Wolfe sighed. "Cassie?" A moment's hesitation. "Devlin? Let's get these doors closed. Then you two help me get it down."

Cassie gave me an affectionate nudge before she let go of my jacket and went to close the double doors at one end of the room. I took the ones at the other end. It wouldn't do any good, but if it would make the man feel better, fine.

Just as I took hold of the door handle, Vanessa pushed in. She was dressed up this time like a French maid of some sort, in a chic little white apron and a chic little black dress with a very low neckline, carrying a covered silver dish. "What?" she asked, affecting innocence. "Is it too late to serve?"

"Get out of here, Vanessa. And take her with you. We've already got enough trouble today."

"*Au contraire.* Close the doors now."

By her tone, she meant business. I closed the doors behind her, and she strolled on into the dining room, unnoticed in the commotion. All the Wolfes were on their feet, tracking the bird; Michael was up now, too, trying to stay out of its flight path.

"Devvy, come here a second," Cassie said. "I think if we chase it that way—" Then she saw Vanessa, and her eyes narrowed. "You could be some help here."

Vanessa smiled charmingly. "A pleasure to be of service, miss. Care for an oyster?"

Mr. Wolfe, swiping at the raven with the carving knife, turned toward the unfamiliar voice. "Who is that woman? Where did she come from?"

"It's a long story, Daddy," Cassie said.

I decided to let her handle that one. Meanwhile, I started walking the perimeter of the room, hoping the raven would follow me.

"Look!" Mrs. Wolfe's hand flew to her throat. "It's following her!"

So far, so good. Now if I could get it outside, maybe I could get it to turn back into Monica, and we could have words. As if it read my thoughts, the raven landed on my shoulder.

"Thank you," I told it. "We'll just go out back now, and then we'll talk. Deal?"

By way of answer, the raven gave me a friendly peck on the jugular.

"Oh, for crying out loud," Lucy complained.

"Quiet," Cassie said. "Devvy, I'm coming with you."

Another peck. It hurt this time.

"I don't think it wants you to. But come anyway. I might need some help." Slowly, I started walking toward the doors at the other end of the room, which were closer to the back door. The raven tightened its talons on my jacket. Irrelevantly, I wondered whether some alterations place in Greenville could repair claw marks.

We were halfway to the door, which Cassie was holding open, when Vanessa stepped into our path and the raven screeched—a horrible noise, especially so close to a person's ear.

"Hello, Monica," Vanessa said. "Oyster?"

The bird let go and made a direct line for her. There was a terrible flash of lightning, followed by a terrible clap of thunder, followed by the crash of the silver dish's cover on the floor, where the raven had thrown it. The next thing I knew, it had an oyster in each foot—which it promptly shelled and dropped down the front of Vanessa's little black French-maid dress.

Vanessa howled in outrage and started pelting the raven with oysters, half-shells and all. Her intention was better than her aim, though; one landed smack on the top of Mrs. Wolfe's beautifully coiffured head. The woman looked stunned for an instant— but only for an instant. Blue fire flashed in her eyes as she searched the table for something airworthy. And in that second, I finally saw my beloved in her mother.

Mrs. Wolfe launched a dinner roll, knocking off Vanessa's little cap. Vanessa, not amused, scooped up the roll and lobbed it back.

"You can't do that to my wife," Mr. Wolfe snapped.

Vanessa laughed. "'Can't,' hell. I've got an oyster with your name on it, too, you old tightass."

"I beg your pardon?"

"Tightass," Vanessa repeated—and nailed him in the forehead.

The food fight was on.

Cassie still had the doors open at the other end of the room; I crossed the battlefield, stepping around oyster and turkey parts, to close it for her. Without a word, she wrapped herself around me and buried her face in my shoulder so she couldn't possibly see.

"My family for Christmas," I promised, holding her tight.

Chapter Five

We sat around the long table in heavy silence. I'd taken care to see that Cassie got the only clean chair; that dress was one of her favorites, and I doubted that cranberry sauce and gravy would come out of wool.

Frankly, I doubted that they would come out of wallpaper, Oriental rug or upholstery either. The Wolfes were fairly well totaled too, including Lucy, who'd turned out to be an easy target but a deadly shot with turkey wings. Part of one was still lodged over her husband's left ear, just where he had a tuft of real hair. The toupee itself was in the gravy boat—a good enough place for it, in my opinion.

As for Monica and Vanessa, they'd disappeared at the height of the battle they'd started, which was just like demons. But at least we had some quiet time now.

Cassie gave her parents another reproachful look. Mr. Wolfe frowned and straightened his tie, dislodging a clump of stuffing.

"Maybe we should let Buster in," I said, watching it scatter on the rug.

"No, we should let *goats* in," Cassie corrected. "We probably need a couple hundred of them. Go call directory assistance, honey. There must be goat ranches around here somewhere."

"That's enough, dear," her mother said wearily.

"She thinks that's enough," Cassie told me, feigning amazement. "I wonder what she thinks would be too much. I put on my best perfume for this dinner, and now just look at this place. Of course, the *goats* won't care, but—"

Mr. Wolfe frowned. "Cassandra Reneé, that'll do."

"Now they're doing middle names," she continued, still addressing me. "I always knew I was in trouble when they did that. Know one thing I always got in trouble for? *Playing with my food.* Throwing peas at my sis—"

"She's too big to spank," her father told her mother, shrugging.

"—at my sister. Just so you know, she always started it."

Across the table, Lucy actually stuck her tongue out at Cassie. Cassie did it right back.

"Girls," Mrs. Wolfe scolded, "how many times do I have to tell you that isn't ladylike? Young ladies..."

Her voice trailed off as both her daughters glared at her. No doubt this was an ancient irritation. No doubt it was extra-irritating now, coming from a woman who'd been throwing cranberry sauce at people a few minutes ago.

"I am not a lady," Cassie said grandly. "I'm a professional advertising executive. I own lingerie that would make Great-Aunt Emily spin in her grave."

What that had to do with anything was debatable, but it was certainly true. Feeling the family's concentrated attention, I tried to look nonchalant—and to think about anything else.

"But that doesn't matter today, does it? No. It's only Thanksgiving. I only brought home the person I love, and you only acted like *this.* It's a miracle no one was killed."

"All right, Cass," I said, sensing where this was going. "It's over. Let's not—"

"Over? Oh, no. I'm just getting started. You." She targeted her sister. "You've been acting like Devvy's some kind of slimy green thing in a petri dish, and *you* call *her* rude. And *you.*" Now she had Michael in the crosshairs. "I don't like you. I never, ever did. As of today—"

Michael, who'd pursed his tiny lips as soon as she started on him, unpursed them with an audible pop. "For God's sake, you can't expect me to approve of this...this...*arrangement*. It's unnatural."

"So are half your parts," Cassie shot back.

Both her parents gave her the two-name warning again. But Lucy was smirking.

"Well, it *is* unnatural," he insisted to the room at large. "She's a girl."

Cassie tossed her head impatiently. "Thank you for that news flash, Michael. For your information, I know the difference. For your *further* information, you don't count. Now get that wing off your head. You're disgusting."

"We don't have to sit here and listen to this," Lucy said. But neither of them moved.

"As for you two," Cassie told her parents, "you are just beyond belief. You've done everything but put Devvy out in the doghouse, like she wasn't even civilized, and then *you* act like animals. Really, really *bad* animals."

The Wolfes just sat there too, taking the Fifth.

"I hope you're happy. There are little children in the other room. How are you going to explain this to them?"

"Oh-oh," Mr. Wolfe said, startled.

Cassie nudged me. "'Oh-oh,' he says. My father, the bombardier, says, 'Oh-oh.' I think it's a little late for 'Oh-oh,' don't you?"

"Yes, but—"

"Maybe you can take them all out back and hose them off while I set this room on fire. I really don't see any other way."

She had a point. But she was forgetting one very important thing. "There's always another way," I told her. "Mrs. Wolfe?"

The woman tried to smile. "Yes?"

"Do you have a back staircase?"

"Yes, we do. Why?"

"I'll bet if you sneak upstairs and clean up, and we watch the kids for a while, they'll never know."

The four miscreants looked at one another. Then Michael snatched his hair out of the gravy boat. A heartbeat later, they were all scrambling out the back double doors and up the stairs. Cassie and I waited. Feet pounded down the hall overhead; doors slammed; water started running.

"You told me to cut them some slack," I explained, in defense of the way she was looking at me.

"That was before."

"Let it go, Cass. Vanessa started it. And I'll remind you whose demon she is."

"Don't go anywhere near there. *She's* not the one who flew down the chimney in the first place."

I considered. "All right, Monica started it. But we still have to finish it. We can't leave this room like this. What do you want to do? Demons or maid service?"

"There's always both," Vanessa said.

We turned. She was right behind us, still in maid costume, but in a clean one now.

"You've already been enough help," Cassie snapped. "You don't look like a very good maid anyway. And while I'm already yelling at you, what is *up* with these little getups of yours? Have you been playing with my old Barbies or something?"

"Exactamento."

"I don't think there was ever a Hooker-Maid Barbie, Vanessa."

The demon shook her head sadly. "Pity. It would've been popular. Can I ask you something?"

"No."

"What's the deal with Barbie feet?"

Cassie looked at me, exasperated, for help with the translation. "They're a weird shape," I said.

"Of *course* they're a weird shape. The little shoes wouldn't stay on if they weren't. What's her point?"

"Her point," Monica said, "is exactly the shape of her head."

Cassie and I were far past surprise for one day, so we took her sudden appearance for granted. For her part, Vanessa just rolled her eyes.

"She could have at least shelled the oysters first," Monica continued. "She could have cut your mother's head right off, Cassandra. You're lucky she throws like a girl."

"Ooooh, that hurts," Vanessa said, smirking. "But look who's talking anyway. You missed the old man by a mile with that pie."

"I winged him, Blondie. Don't talk to *me* about—"

"Winged him? You couldn't have hit him if he were ten feet wide and yellow."

"Enough," I told them.

"Stay out of this, Devlin," Monica said, pushing the sleeves of her long black gown up. "I'll fix all of them for you later. I promise. But first, I'm going to fix *her.*"

Cassie sighed. "You handle this, honey. I'll go keep an eye on the kids."

"Why do I always have to do everything?" I complained.

"Because the witch is *your* fault."

Monica shot a menacing look at her but let her leave the room. That left me and two demons—and a mess that could take years to clean up. As I scanned the room again, wondering where to start, I noticed that the chandelier was dripping. There seemed to be most of a turkey carcass wedged up there, cavity end down. How could *that* have happened?

"Now," Monica said, closing in on Vanessa, "you pay for this, you amateur bitch. Turn me into a gull, will you? How would *you* like to be the next Mrs. Michael Jackson?"

Mockingly, Vanessa whistled a few bars of "Beat It"—which did it for me. I shoved them apart and held them off, too mad to care what they might turn *me* into for it. "Get this straight, both of you. I don't care what you are. I don't care why you hate each other so much. I don't care who started it. I just want it to stop. *Right now.* Understood?"

"Don't forget that you're mortal," Monica said dangerously.

"And don't *you* forget that I'm not stupid. You can't win if I don't let you. All I have to do is go straight again—"

She barely bit back a hiss of surprise. "You wouldn't dare."

"—and you're gone. Isn't that right, Vanessa?"

"I don't think you should," she said, looking concerned. "Cassandra would kill you."

"Then I'd be out of my misery either way, wouldn't I?"

Both demons considered the implications. While they did, I tried not to think. Cassie *would* kill me, all right, which would cost her the moral edge she'd just gained over her family.

As if on cue, the turkey carcass plopped down out of the chandelier at that moment, landing on the table with an awful half-squish, half-thud. Vanessa's nose wrinkled in disgust.

"You're bluffing," Monica told me.

"Maybe. But don't bet the rent. You two are a lot of trouble."

Vanessa shrugged. "You're right about her. She's always been no good."

"You're just as bad," I reminded her. "If you'd stayed at the beach like you said, none of this would have happened."

"Oh, I don't know about that, Devlin. You hate that Michael person. He hates you. Somebody would've thrown something sooner or later."

"I don't doubt it. But probably not on *this* scale." Pointedly, I surveyed the ruin of Mrs. Wolfe's beautiful dining room. "Now let's talk cleanup."

It was Monica's turn to smirk. "That would be a job for Hooker-Maid Barbie here."

"That would be a job for *both* of you. Humans couldn't possibly get this place cleaned up before the board of health found out. I figure between the two of you, you can manage."

"That sounds like a threat, Devlin," Vanessa said, with a bit of edge.

"It's not a threat. It's a fact. You two put this room back together on the double, or I give the straight thing another chance."

I held my breath, waiting to see whether the demons would buy it. Finally, Vanessa threw up her hands.

"All right, c'mon, Monica. It won't kill us. Where do you want to start? Ceiling or floor?"

In grudging silence, my demon lifted a finger, literally, and the ceiling was clean again.

"Thank you," I said. "Now I'm going to go get Cassie, and we're going to get out of this madhouse for a while. Can I trust you two to be gone before her family comes back down?"

Vanessa snorted. "Like we'd even want to be caught dead with *them* again."

"I don't know about this. We're just letting them walk out of here," Monica said.

"They'll be back. The weekend's not over."

That seemed to pacify her. With a martyred sigh, she pointed to the chandelier, which started tinkling as the crystals started coming clean. Satisfied, Vanessa set to work on the windows.

I left them then, hoping that I hadn't just made a big mistake.

Chapter Six

Cassie said she wanted me to have one good memory of Thanksgiving, so she took me to Country Club Plaza that night for Plaza Lights.

We'd driven through the day before, on the scenic route. From the street, the Plaza had looked both interesting and expensive, which was all I asked of shopping districts. But it was even more interesting close-up—blocks and blocks of 1920's ersatz-Spanish mall, bristling with ornate towers, balconies, courtyards and fountains. Lots of fountains. It didn't take long to run out of coins.

Cassie told me Kansas City had more fountains than Rome and more miles of boulevards than Paris. When I asked what that proved, she stopped speaking to me for two or three minutes. So I took it back. In all truth, I'd found the city surprisingly beautiful, and I liked the look of this Plaza. Maybe we'd come back in the summer.

Without telling her family, of course. Also without these crowds—the streets were positively mobbed—and without the caroling.

The up side was that all these people could function as windbreaks. It was getting seriously cold. We'd put on heavy sweaters when we changed clothes and thrown on coats when we left, but they weren't enough now. Cassie was starting to shiver a little, which concerned me. All these stores and not one of them open, or I'd have found her something warm, damn the cost. Then I spotted a coffee vendor down the block.

"Put this on," I told her, stripping off my leather coat. "I'll be right back."

"What? Are you crazy?"

"Hard to say. Wait here. I'll be back in a minute."

Cassie grumbled something about having to drag my frozen corpse to the morgue, but when I looked back, she was draping the coat over hers like a cloak. Good. She got really crabby when she got sick, which I didn't need.

A few minutes later, I came back with two large coffees, almost too hot to hold through the thin foam cups. She wrapped both hands around hers and closed her eyes in bliss.

"It's just plain coffee," I remarked. "That was fastest."

"I don't care if it's battery acid; it's *hot*. Thank you, honey."

The people nearest us pretended not to have heard that. I gave them a look that made them pretend not to see us, too. Reassured that we wouldn't be an issue, I peeled back the plastic tab on my cup lid and soaked up the escaping steam. God, it was cold out. "So what happens here? Where's the tree?"

"It's not about a tree. See those lights?"

I looked where she was pointing. The tops of the buildings were strung with lights—probably miles of lights, if they'd wired up the whole mall.

"There's a little ceremony," she said, "and then the lights get turned on. It's really kind of pretty."

"So we don't have to stand anywhere special? We don't even have to stand?"

"No, but—"

"Come on. I remember a place."

She didn't argue, for once. We crossed a few streets and wound up at the Neptune fountain. There was just enough room left on the base for one small person to sit all scrunched up; I hovered meaningfully over people until they made enough room for Cassie.

"You're not sitting?" she asked.

"We'll take turns."

She seemed about to argue, but that was when they turned the lights on, and everything got very festive for a while.

Being coldhearted and evil, I was mostly immune to Christmas lights. Still, the effect was prettier than I'd expected, and so was Cassie's expression. All this carrying-on seemed to take her back to childhood somehow. Looking at her, I suddenly saw a blonde little girl in bunny slippers and a flannel nightgown, up early Christmas morning, all wide-eyed wonder that the milk and cookies were really gone...

Damn, I was doing it again. A few weeks ago, I'd pictured her on a Schwinn with pink streamers, and now this. What was wrong with me, anyway? The cherub in my head had nothing to do with the real Cassie, who most likely had ripped into packages first, asked questions later and taken no prisoners.

"Hey," she said softly.

I could barely hear her over the crowd noise and the music. "What?"

She got up and moved close enough for private speech. "You had the weirdest look on your face just now."

"What look?"

"It was like you were a little kid on Christmas morning, and you knew you weren't going to get what you wanted."

Startled, I just stared at her.

"I had this really clear picture. You had on a flannel robe and fuzzy slippers, and no front tooth. It was adorable, except that you were so sad."

"Sad?"

As discreetly as possible, she gave me a little hug. "Never mind, Devvy. It's been a long day. Let's go back."

There was more to that, I was sure, but it was much too cold to argue. Obligingly, I turned to follow her through the crowd to where we'd parked the car. Then something occurred to me.

"Hold up," I said, fumbling in my pocket for the coffee change. It wasn't much, but it was all I had. Leaning over a young couple, I tossed the coins into the fountain and just stood there a minute watching the water.

Cassie tugged on my sweater sleeve. "What was that for?"

All I could do was shrug. It had felt a little like asking for something, but I didn't know what.

"Well, if you wished you wouldn't see my family again, you just wasted your money. Look."

I did. There they were, the whole pack of Wolfes, about to cross the street right in front of a horse-drawn carriage. Michael still looked peevish, although for all I knew he always looked that way.

There was nothing to do but grab Cassie and push off in the other direction.

We made lousy time, but we got out of the Plaza alive.

First thing back at the house, we found matches and made a fire in the den. We were still cold to the bone, so we found some brandy, too. Then, to make absolutely sure of our survival, she took the stadium blanket off the back of the couch and wrapped it around us both.

"Only until your parents get back," I said.

"For as long as it takes," she countered, reaching for the snifter she'd set on the coffee table. "This is for medical purposes."

Her close presence under the blanket didn't feel medical, but whatever. In silent accord, I clinked snifters with her, and we drank. The brandy burned all the way down, but it burned good.

"Will you tell me something?" she asked.

"Sure."

"What did you wish for? Back at the fountain?"

That seemed like a strange question. She was serious about it, too, which was just as strange. "I'm not sure, Cass. Nothing in so many words. I just had a feeling."

"So did I."

That was all, but something unspoken hung over us. I couldn't tell whether it was good or bad, but it was big. She reached over to pat my thigh and just left her hand there, fingers tracing idly.

It hit me then how cold I'd been, how tired I was and how much I wanted this day over. Taking a careful grip on the snifter so it wouldn't spill, I put my head back and closed my eyes. The house was absolutely still except for the tick of the clock on the mantel and the crackle of burning wood. Falling asleep seemed both possible and desirable.

Then warm fingers touched my face, and a warmer mouth touched mine. Cassie made it last a while. "Don't go out on me," she murmured. "Want to go upstairs?"

Yes, eventually, but the very effort of moving, much less climbing stairs, was too much to think about just then. Reaching deep for some physical reserves, I pried one eye open. "This is the first time I've been comfortable all day. Ten minutes?"

Her lips curved into a gentle smile. "Fine."

Relieved, I let the eye close again. Cassie was still there, but it was probably safe to relax for a few minutes. I felt her tuck the blanket closer around both of us. Then she kissed me again, very softly, still taking her time, and my mind and body fought a short battle. The body won. That decided, I started to put the snifter on the end table, but Cassie took it and did it herself, reaching over me.

This maneuver put her in a compromising position, which I helped her get much farther into. Straddling me now, she bent back down. My hands ran up her thighs and around her hips, lingered a while, then moved of their own accord. While I fumbled with the buttons on her sweater, she pushed my pullover up and unbuckled my belt. It had a difficult catch, which was just as well, because just as she got that done, her family walked in.

We might never have noticed if Mrs. Wolfe hadn't made some noise fainting.

Cassie jerked up and back to see what had happened, pulling the blanket back in the process—and Michael slapped his hands over his eyes. Too late, I realized that she'd unhooked her bra before we were interrupted. It was one of those front-closing models, and a good part of her was on full display.

Our eyes met. For a second, she looked a very guilty sixteen, caught making out on prom night. But I must have looked guiltier, because she suddenly laughed and started buttoning her sweater back up.

Right. Good point. Quickly, I took care of my own predicament. Then, with trepidation, I checked the family's reaction. Mrs. Wolfe was out like a light on the Oriental rug; Mr. Wolfe had just managed to catch her head, but the rest of her had knocked over a small table. He was too busy with her to pay us any mind at the moment. And Michael had turned his back on us, hands still over his eyes, as though he'd just happened onto a crime scene.

But Lucy didn't look shocked, horrified or even particularly upset. She was patting her husband's shoulder reassuringly but almost smiling at her sister. Cassie sighed deeply and shrugged at her, which got her a real smile. There might be some history in that, I thought. Both of them had probably been caught like this before, and sisters generally stuck together in sticky situations.

All right, neither of them would have been caught exactly like *this*, but that wasn't the point.

"I suppose this makes us even," Cassie said, twisting around to sit on my lap. "One food fight for one make-out session on the couch. All right, Daddy?"

He mumbled something indistinct, still patting his wife's cheeks in an effort to bring her around.

"I'm going to take that as a yes. Michael?"

"Are you decent?" he asked sharply.

She rolled her eyes in amused exasperation. "Yes."

Mistrustfully, he turned. By his expression, he'd expected "decent" to mean we were at opposite ends of the county. But he didn't make a point of it. "I'm just glad the children didn't see that."

"Well, thank God," Cassie said, her tone dripping venom. "It's bad enough that they see animals having sex on the Discovery Channel. Where are the little angels, anyway?"

"They wanted to say goodnight to Buster," Lucy explained. "I imagine they let him out back to pee."

Michael winced. "We've discussed that word, dear."

"Pee," she said clearly and distinctly, looking him straight in the eye.

Cassie nudged me, delighted. But given this family's recent history, I wasn't sure how much more fun I was up for.

"We'll talk about this later," Michael promised his wife. "Right now—"

Lucy cut him off. "Right *now*, I think you should get that bug out of your butt. I've about had it with you today."

"Let's get out of here," I told Cassie.

"Not a chance. Here." Retrieving our snifters, she handed me mine and then clinked hers against it. "Cheers."

"—your attitude," Michael was saying. "Sometimes you surprise me, Lucy. Not good surprises, either. The kind of surprises that make me wonder why I stay married."

That really was all I wanted to hear. "If you'll excuse us, I think—"

"Keep out of this, Devvy," Cassie said happily, hooking her free arm around my shoulders.

"Why *you* stay married?" Lucy snorted, sounding very much like her sister at times of high emotion. "You look more like the Pillsbury Doughboy every day. I'll have you know that men still whistle at me on the streets."

"They're hailing taxicabs, Lucy," he said patiently.

"Oh, taxicabs my ass. Do you ever wonder what I do when you're out of town? Do you ever wonder why Jeremy is just a little *cuter* than the other kids?"

The shot of brandy that I'd just taken for fortitude almost went down the wrong way. Cassie patted me on the back, but a little absently.

"He's got my ears," Michael insisted. "He's got my feet."

Ears? Feet? Did parents really get this anal? Then I considered the source. Yes, they did if they were Michael. To prove my point, he started ticking off a list of features, each of which Lucy argued about.

At the same time, Mrs. Wolfe began to stir on the rug. "There, there, Elizabeth," Mr. Wolfe said anxiously. "You're all right. Just a little spell."

"What happened?" she asked him. "What's going on?"

He patted her face again. "Never mind."

I would have liked to have heard more of that, but things were heating up at our end of the room. Lucy was informing her husband that she had her lawyer's number on speed dial, he was telling her that his lawyer would eat her lawyer's lunch any day she named, and Cassie was drinking to each point her sister won. By now, she was getting a little looped. So was I, what with keeping her company.

Then things got personal. Out of the blue, Lucy went off on her husband for going off on Cassie and me. "She's my sister. I love her no matter *what* she sleeps with, and what you think doesn't—"

"She's turned queer, Lucy," Michael shot back. "Your own sister. The aunt of your children. You're fine with that?"

Damn, I wasn't. Cassie was laughing, but I didn't see anything funny about it. "Let's not be using that word, boy. She hasn't 'turned' anything."

He rounded on me, his face even redder. "The hell she hasn't. You two were groping each other like weasels in heat, and if that isn't—"

"Weasels in heat," Cassie repeated thoughtfully. "How do you happen to know what that looks like, Michael?"

"What are they saying?" Mrs. Wolfe asked, still on the floor.

Mr. Wolfe promptly covered her ears. "Nothing, Elizabeth."

"Don't listen to him," Lucy told us. "He's just jealous of Devlin. Isn't that right, pumpkin?"

"I beg your pardon," he said stiffly, "but I most certainly am not—"

"Of course you are. You've been jealous of everyone she ever brought home. Don't think I don't know you want her yourself."

"Oh, God, kill me now," Cassie moaned, sinking down on my shoulder.

Michael glared at me significantly. "She's just saying that. She's just trying to make me look bad."

"Works for me," I said, raising my snifter to Lucy, who smirked in return.

"I do *not* want to sleep with Cassie," he insisted. "She's my sister-in-law, for Pete's sake."

Cassie lifted her head enough to blister him with a look. "She doesn't want to sleep with you either. And believe me, you could *be* the last man on earth."

"That's enough," Mr. Wolfe announced. "We don't have to discuss these things."

Michael wasn't done. "With all due respect, Dad, I really think we should have this out. I think..." Suddenly, he froze in an attitude of listening. "The kids. Quick—everybody act normal."

Pointedly, Cassie got even closer to me.

"The kids," Michael pleaded. "They don't need to see this."

"Don't they?" she asked. "Well, let me just check with your wife and see what *she* thinks. Lucy? Do the kids need to see this?"

"I don't know why not," Lucy replied. "They see everything else."

Michael practically burst a blood vessel, but it was too late; the children were already stampeding into the den. They took in the scene—their grandmother on the floor, their aunt on my lap—and didn't react in the slightest. The two little boys tried to tackle their father, and the little girl tugged on the hem of Lucy's sweater, wanting to be picked up.

"They look traumatized, all right," Cassie remarked. "We're going to bed now. Can I say *that* word in front of them?"

They were still arguing about it when we left the room.

She was already in bed when I came out of the bath, looking very much asleep. That worked for me; I was dead tired. On top of that, we were still in her parents' house, and I'd had enough of fighting City Hall for one day.

Wearily, I switched off the light and climbed into bed. I'd barely closed my eyes when she rolled over to snuggle up. That worked too. Pulling her closer, I kissed her hair and then settled in for the night.

"You're awfully quiet," she said. "Are you all right?"

"Fine. Just tired."

"You don't sound fine. You're not having a good time, are you?"

There were many possible answers to that question, all of them wrong. But the stress of the day had been too much, and all I could do was start laughing.

A little anxiously, Cassie raised up and put her hand on my forehead. "Are you sure you're all right?"

"Am I all right? Well, let's see. So far this weekend, I've had to deal with your parents, your sister, the prick she's married to,—"

"I don't think it's all his."

"—flying turkeys, hyperactive children and a psychotic dog. Not to mention Vanessa. Not to mention Monica. Not to *mention* that we just committed foreplay in public. Of course I'm not all right. Are *you* all right?"

"Yes. And I'm having a great time." With a sigh of relief, she snuggled back down. "This isn't what you expected, is it?"

"I don't know how anyone could be *expected* to expect something like this."

"It's all right, honey. My family's crazy."

"Well, yes. But I don't blame you. So is mine."

"See? We're a perfect match."

Wisely, I kept quiet.

"I love you," she said.

"I love you, too. Get some sleep now."

"Devvy?"

Good thing I *did* love her. "Cass?"

"Can I do something?"

"What?" I asked suspiciously.

She laughed. And then she started to sing, very softly, a song that I never dreamed she even knew.

My eyes shot open. "How do you know that? I didn't think you even liked Cowboy Junkies."

"You do. And I love you. Problem with that?"

"No, but you mean you—"

"Shhhh," she said, and sang the next two lines.

Cassie wasn't just saying it. She meant it. She loved me. She didn't love my taste in music, though, so this could mean only one thing:

This was getting serious.

In the silence that followed, I blinked hard a few times, but it was no good. She raised up and touched my face in the dark, finding the place where the tears were starting to run down.

There was no need for words between us then, or for sleep till a long time later.

Chapter Seven

Friday

Mrs. Wolfe knocked once, as a formality, and opened the bedroom door without waiting for an answer. "Good morning. I thought you might...Oh!"

I watched her nearly climb the wallpaper in panic. It was oddly satisfying. "Good morning," I repeated politely.

"I didn't...I thought...I mean..."

"Cassie's in the shower. Can I give her a message for you?"

The woman's lips worked, but no sound came out. Very peculiar. I was lying in bed fully clothed in pajamas, all buttoned up, not doing a thing, yet she was acting as though she'd stumbled into Satan's reception room.

"She should be out any time now," I added. "She usually takes about twenty minutes. Baths are a different story. Get her in a tub, and she'll stay there for hours. Especially if she has her foam bath fish to play with. Is something wrong, Mrs. Wolfe?"

"No, no, nothing. I just..." Her gaze swept the room, lingering on the dresser, where we'd dumped our jewelry, keys and other effects. "I didn't know you were staying in this room, Devlin."

I tried not to smile. "Cassie asked me to."

"I see. When she said she was staying in here, I naturally thought..." A sigh. "Well. You say she's in the shower?"

That was what I'd just said. She might also have caught a clue from the sound of running water in the bath or the steam leaking around the closed door. But there was no point in oppressing her about it. "She is."

"Well. Would you tell her I'm starting the cookies?"

"Will she know what that means?" I asked cautiously.

"Oh, yes. She likes to lick the beaters. Ever since she was a little girl. So I thought maybe...If you think of it, would you tell her?"

"I'll tell her. I promise."

Mrs. Wolfe answered with a strained smile and then excused herself, closing the door firmly. Barely a minute later, Cassie emerged from the bath, hair wet, wrapped in a towel.

"That felt great," she reported. "Did you miss me?"

"Desperately."

"I left you some hot water. Don't be long."

"I won't. By the way, your mother was just here."

"She was?"

"She seemed surprised to see me."

Cassie sighed. "She'll live. What did she want?"

"She said to tell you she's starting the cookies, and something about licking the beaters."

A snort. "What am I, six years old?"

"I think she was trying to make a peace offering. It might be a start. What kind of cookies?"

"Christmas cookies. She always starts baking the day after Thanksgiving. As if there aren't any bakeries."

I couldn't help it. "'Are there no prisons? Are there no workhouses?'"

Cassie unwrapped the towel from around herself, snapped me with it and then turbaned it around her hair. "I'm getting dressed now. Go on and get your shower. We can have cookie dough for breakfast if you hurry."

I propped myself up a bit, idly enjoying the view as she rummaged in the big suitcase for clothes.

"I mean it, Devvy."

"All right, all right, I'm going." Regretfully, I stretched one last time before getting up. One hand made contact with something dangling off the headboard; curious, I yanked it down to see what it was.

So that was where Cassie's pink nightshirt had gone last night.

"Did my mother see that?" she asked, amused.

"That would be my guess."

"Then you'd better let *me* test all the cookie dough. She might try to poison you now."

True.

"I'm kidding," she said.

"Be sure to tell *her* that."

Cassie crossed the room, kissed me and shoved me in the direction of the shower. It seemed to me that she was taking the threat awfully lightly.

There are two kinds of people in the world, they say: those who divide the world into two kinds of people and those who don't. It had always been my opinion that there were too many kinds for there to be only two, but a few minutes in Mrs. Wolfe's kitchen made me reconsider. In her world, you either baked or you didn't. Period. And if you didn't...

Well, hell's bells, how was I supposed to know how to use a cookie press? I'd never even *seen* one before. Cassie tried to make me feel better by sneaking me some dough, but it was still a bitter failure. Morosely, I retreated from the field and started washing dishes. That, at least, I knew how to do.

"Do be careful with that," Mrs. Wolfe urged as I picked up a mixing bowl. "It's a family heirloom."

"Yes, ma'am." *Family heirloom, hell. I'll bet you bought it at Restoration Hardware, you old—*

"And don't use soap on that pan. It ruins the temper."

Several smart remarks came to mind, but I let them pass. My mother had an iron skillet that she was the same way about. Personally, I didn't see how you could get a thing really clean without soap, but it wasn't like I cared.

Cassie detoured past the sink on her way to the oven. "It could be worse," she whispered. "My sis—"

Exactly at that instant, there was a godawful commotion in the front of the house, which could only be Lucy and her brood.

"Oh, good," Mrs. Wolfe said, sounding as though she really meant it.

Cassie started to say something to that, but suddenly the children were among us, squealing; Buster was barking in the back yard; and Lucy was yelling at everyone to stop yelling. Without quite meaning to, I said a bad word, which got me a sympathetic scratch on the back from Cassie.

There were several minutes of unbelievable chaos in the kitchen, which ended only when Mrs. Wolfe surrendered the first batch of cookies and sent the children outside. "They're not decorated yet," she fretted to Lucy. "I hate giving them undecorated cookies. Are you going to stay a while? Do you want to help?"

Lucy didn't answer right away. It took a second to figure out why she was staring at me: the Christmas apron. Annoyed, I stared right back. It had been Mrs. Wolfe's idea. She and Cassie had on Christmas aprons, too, and in my judgment we all looked stupid, so singling me out wasn't fair.

"I wasn't planning to, Mom," Lucy finally told her, "but maybe I should. I don't have an apron, though."

"Of course you do, dear. We've always had aprons."

Lucy looked at mine again with greater significance.

"Oh, for God's sake, your name's not on it," Cassie told her.

"It's tradition," she said. "I always wear that one."

This was just ridiculous. I wiped my hands on the dish towel and then took the apron off, handing it over in silence.

Lucy lost no time putting it on. "It's nothing personal, Devlin. It's just that...well, this is family."

"Of course it is," I agreed.

"We've had these aprons for years."

"I understand."

"Now, if you were part of the family, we'd probably get you your own apron. But that would be a little weird, wouldn't it? I mean, Cassie never brought a girl home before, so—"

"Get over it, Lucy," Cassie snapped.

"Oh, get off your high horse," Lucy shot back. "I don't care. I just don't know how I'm supposed to act. What am I supposed to do?"

I started to excuse myself, but Cassie yanked me back. "You could start by acting normal," she said.

"Normal? Come on, this isn't *normal*, and you know it. Why, the kids were asking last night if they need to call her Aunt Devvy."

With a strangled little noise, Mrs. Wolfe dropped a cookie sheet and fled the room. For my part, I was too stunned to run.

"Don't make this weird," Cassie warned. "We're not doing that stuff."

"Well, how do I know? I keep reading about it in the papers. How am I supposed to keep up with what we're supposed to call you?"

It seemed to be time for me to get involved. "What do you mean by 'you'?"

"You people."

Cassie tried to keep hold of my sweater, but I broke her grip. "We aren't 'you people.' We're us. What's your problem with that?"

To my surprise, Lucy started laughing. "Got a temper on her, doesn't she, sis?...I don't have a problem. I don't hate you, either."

"Your husband does."

Lucy snorted. "Michael's a pig. He's *my* pig, but he's still a pig. At least I've got three beautiful piglets with him."

The mysteries of attraction were too profound for my understanding—and for Cassie's, too, by her expression. But at least the tension in the room was dropping off.

"He *is* jealous," Lucy continued. "And I think he's scared. I think he thinks it's contagious. One time in college, a lineman came on to him, and—"

"He played football?" I interrupted.

"In college. Anyway, they were all in this tackle, and—"

"I never heard this story," Cassie said.

Lucy shrugged. "Well, you wouldn't have. It's not like it's something we're proud of or would *talk* about or—what? Did I say something wrong?"

Cassie and I looked at each other. Then Cassie let out a long breath. "Never mind. Maybe we should do cookies and not talk. How would that be?"

"Fine," Lucy said abruptly.

We all set to work again. Except for the shrieking and barking in the back yard, it was quiet for a few minutes.

"So do you like men at all, Dev?" Lucy asked.

Cassie slammed the oven door shut perhaps harder than she meant to. "What kind of question is *that?*"

"It's all right," I told her. "It's a fair question. Lucy, you really want to know?"

"Considering that you're sleeping with my sister," she said, "I might even have a right to know."

While Cassie sputtered, trying to come up with something bad enough to say, I debated how to handle it. Well, truth never hurt. "No, you *don't* have a right. But since you asked, and since you're her sister, I'll tell you anyway. Yes. I do. I like a lot of men, and I even think some of them are attractive." Feeling the heat of my beloved's annoyance, I turned and gave her my very best smile. "Not half as attractive as Cass, though. I've never seen anything so gorgeous, have you?"

That mollified Cassie—a little—but didn't throw Lucy for a second. She leaned on the counter on both elbows, all rapt attention. "Really? Wow. This is interesting. So what men *do* you find attractive?"

"This could start an argument," I remarked. "Cassie and I have different opinions. She thinks Ricky Menudo is cute, for—"

"Martin," Cassie corrected.

"—example, but I go for Johnny Depp myself. Or Tom Cruise. Kevin Kline." I considered a minute. "Mel Gibson."

"Well, *duh,*" Lucy said, laughing. "Who doesn't?"

"I like John Travolta, too," Cassie said thoughtfully. "Devvy hates that. Then there's Kenneth Branagh. We agree on him, don't we, sweetie?"

I just smiled.

Lucy shook her head. "I'll be damned. What about Sean Connery?"

"The older one. Not James Bond."

"You're a girl, all right," Lucy said approvingly. "I hear Buster likes you, too. And I know *he's* not gay."

Cassie ignored that, still thinking. "Brad Pitt."

"Too pretty," I told her. "Tim Daly."

That stopped conversation.

"The guy from 'Wings'?" Lucy asked.

"Yes, the guy from 'Wings.' I saw an interview with him once, and…I don't know; there was just something about him."

"Let's change the subject," Cassie snapped.

Lucy started laughing again. "Jealous much?"

Cassie glowered at her and went back to work with the cookie press.

"So you two really like each other," Lucy told me.

"We really do," I assured her.

"Yeah, I guess you do. Well. Tell me something, then. What's it like?"

I didn't like where she might be going with that. "What's what like?"

"Later," Cassie told her. "Mom might come back in any minute."

"Well, I'm curious. Not curious *that* way, but still. Is it any good? Do you get off?"

Cassie gave her sister a murderous glare. "I said later."

"Oh, come on, you can tell me. So how do you even *do* it, anyway?"

Cassie lost control of the cookie press, sending dough flying across the kitchen. A glance confirmed that she was in no mood to be rational, so I jumped in before she could. "Look, Lucy, this is private. If you don't mind—"

"You were practically having my sister in public last night," she retorted.

There was no defense for that, but Cassie tried anyway. "You weren't supposed to be back yet. You *never* get back from Plaza Lights that early."

"Doesn't matter. You could've gone up to your room. It's not like we would've walked in on you there. For crying out loud, she had you half-naked on the couch."

Outraged, I was about to change the subject in no uncertain terms when a gasp from the doorway made us all turn. Mrs. Wolfe was standing there with her hand at her throat, visibly unsteady on her feet.

"Mom?" Cassie asked.

Mrs. Wolfe opened and shut her mouth a few times, with no result, and then simply turned and walked away. We heard her heels clacking on the stairs in an irregular pattern, as though the effort of climbing were too much.

Cassie untied her apron, wadded it up and hurled it at her sister as hard as she could.

"It was just a question," Lucy protested.

"I'm going to get you for this," Cassie growled. "In the meantime, *you* finish the cookies. Come on, Devvy. We're going shopping."

We didn't need to shop, but that wasn't the point. We lost ourselves in the crowds at the mall, looked at everything, argued about jewelry and gradually forgot our troubles. After about an hour, we stopped for lunch. Except for some cookie dough, we hadn't had breakfast, and it was time for a little something.

There was a line outside the restaurant, but Cassie knew one of the managers—very, very well, it seemed, as eager as he was to hustle us a table. I eyed him speculatively over the wine list. Wouldn't have thought she would ever have gone for a man with an earring, but he wasn't as bad as her usual.

"We're old friends," she explained after he finally left to fetch us a waiter.

"Did I say anything?"

Cassie smiled but didn't answer. Which was just as well, because all of a sudden two waiters were hovering all over us. Yes, she'd slept with the guy, all right. But at least she was getting good service now.

We hadn't even started ordering when a third waiter showed up with a bottle of wine. "We hadn't decided yet," I told him.

"It's from the party at Table 10. Would you care to taste it?"

He was already pouring, so I didn't argue. Then I realized that Cassie was very quiet. She was staring at whoever was at Table 10, wherever that was, so I turned to see what was wrong. They looked harmless enough—just two ordinary-looking couples out for a day at the mall. One of the men was smiling at Cassie, but she wasn't smiling back.

"Something wrong?" I asked.

She didn't take her eyes off the other table. "Did I ever tell you about Charlie Foreman?"

"No. What about Charlie Foreman?"

She didn't answer. Uneasy, I turned again. The man was on his feet now, headed our way, and we were clearly about to be boarded.

"Work with me on this," Cassie said softly.

Chapter Eight

He was nothing to look at, really—so ordinary that I probably couldn't have picked him out of a police lineup unless he were on fire. Everything about him was vanilla, from the thinning no-color hair to the buttoned-up Oxford shirt he had on with his Levis and sneakers. My guess was insurance agent or wholesale carpet dealer. Not Cassie's type. Not even close.

But the closer he got to our table, the greater the disturbance in the Force. There was something about his smile I didn't like. It practically screamed cat and canary, which meant there was something I didn't know, which meant I was going to hate whatever was about to happen.

"Hello, gorgeous," the man told her.

Under the table, Cassie kicked me—fairly gently, but not accidentally. "Hi yourself. How are you?"

"Great. Can I?" Without waiting for an answer, he made himself at home in the chair next to her. "Jeez, Cassie, you look great. So what have you been up to?"

To my alarm, she gave him the full treatment: the little tilt of the head, the little half-smile, the batting eyelashes. "Nothing special. Thank you for the wine, Charlie. That was sweet of you."

"What can I say—I'm a sweet guy." He smirked at his own cleverness and hitched his chair a little closer. "So what's going on? You married yet? Or do I still have a chance?"

I cleared my throat significantly. Cassie shot me a silent warning.

"Sorry," I said. "Sinuses."

Charlie smiled ingratiatingly and stuck his hand across the table. "Charles Foreman. Old friend of hers. And you are...?"

"Devlin Kerry." With great reluctance, I accepted the clammy handshake. "Also a friend of hers. Not quite as old."

Not knowing how to take that, he let go in a hurry. Cassie, however, knew exactly how to take it and kicked me under the table again. "She's visiting us for Thanksgiving," she explained. "Her boyfriend dumped her last week, and she didn't want to go home this year. You'll have to excuse her; she gets a little *irritable* these days."

My boyfriend? And *I* got dumped? Shading my eyes with one hand to block his view, I raised an eyebrow at Cassie. Stubbornly, she raised one back.

"Too bad," Charlie said, too sincerely to mean it. "What about you? Your boyfriend didn't mind that you didn't bring him home instead?"

"Oh, no. He's very special," Cassie replied. "He goes along with whatever I want. Isn't that right, Devvy?"

In silence, I contemplated the menu.

Charlie shook his head. "Can't blame the lucky bastard. *I'd* sure go along with anything you wanted."

I felt Cassie's smirk but refused to look up.

"Isn't that sweet," she said.

"I'm not just saying that. If you wanted to, say, go out tonight, I could go along."

That got my full attention—and so did the arm that he'd just draped over the back of her chair. Mostly unconsciously, I fingered the blade of the bread knife, testing the edge.

"You know what? I'm at a hotel this year. Too much commotion at the folks' house. So we can be alone. Say, 8 tonight? My room?" He leaned even closer to her. "Just like old times."

Cassie looked stricken. "I really can't, Charlie. I have company."

"Bring her. I've got a friend, if that matters. How about it?"

I was no longer working with this situation. Cassie and I were going to have a long talk about how her past affected our present, but first, I was going to hand this little weenie his head.

Then a set of long, sharp fingernails ran lightly over my shoulder, and Vanessa took the vacant chair next to me. "Sorry to be late, darling," she purred. "There is the *most* annoying traffic today. Did you order yet?"

If Cassie had looked stricken before, it was nothing compared with now. That made two of us. Vanessa smirked across the table at Charlie, who was gaping as though she'd walked in stark naked—which wasn't far off, given how low her sweater was cut in front and how tight her jeans were. It was no consolation to me that she'd at least showed up in civilian clothes.

"You must be Cassandra's boyfriend," she told him.

"I like to think so." Leaving his arm on Cassie's chair, he leaned forward and offered his hand. "Charles Foreman."

Vanessa took it in a way that had nothing to do with a handshake. "Vanessa. Devlin's lover."

Cassie, who'd chosen the wrong moment to try the wine, started choking. Solicitously, Charlie began to thump her on the back.

"Any more of that wine, honey?" Vanessa asked me.

"Don't 'honey' me," I snapped, keeping a close eye on Charlie. He didn't seem to be affected by the premise at all. What was wrong here?

For her part, Cassie seemed affected to the point of wanting to lunge across the table, but Charlie held her down. "Easy," he said. "Steady there. You're all right."

I wasn't. "This isn't what you think," I told him. "She just made that 'lovers' thing up. We don't even *like* each other."

Briefly, he looked over at me, then at Vanessa, who put a proprietary hand on top of mine. I shook her off as hard as I could.

But he only smiled. "Hey, I'm cool. You don't have to lie about it."

"See, sweet pea? I told you it's all right." Vanessa tried to put an arm around me, but I whacked her away.

"It is *not* all right," Cassie informed her. "You are *not* her lover."

"I don't see why not. She doesn't have a boyfriend. You said so yourself."

Cassie shoved Charlie off her before she answered—and he got that gotcha look again, for some reason. "Never mind what I said. How do you even know wh...oh, never mind. Devvy wouldn't touch you. She has better taste than that."

"Vanity, Cassandra," Vanessa chided.

Ominous silence fell on the table. Suspicious, I checked Charlie's table. They were watching—and, clearly, listening—with great interest.

"About tonight," Cassie said, her voice strained. "Maybe I can make it after all. Where are you staying?"

Vanessa held me down, but barely. Charlie noticed that, too, and started laughing.

"Excuse me?" I asked coldly.

Cassie tried desperately to ignore us. "I can probably get away for about an hour. What's your room number?"

"Forget it, Cassie," he said. "The jig's up. I knew it. *Knew* it. Hey, Pete!"

We all turned; the man at his table made a show of cupping a hand to his ear.

Charlie grinned big at him. "Pay me!"

Cassie went white, which told me everything I needed to know. Without caring whether all of Kansas City was watching, I scraped my chair back, went around the table and yanked him up by the shirt collar. It didn't take much; he was about the size of a mouse.

"Hey!" he yelped. "What's the matter with you?"

With another good shove, I started walking him out of the restaurant. "You're the matter. And you're leaving."

"You don't *look* like a dyke. Hey, watch where you're—ouch!"

"Keep moving," I ordered, keeping his collar pulled tight. Served the little creep right for using the D word...and for buttoning his top button without a tie this long after the '80's.

A beefy hand grabbed my shoulder from behind. The man it belonged to started to tell me to take my filthy paws off his buddy, but the threat ended in a strangled squeak, followed by a thud. Keeping hold of Charlie, I turned to see what had happened. His friend Pete was flat on his back on the carpet, eyes rolled back in his head.

I scowled at Vanessa. She smiled back at me and then blew on her index finger. Smoke rolled off it.

Damn.

How we got out of the restaurant, I'm not sure; things got a little confused for a while after that. But no one pressed charges, no one paid damages, and I doubt anyone ever paid for the wine.

Cassie hadn't said a word for a very long time. Usually, that meant she was furious, but she just seemed shell-shocked. So I drove the rental car, and she curled up all the way on the other side, hugging the armrest.

Vanessa had insisted on coming along; I made her sit in the back. She didn't argue. In fact, no one said anything until we were a mile or so down the road.

"Where are we going?" I asked Cassie.

She didn't answer.

"Stay on this street for a while," Vanessa directed.

I glanced at her in the rearview mirror. She had the red-eyes thing going again, but it wasn't the same as Monica—more like the difference between a pit bull and a poodle.

That reminded me. "Where's Monica?"

"She left," Vanessa said.

"Left?" I checked the road again, to make sure no traffic was within crash range if something happened. "What do you mean, she left?"

"She said she couldn't do anything here. It's true, you know." Vanessa sounded rather proud. "This is Cassandra's turf. I have a home field advantage."

It occurred to me to ask whether Monica would have a home field advantage if I took Cassie home for Christmas, but I was just smart enough not to ask in front of her. She was upset enough already.

"Anyway," the demon added, "she said she wanted to get a head start at the office."

"Meaning what?"

"Well, Devlin, she *is* your admin now. Have you forgotten?"

Yes, I had, and so had Cassie. She raised her head a few inches off the door panel, gave me a piteous look and then put her head back down. Uncertain, I reached over and patted her shoulder.

"She'll want to go through your files, I imagine," Vanessa continued. "Get up to speed on your clients and read your e-mail and return your phone calls and all that. I hate her, you know, but I've got to hand it to her: She's thorough."

"We'll talk about this later," I told her, meaning it with all my heart.

"What would you rather talk about, then? Politics? Religion? How about sex?"

"How about what just happened back there?"

"Sex it is. Good." The demon got comfortable, stretching out sideways in the backseat. "Do you know who Charlie Foreman is?"

"I sort of figured him for a rug salesman," I said.

"Pharmacist. But that's not important. He went to high school with your sweetie there, and that's where he found out."

"Found out what?"

"That she was going to be gay."

That got no reaction from Cassie at all. I reached over again and rubbed the back of her neck one-handed, for comfort. She usually loved that, but it got no reaction either. "Vanessa, I hate when people think they can pull my chain. So don't—"

"I'm not a people. I'm a demon." In the mirror, I saw her pull out a nail file and set to work grooming her claws. "Now, are you going to keep interrupting, or are you going to let me tell the story?"

"Do I have a choice?"

"No," she said. "It started freshman year. The little geek started hitting on her as soon as he got a couple of hormones. He was just like..." The demon paused, frowning. "What's that stuff that sticks together? Hellcro?"

"Velcro," I said, not amused.

"Are you sure? Well, I'll humor you anyway. He was just like Velcro. *Stupid* Velcro. Cassandra kept telling him to get lost, but he wouldn't. Not that she thought about him all that much—she was too busy dating the football team." Vanessa leaned farther across the seat to speak confidentially. "She always had awful taste."

"Never mind," I told her. "Go on."

"I *am* going. What was the worst thing you could call a person in high school?"

I had to think about that one. "Depends where you went. Where *I* went, the worst thing you could be was a Delbert."

"Sexually," Vanessa prompted.

"You mean like the majorettes? We called them the Whore Corps. I don't like to repeat what we called the cheerleaders, because Cassie *was* one, and she's sitting right there, but—"

"Don't be stupid on purpose, Devlin. Queer bait. *That* was the worst."

Oh. Right. That was a bad one. But still... "What's your point?"

"Not my point. *The* point."

"Don't make me stop this car," I warned Vanessa. "Either tell the story, or I'll—"

"He blackmailed her. He thought he saw her doing something she wasn't *really* doing with another cheerleader, so he said he'd tell everybody she was queer bait if she didn't go out with him. So she caved."

"But that's crazy," I argued. "She was straight as an arrow in high school. She was only with one other woman, and that was in college. Only *one time.*"

"Since when do rumors have anything to do with the truth, Devlin?" Vanessa asked. "Although in this case, they did and they do. She knew a long time ago how she was going to be. She just didn't know who *you* were going to be."

I checked Cassie again. Nothing. "What are you saying? She slept with that little pissant just so people wouldn't talk about her? Because she had some kind of hunch?"

"She never slept with him. She just let him tell everyone she did."

"But he said—"

"And you believed him? Tsk, tsk, tsk. It was high school, Devlin. A rumor about sleeping with boys could ruin a girl's reputation. In a good way. A rumor about being gay, on the other hand..." She filed her nails in silence for a few seconds. "Well, you remember high school."

Grimly, I gripped the steering wheel tighter. There'd never been any proof in my case, either, but there had been rumors.

"Want to talk about it?" Vanessa asked hopefully.

"No."

"Oh, all right. We'll just talk about Charlie some more. Want to know what else I know about him?" She was hanging on to the back of my seat now, radiating eagerness.

"No."

"Oh, come on—this is the good part. Even *she* doesn't know this."

"Let me guess," I said wearily. "He cheats on his wife."

"What wife?"

"Or his girlfriend. Whatever. The woman he was with at the restaurant." *Trouble,* I thought, rubbing the bridge of my nose. Vanessa was working up to something, which was just like her. "You know, that bothered me. It was bad enough that he was hitting on Cassie at all, but doing it right in front of his—"

"You mean Pete?"

I frowned at her in the mirror. "No, I mean the woman he was with."

"He wasn't with a woman." Small red sparks danced in her eyes. "He's gay."

Cassie sat up abruptly. "What?"

"Mr. Queer Bait is queer!" Vanessa bounced on the backseat gleefully, getting control of herself just as I drew breath to tell her to stop it. Then she leaned forward again. "And so is his friend, and so are the women they were with. How do you like *that?*"

I risked a quick look. Cassie had gone a very bad shade of white again.

Vanessa was clearly savoring the moment. "There were two whole tables of people just lying their heads off today in that restaurant, and the amateurs took *you* to the cleaners."

"He chased me for years," Cassie protested. "He really meant it."

"Of course he did. He didn't want to be called 'queer' either. That's why he went so far the other way. You'd know something about that. Wouldn't you, Cassandra?"

A few beats of silence.

"All that closet stuff is a crock," she added. "The best place to hide is in plain sight. Isn't that right, girlfriend?"

"Devvy, make her stop," Cassie ordered.

"She's *your* demon," I reminded her.

She pondered that. Then she curled back up against the armrest. She didn't say another word for hours.

We spent a tense, mostly silent evening avoiding her parents. That was easy. Mr. Wolfe was dug in with a stack of newspapers in the den; Mrs. Wolfe was in bed, allegedly nursing a migraine; and it was a very, very big house.

When we finally went upstairs, Cassie stopped short of the guest room door. "Not tonight," she said quietly.

"I know. I wasn't asking."

"No, I mean..." She took a step back. "I think I want to be by myself tonight. In my old room. Do you mind?"

No, I didn't, not really. But for some reason, that really hurt. Trying not to let it show took all that I had. "Will you be all right?"

"I'll be fine. I just need to be alone for a while."

Mechanically, I nodded. "What about Vanessa? Isn't she sleeping in there?"

"She can sleep hanging upside-down in the attic for all I care." Cassie sounded downright poisonous—the first flash of emotion she'd shown since the restaurant. I decided to take it as a good sign.

So I kissed her goodnight—platonically, on the forehead—and went to bed in the guest room. Alone.

Something woke me a couple of hours later. Half-expecting a burglar—or, worse, Buster—I reached for the bedside lamp with the idea of using it as a weapon. Just in time, I recognized Cassie's perfume.

She didn't say anything at first; she just climbed into bed and held on tight. In sheer relief, I did the same.

"I thought not tonight." I hoped it sounded casual.

"No." She held on tighter.

"Is something wrong? Did..." An unpleasant thought surfaced. "Did Vanessa say something?"

I felt her shake her head. All right, we could talk tomorrow. All that mattered now was that she was here.

One thing was sure, though: I was going to have Vanessa help me out Charlie Foreman before we left town. It probably couldn't happen to a nicer guy.

Chapter Nine

Saturday

Cassie was more or less herself again in the morning, so we got off to a good start. That was only asking for trouble, of course. Being around the Wolfes was like being forced to play with a jack-in-the-box—a contraption I'd hated when I was little and still didn't like much. Nothing good could come of a thing that started with "Pop Goes the Weasel" and ended with a plastic clown, in the toy box or in the larger world.

But Cassie's family was even worse. You never knew what was going to pop up, or when, or what it would want when it did; and nine times out of ten, it led to some kind of violence.

The day did start harmlessly enough, though.

Her parents had finished breakfast by the time we got downstairs, and they made a point of sticking around to have coffee and small talk with us. Very small talk: the weather (lovely), the stock market (favorable), the Chiefs' chances in the playoffs (who knew). Mrs. Wolfe and Cassie even had an animated conversation about winter handbags, which drew her father and me together in silent sympathy. It wasn't that I didn't care, even though I didn't, but I had a couple of perfectly good purses already.

Shoes were different. But everybody knew that.

When they tacked off to fashion organizers ("The cutest little credit card case," Mrs. Wolfe was saying, "and in five colors!"), Mr. Wolfe shook his head, folded his paper and engaged me directly. "So. Devlin. Cassie tells us your agency is having a very good year. Business is good?"

I muttered vague agreement, troweling maple-walnut cream cheese onto a bagel.

"She says you're looking to diversify."

Diversify? I gave her a narrow look, but she was lost in Gucci, Pucci and Coach, and not going to pay me a bit of attention for a while.

"Your client base," he prompted.

Thank God. "We'd like to. An agency always likes to have a range of clients."

"She says you specialize."

I almost choked to death on coffee. Absently, Cassie smacked me between the shoulder blades while Mr. Wolfe attempted not to notice.

"Specialize?" I coughed again, to clear the last of it. "Well, not exactly. We work in teams at J/J/G, and some teams are better with some types of accounts, but—"

"I would imagine that you'd want to diversify, if you specialize."

"Very true."

"Do you handle many financial services accounts now?"

Cassie was right: Talking to her father was like being drafted into Rotary. If this was what old boys' clubs were like, the old boys could keep them. "You'd have to ask Cassie; she's more up to speed on the overall client base. I know Walt's team has the First Third account, and I think we have an S&L somewhere, but—"

"Are they all local?"

"Most of our clients are local, yes. We have a few regional accounts. Most of the big ones go to Bates, though. They've got an office in town."

"Could your team handle out-of-town banks?"

I didn't believe it. Yes, he'd behaved badly all weekend, but throwing business to the agency might be an excessive make-good. Still, I could live with taking advantage of guilt. "I imagine we could. J/J/G made its rep on lifestyle accounts, but banking wouldn't be a big stretch. Everybody banks, right?"

At this point in any pitch, Cassie always reminded me to smile. So I did. It was nice to remember for once and not get an elbow somewhere.

To my surprise, it worked. Mr. Wolfe didn't exactly smile back, but his features loosened a little.

"We'll be in touch," he said. "Who do we contact?"

"Nathaniel Jenner. He's the head of..." No, wait—Jenner was on medical leave, thoughtfully arranged by Vanessa. She did have her good points.

I backtracked. "On second thought, you may want to talk to Jack Harper. He..."

Wrong again. Vanessa had checked him in at Research Psychiatric, in a room just down the hall from Kurt, who had checked in on his own. Hell's fire, who was left?

"Is something wrong, Devlin?" Mr. Wolfe asked.

"No, sir. There's been some reorganization at the agency. I'm just trying to sort it out. Excuse me one second." I tapped Cassie on the shoulder. "Cass?"

She broke off her conversation, whatever it was—I'd just caught the terrible phrase "leopard print"—and turned to me. "Is it important?"

"Your father is thinking of throwing the bank's account to us," I said. "He wants to know who to contact. With the *reorganization,* I'm not sure what to tell him."

Cassie was a very fast thinker, which was one of the things I liked most about her. "Rita Sanchez," she said promptly. "So is that true, Daddy?"

"I don't see why not. We're not satisfied with our advertising."

"Might be a conflict of interest," I remarked.

She shrugged. "Chip can handle it. I was going to talk to Jenner about giving him a raise anyway."

"Then it's settled," Mr. Wolfe said.

Amateur, I mused. But no new client wanted to know what really went on in advertising, and half of them never figured it out even after they saw it firsthand.

Cassie pushed her chair back and went around the table to give her father a hug. "You're not so bad for an old fogy," she informed him, mussing his hair. He tried to act like he didn't like it but didn't quite pull it off.

Mrs. Wolfe and I watched this heartwarming moment with polite interest. Then she smiled at me. Clearly, there'd been marital conversation the night before. I wondered whether Vanessa had eavesdropped and whether she'd tell.

Scratch that—of course she'd tell. The question was whether it was worth giving her another IOU. I'd been careful not to rely on her, but services rendered always had their price.

"We'll be decorating the Christmas tree this afternoon," Mrs. Wolfe happily informed me. "I hope you don't mind."

"Not at all."

"The children get so excited."

"The children?" I asked, uneasy.

"Oh, yes. They always have such a good time. They have a little Santa hat for Buster, and—"

I deliberately didn't hear the rest. If this was the price of getting a big account, it might be time to consider another line of work.

The Christmas tree arrived just before Lucy's family did, which was very bad timing. While the men from the tree farm struggled to get the monster fir upright in the stand, the children tried to "help." I was sure there would be bad language before it was over, and I may not have been the only one who thought so, because Mrs. Wolfe kept nudging up the Christmas music on the stereo.

It would make perfect sense. My brothers and I learned to swear by watching our father put up Christmas trees, after all.

"Kids! Settle down!" Michael ordered.

Naturally, they ignored him. So he parked himself in a club chair and scowled at me. Then, for good measure, he scowled at his wife, who was chatting with me at the moment.

"His face is going to freeze like that one of these days," she predicted. "What's the matter, Michael? Are they ignoring you again? Are you feeling...oh, I don't know...*impotent?*"

Cassie had gone out to bring Buster in and arrived back just in time to hear that. She practically fell over laughing...and lost her grip on Buster's collar. The dog streaked right for me, making contact at high speed. Michael liked that, and so did his shrill little spawn. The tree farm workers practically dropped the tree.

"Honestly," Lucy said, offering me a hand up, "I think that damn dog is oversexed. Are you all right?"

"This is really starting to get on my nerves," I complained, wondering whether I would get out of the weekend with even a shred of dignity intact.

"OK, sweetie," Cassie said calmly. "I'll take care of it. I'll take him out back and shoot him...Daddy? Can I borrow a gun?"

Mr. Wolfe shook his head at her, not in answer but in reproach.

"I don't know why he keeps picking on *me,*" I told Cassie, who was dutifully trying not to laugh. "It's not like I don't shower."

"I know," she soothed as she rubbed my back.

"It's not even like I don't like dogs. I *love* dogs."

"I know."

"But this is getting—"

"Do you two have to keep *handling* each other all the time?" Michael asked abruptly.

This time, the workmen lost the tree altogether. The crash was the only sound in the sudden silence, except for the Christmas music. Acting purely on instinct, Mrs. Wolfe turned it up another notch.

"Excuse me?" Cassie replied in a tone that could have flash-frozen Havana.

Michael didn't answer.

"Here we go again." Lucy sounded aggrieved. "Honey, I want you to stop this right now. You're not *that* big a bigot. You have black clients. You're just giving Dev the wrong idea about you."

She said a few more things after that, but I was still working on the part about the black clients. Unbelievable. Under her breath, Cassie was muttering something that sounded like "Shut up, Lucy. Shut up *now*, Lucy."

Michael still hadn't said anything. But he was looking at his wife as though she'd sprouted antlers.

"We have Christmas cookies," Mrs. Wolfe offered with desperate cheer. "Would anyone like a cookie? Some coffee?"

"You're not fooling anyone, Michael," Lucy snapped. "This is *really* all about you wanting to screw my sister."

The workmen froze on the spot.

"Christmas tea?" Mrs. Wolfe pleaded.

"Stop that, Elizabeth," Mr. Wolfe said firmly.

Cassie slumped onto my shoulder and said something indistinct into my sweater.

Lucy wasn't done yet. "Now, if you want to punch Dev in the nose or something, you go right ahead. She's a girl, so it wouldn't be very gentlemanly of you, but you're not acting like a gentleman anyway, are you? No, you're not. I don't think my sister wants you, but you just go right ahead and do the caveman thing, and I'll just call my lawyer. That work for you, snookums?"

Damn, these Wolfe women were good. I was proud to be there with them, ruining the family Thanksgiving.

"I think you've lost your mind," Michael told her flatly. "I worried this would happen someday. We're calling Dr. Owens first thing Mon—"

"Hold that thought. Kids?"

The children looked up. They'd been trying to wrestle a Santa hat onto Buster, which had mercifully kept them preoccupied.

"Why don't you go out back and play with Aunt Devvy for a while?" Lucy suggested.

"Now, just a goddamn minute," I said, truly annoyed. "I am *not*—"

But Cassie just started laughing again. "Great idea. Come on, kiddos—your mommy and daddy want to get rid of us. What if Aunt Devvy pushes you in the swings?"

Bristling, I pushed her off me. But suddenly there were shrieking children and a hyperactive dog all around us, and it was too late. Cassie gave me a smug little look, knowing she'd pulled off her fast one.

She thought fast, all right. Sometimes it was one of the things I liked *least* about her, too.

When Cassie and I finally came back in, the tree was up, the tree guys were gone and the battle was over. Only just over—you could practically smell gunpowder over the pine and holly. We hung back in the doorway and surveyed the damage.

Michael, his tiny lips pursed into a fish mouth, was sullenly holding a string of lights for Mr. Wolfe, who was up on a ladder. Mrs. Wolfe had collapsed into a chair with a dazed expression but was still alert enough to give frequent helpful advice to her husband, who wasn't saying much but was definitely getting a bit of the fish look too. And Lucy was stretched out on the couch, eating cookies with evident relish. Every so often, Michael would shoot her a disapproving look, and she would deliberately cram a whole cookie into her mouth.

Why, I wondered, did anyone ever get married?

"Need some help?" Cassie asked.

The range of expressions when they noticed us standing there was fascinating.

"Ask your mother," Mr. Wolfe said peevishly. "She's the expert."

I flashed on Christmas trees past, and on my own parents' conduct, and instinctively took a long step toward the door, but Cassie grabbed hold of my sweater. Lucy saw, and smiled.

"Where are the kids?" she asked. "You didn't sell them, did you?"

"No takers," I said. Lucy and Mr. Wolfe found that amusing; Michael and Mrs. Wolfe did not.

"They're still out back," I added, resisting the urge to bat Cassie's hand away as she steered me back into the room. "Trying to push Buster in a swing. I don't think he's having a good time, but he's wearing the hat."

"It's all right, then," Lucy told us. "It'll end in biting, and then they'll be sorry. But it takes a while to get Jeremy that mad." She popped the last piece of cookie into her mouth and got up, brushing off crumbs. "C'mon, Cassie—let's get out the ornaments. I get to hang the red ones."

"Divide them up, girls." Mrs. Wolfe was still reclining in the big chair, but she delivered the order with military precision. "We're not going to have this argument again, and I don't want any more scenes in this house this weekend. Do you understand me?"

I don't know what got into me, but after three days of hell on the prairie, I'd finally found an ally. Without thinking, I crossed the room, put a hand on either side of Mrs. Wolfe's head and kissed her on the forehead. She looked as startled by it as I was.

"Oh, Christ," Michael spat.

"Sorry," I said quickly. "Nothing personal."

She blinked a few times. Then, against all odds, she smiled. "Make sure they let you hang some of the red ones, too, Devlin."

"Yes, ma'am," I said.

Well, I'd be damned.

There was only one more ordeal to get through in Kansas City, I thought. It would necessarily be a bad one: Lucy and Michael's children were in a Christmas concert that night. But the next day, Cassie and I would get on a plane, and it would all be over.

So we got dressed up after dinner and drove to the concert. I figured if it was bad enough, and the auditorium was dark enough, I could at least catch up on some sleep.

But even Ebenezer Scrooge finally broke, and so did I. It might have been the Christmas decorations. It could have been that the concert wasn't bad. What it probably was, though, was the little girl in the white dress.

I'd noticed her early in the evening. She was with her parents in the balcony, in the tier of seats closest to the stage, and she couldn't sit still. Every few minutes, she ran between her mother and the balcony railing, which she would hang on to gape in wonder at the goings-on below.

Every time she did, I couldn't help smiling. She had on a fancy white dress, with a little red bow in her hair, and in the lightspill from the stage, she looked like a tiny angel playing hooky to hear the music.

Cassie nudged me. "What are you smiling about?" she whispered.

I pointed out the girl, who was busy directing the choir at the moment. Cassie laughed and reached over to squeeze my hand.

When we came to the audience participation number—"Hark, the Herald Angels Sing," which is never a good audience participation number because of the high notes—we all stood and did our best. Most people fumbled in the half-dark with their programs, trying to read the lyrics, but I didn't need them. Neither did Cassie. We'd done enough church time as children to know the church carols by heart.

The little girl in the balcony didn't know the words, but she sang her heart out anyway. Just looking at her made me happy, for some reason.

That night, after Cassie had fallen asleep, I thought about the girl. I had a very clear picture of her, white dress shining in the stage light and a beatific smile on her face as she hung over the railing. I left that picture lighted in my head as a benediction and finally dropped off to sleep myself.

Chapter Ten

Sunday

Our flight home left Sunday morning, so we were up at dawn, throwing things into suitcases. I was ready. Not just because I wanted to get out of that house before anything else could happen, but also because it was time to go back to work. We'd been away for two weeks, after all.

Cassie said she'd loosen up my work ethic sooner or later, even if it took a crowbar.

We were almost packed when it dawned on me. "Cass?"

"Hmmmm?"

"Can I see your old room?"

Her head popped out of the bath, where she was gathering up the last of her many, many hair appliances. "What?"

"Your old room. I haven't seen it."

"You won't like it," she cautioned. "Are you sure?"

I shrugged. "How bad can it be?"

Stupid question. I knew it the second I asked, and when Cassie opened the door to her room, I knew we were in trouble. My first clue was Vanessa. She was floating a couple of feet above the bed, wearing a pink sleep mask, fuzzy pink slippers...and nothing else. I winced.

The demon snorted. "Oh, don't be a baby. I'm just having a little fun with you."

"Not *that* much fun," Cassie insisted. "Devvy, don't look."

I didn't. But everywhere else I looked was bad, too. The infamous vanity table. The cheerleader costume hanging in the closet. The Barbies—dear God, the Barbies. And, just as Vanessa had threatened, the Rick Springfield poster tacked up on the wall.

"No stuffed animals?" I heard myself ask in a very small voice.

"On the bed," Cassie admitted. "But don't look yet. Get dressed, Vanessa. *Now.*"

"All right, if you're going to be like that," she said sulkily. "How's this?"

Cassie started sputtering in outrage, so I took a chance and looked. Vanessa was still floating over the bed, but now fully dressed. As a nun.

Cautiously, I walked over to examine her getup. When I met her eye, Vanessa winked.

"I'm not wearing anything under this," she said.

That was all Cassie wanted to hear. She pushed me away, grabbed a double fistful of Vanessa's habit and yanked her out of the air. The demon landed on the carpet with a thud. "Hey!"

"Don't 'hey' me," Cassie told her, with some heat. "You're not funny, Vanessa."

"Just think about it a while. It'll come to you." She stood up, making a show of straightening her wimple. "You humans are so touchy about your childhoods. You pay good money to tell doctors how your mothers warped you, and all it does is buy swimming pools for the doctors."

I was lost again. It was starting to feel like my normal condition. "What does that have to do with anything?"

"Monica's right," Vanessa said, a little sadly. "You're hideously literal. Here you've been in the middle of a psychodrama all weekend, and you haven't seen a thing. Don't make me explain it, Devlin; I hate being bored. Besides, I don't think I can."

"Try," I growled.

Vanessa heaved a sigh and flounced past Cassie to perch on the edge of the bed. Inevitably, she started to reach into her cleavage for the nail file—which required some unbuttoning, with that habit in the way—but Cassie was in no mood.

"Get one off the vanity table," she ordered.

Pouting, the demon pointed a talon at the table. Things obediently lifted off and flew toward her: files, emery boards, cuticle scissors, little bottles of pink polish. Alarmed, I pulled Cassie back. Vanessa selected the longest, sharpest file and set to work.

"You were saying...?" I prompted.

"Just look around you," Vanessa said. "This is what she was: a nice girl from a nice family. She was going to be an insurance salesman's wife, sure as she was alive. She did everything she was supposed to do. Including sleeping with the football team, but her parents didn't know that."

"I did *not* sleep with the football team," Cassie complained. "Just the quarterback."

Vanessa smirked knowingly. "That's how rumors get started."

"She's crazy," Cassie told me.

"Don't look at Devlin," Vanessa said. "*She* slept with a defensive tackle."

Cassie gave me a look that could take paint off a battleship.

"He was cute," I protested.

Vanessa laughed. "Dumb as a box of rocks, too. The only time he ever recovered a fumble, he started running toward the wrong end zone. His own teammates had to tackle him. Remember that, Devlin?"

I remembered, all right. It had been homecoming, and I'd had to go to the dance with him after that. God, the humiliation.

"That was the night you started thinking boys might not be all they were cracked up to be," she added.

I would have argued with her, but Cassie was still giving me that look. "Never mind. We were talking about Cass."

"What's the difference? You both hate being embarrassed. And now just look at the two of you."

"Cut that out. *You're* sitting on her bed in a nun costume."

"It's a metaphor."

My head was starting to hurt. "I *get* it, Vanessa. What about her parents?"

"They don't get it."

Cassie said a bad word and walked over to the window, glaring out at nothing in particular.

"They think this is all your fault," Vanessa continued. "They're trying, but her father still kind of hates you. And don't even get me started on that brother-in-law of hers. He's such a chauvinist, someone's going to make bacon out of him one of these days."

"And die of ptomaine," Cassie said, still glaring out the window.

"Don't worry about him. I'll fix him. It'll be fun." Vanessa filed in silence for a few seconds. "Speaking of fixing people, aren't you going to ask me about Charlie Foreman?"

Cassie didn't say anything. All right, then, it was probably OK to bite. "What about Charlie Foreman?"

"I've already fixed him."

Good, I thought.

"Aren't you even going to ask how?" the demon asked.

Lead me not into temptation, because I already know the way. "No."

Vanessa smiled evilly and switched the file to her other hand. "I'm going to tell you anyway. He's having boyfriend trouble. Now humor me and ask me what kind of trouble."

Cassie turned. "Stop picking on her. She's barely had coffee this morning. Just tell us, so we can—"

"His boyfriend found God last night."

"What?" Cassie asked.

"It came to him in a dream. He was visited by a nun." Vanessa clasped her hands to her chest, gazing toward the heavens with a vacant expression of rapture. "And yea, he didst repent of his wickedness. Yanked off the nipple rings and called—"

"Too much information," I advised her.

"—one of those church help lines. He's on his way to be saved right now. He made Charlie go with him. Did you know that churches can cure deviance?" She started filing again, looking gleeful. "That trick might have worked on *you* a few months ago, Devlin. You're lucky Monica's too vain to stoop that low."

"I hate to be a bother," Cassie said icily, "but we have to finish packing. So if you have anything else to say to us..."

"It can wait." Vanessa gave her claws one last swipe and started to tuck the file into her habit, but Cassie pointed meaningfully at the vanity table. The demon shrugged and sailed it over. "I'll leave you two now. Don't forget to show her your trophies, Cassandra. She'll be *très* impressed."

"Trophies?" I asked.

But Vanessa was gone, and where she'd been sitting on the bed was a pink stuffed animal.

Correction—a pink stuffed demon.

Cassie caught on at the same time I did. Without a word, she grabbed the thing, marched over to the window and threw it open. The toy demon followed. I heard it bounce on the rooftop, making little squeaks of protest.

Then she slammed the window back down with a bang that rattled everything in the room. "I hate her. As soon as we get back home, we're calling an exorcist. I *mean* it. I think—"

"Trophies?" I repeated.

"They're not trophies. They're just souvenirs." She shook her head, disgusted. "Honestly. She's trying to make me out to be some kind of schoolgirl slut."

I didn't say anything.

"Oh, c'mon, I wasn't *that* bad. Here. I'll show you."

She walked across the room to the little desk against the far wall. Over the desk was a cabinet of the type normally used to display porcelain knickknacks. But the cubbyholes were filled with jewelry. Lots of jewelry. Enough to stock a small store.

I frowned, scanning the inventory. Boys' high school rings. Boys' ID bracelets. First Promise rings with the fake diamonds. A couple of solitaires that looked suspiciously like—

"Engagement rings," Cassie confirmed, following my glance.

"You kept them?"

"Well, of course I kept them. They were stupid enough to give them to me, weren't they?"

"Tarantula," I said.

"Me? I gave back all the other stuff. You should've seen my friend Amber. She still has about twenty stereos and a couple of big-screen TVs."

I brooded on that for a minute. What would a girl have had to do to *get* a big-screen TV?

"Are you upset?" Cassie asked, very softly. "I know it looks bad, but—"

"No. It's OK. You were normal."

She touched my face, concern in her eyes. "'Were'?"

"Well, you went into advertising after that, didn't you?"

Cassie started laughing. Then she hugged me as hard as she could. "You're crazy, Devvy."

"So are you. Now let's go home."

We hadn't made it halfway down the stairs when we heard the awful unrest that could mean only one thing. Well, technically, three things.

"I wish Lucy could keep a babysitter," Cassie grumbled.

"Probably not enough money in the world for that." Apprehensive, I shifted the big travel bag to the other shoulder. "What do you want to do? Sneak out back and go around the house?"

"That would be rude."

"Yup," I agreed, turning to go back upstairs.

She grabbed the strap and yanked me to a halt. "Not so fast, Devvy. We have to at least say goodbye to my parents."

"They're your relatives. *You* do it. I'll send them a Christmas card when we get home."

Cassie fixed me with her most terrible glare. "Do you want me to be like this at *your* parents' house at Christmas?"

In silence, I weighed the options. There weren't many. I would back her no matter what, but I knew how she could get, and I'd never hear the end of it from my family if she did.

"I didn't think so," she said. "Now come on. Five minutes, and then we'll go."

Without waiting for an answer, she swept on down the stairs, banging into both railings with her luggage but refusing to notice. Easy for her. I was hauling more suitcases than she was.

"There they are," Lucy reported, catching sight of us from the foot of the stairs. "Kids! Come say goodbye!"

Cassie managed to set her suitcases down before the children charged her. That was all very well and good. But I was still a couple of steps from the bottom when Buster galloped in. He skidded to a stop at the foot of the stairs, tongue hanging out, tail wagging.

"No," I ordered, looking him straight in the eye.

He didn't move. Carefully, I started to take the next step down.

I never saw him coming. There was just a dog-colored blur, and then there was a sharp snout in a very personal place. After that, the world went sideways.

"Damn you, Buster, I'm having you neutered," I heard Cassie growl.

If he understood, Buster didn't care. He was standing over the wreckage, breathing in my face, and I was fairly sure he was laughing.

"Wow! That was cool!" Chad told me. "Can you do that again?"

Cassie, who'd just shoved the dog halfway to China, told her nephew to go away. She was starting to tell Lucy a thing or two on top of that when her parents hurried in.

"What was that noise?" Mrs. Wolfe asked.

Don't worry, Mrs. Wolfe; it was nothing. For my next trick, I'm going to saw that damn dog in half.

Painfully, I got up, with a little help from Cassie and even less from Michael, who was helping only because his wife had given him a look. Cassie gave him one, too, for good measure. "Are you all right?" she asked.

Who knew? "Fine," I said.

"We'll just put the dog out back," Mrs. Wolfe said apologetically, glancing at her husband.

Mr. Wolfe smiled faintly and took hold of Buster's collar. "Around here," he said, "'we' means me. Come along, Devlin. Let's have a talk before you leave."

Still dazed from the fall, I didn't argue. Cassie instantly fell into step with us, but her father shook his head. "Alone," he added.

"You'd better not kill her," she warned. "I'm not kidding, Daddy."

I hoped it wouldn't come to that. But all bets were always off in that household. Numbly, I followed Mr. Wolfe and Buster to the back yard.

Chapter Eleven

Mr. Wolfe kept his own counsel for the whole walk out back and for a while after. Scooping up an old tennis ball, he played catch with Buster for a few minutes without saying a word. I watched with growing impatience. Cassie and I had a plane to catch, so if he was going to kill me, he'd have to start soon.

"Good boy," he finally said when Buster brought the ball back for the dozenth time. "You're a very, very good boy."

Buster wagged violently in agreement.

"Did you have dogs when you were growing up, Devlin?"

"A couple."

"I think it's good for children to have pets. Teaches them responsibility."

Theoretically, I supposed that it did. The main thing I learned from having a dog, though, was that my mother got bent out of shape if it got in the house, even when I *told* her we were just going to watch cartoons. "I'm surprised that your grandchildren don't have a dog, as much as they like Buster."

"He *is* their dog. They didn't take care of him."

There was no point pursing that topic. I smiled uncertainly.

"You don't seem to like him much," Mr. Wolfe said.

"It's not that I don't like him. It's just that he keeps doing that thing with his nose."

"He's trying to get your attention."

As ways of getting attention went, there was no beating Buster's strategy. Still... "I'm not sure I follow you."

He threw the tennis ball again, sending the dog barreling over the lawn after it. "The way to handle him is to say hello to him first. If he thinks you're ignoring him, he'll do 'that thing with his nose.' As you call it."

"I haven't ignored him," I protested. "He hasn't ever given me a *chance* to ignore him."

"This is dog logic. It isn't supposed to make sense to us. When you see him coming, say hello right away and pat him on the head. That'll make him happy, and he won't bother you anymore." He broke off to accept the tennis ball back from the dog. "Good boy."

I watched him throw the ball to the other corner of the yard. "With all due respect, Mr. Wolfe, why couldn't you have told me this the very first day?"

"I don't like you much, Devlin. I didn't see any reason to tell you."

"As long as we're being honest," I said, "I don't like you much either."

To my surprise, he smiled—genuinely. It didn't last, though. "I love my daughter. I want the best for her. Frankly, I'm not sure you're it."

"Neither am I. But that's *her* choice to make. Not mine. Not yours."

"Cassie's choices never give me much confidence."

"Likewise."

"She has unfortunate taste in men."

"The worst there is. But I'm not—"

"Yes, I know. That's the problem." He bent down to take the tennis ball from Buster again, but this time, he didn't throw it. "I have no guarantee that her taste in women is any better."

This conversation was beginning to get on my nerves. "There are no guarantees in life. Now, if that's all you wanted to say to me..."

"No."

I waited.

I waited some more.

Finally, I couldn't stand it. "Mr. Wolfe?"

"I feel very peculiar asking this," he said, "but I feel that I have to. What are your intentions toward my daughter?"

"My intentions?"

"I don't want her throwing her reputation away on you if you're just having a good time with her."

My God, he wanted to know whether I was going to make an honest woman of her. Was it ever too late for *that*. Even if I could, of course, which of course I couldn't. "I'm not sure what you're asking."

He frowned at Buster, who was starting to paw his trousers. "I'm asking what's in this for Cassie."

"That's a question for her to ask," I said, annoyed. "Are you going to throw the ball to the dog now, or what?"

Silently, he flipped it over to me. It was damp. Yuck. More to get rid of it than to pacify Buster, I lobbed it toward the back fence.

"You're not going to give me an answer," Mr. Wolfe observed.

"I'll give *her* an answer. If she asks. Which she hasn't. If you'll excuse me..."

"One more question."

Making a production of it on purpose, I checked my watch. "We'll be late if we don't leave soon. What's the question?"

"How are your parents going to behave when you take Cassie home?"

I sighed. "I don't know. Probably no better than you did."

"I won't have that," he warned.

"Neither will I. Don't worry about it. Between the two of us, we can handle my family." I thought that over for a second. "Except maybe my mother. You'd get along with her, you know. She hasn't approved of anything since the '50's."

Unexpectedly, he laughed. "All right. You pass."

"Sir?"

"Her mother and I wanted to see what you're made of. We still don't like it, but we suppose you'll do. At least this weekend didn't scare you off."

I gave him a very narrow once-over, searching for signs of insanity. "The food fight came close. Was that a test, too?"

"Ah. Yes. That." He looked away sheepishly. "We didn't plan that part. But I'm glad you brought it up. About that woman."

"You mean Va—the maid?"

"We appreciate the thought, but it wasn't necessary for you and Cassie to hire us a maid for the day."

No, and it never would have occurred to us to do that, either. But we'd needed a cover story. That one was the best we could come up with. "Our pleasure."

"We did think it was odd for a maid to be throwing food. But Cassie said she did it so she could make extra money cleaning up after dinner. We understand now. That's good entrepreneurial thinking."

No, it was fast thinking on the part of a skilled professional liar: his daughter. I was very proud of her. "She's an operator, all right."

"We still thought we saw a *few* odd things. But..." He shrugged. "Never mind. We were talking about the maid. I'd like to give her a tip for doing such a good job. Elizabeth says the crystals on the chandelier are as clean as she's ever seen them."

"Don't bother. We'll be paying her enough," I said with conscious irony.

"There was cranberry sauce on the ceiling, Devlin. I think getting it off is worth an extra fifty."

"Whatever. But make your wife pay. I saw her do it."

Mr. Wolfe smiled again. "Cassie might turn out like her mother, you know."

"Takes more than that to scare me."

"Wait twenty years," he advised. "Let's go back now. You've got a flight to catch."

It almost ended the way it started. All our luggage was parked by the front door, waiting to be carried out, and no sooner did I pick up a bag than Mr. Wolfe took it. I took it back. He reached for it again. Only Cassie's quick intervention stopped a scene.

"I thought we agreed to a truce," I told him through gritted teeth.

He glared right back. "We also agreed we don't like each other."

That much, we *did* agree on. Grudgingly, I put out my hand. Grudgingly, he shook it.

Then Mrs. Wolfe, vigilant for trouble, stepped in to say how glad she was I'd been able to join them for Thanksgiving, which gave Cassie a chance for a private talk with her father. Out of the corner of my eye, I saw that she was doing most of the talking. It was too bad I couldn't hear what was going on, but she'd tell me all about it on the way to the airport.

Which reminded me to check my watch again. Damn, we were going to be late in a couple of minutes. "Excuse me," I told Mrs. Wolfe. "Cass? It's almost quarter after."

Cassie sighed, gave her father some parting advice and then went around the room hugging people goodbye. Wanting a piece of the action, Jeremy toddled over to me and held out his hand. I bent down and started to shake it, but he jerked it back, scowling.

"He wants you to give him five," Lucy explained. "Jeremy? Try again, honey."

Patiently, I waited for him to stick out his hand again; he was occupied with gnawing his thumb at the moment. Finally, he did.

"Attaboy," I said, giving his hand a light smack. "Now give *me* five."

He did—harder than I expected.

"Give me ten," I suggested.

He did.

"Give me fifty."

Lucy laughed. But Jeremy just stood there, looking troubled. The next thing I knew, he grabbed his mother around the legs and burst into tears.

"Hey, kid, I'm sorry," I said, concerned. "It was just a bad joke. I make them all the time. Ask your Aunt Cassie."

At the sound of her name, Cassie turned, saw her nephew in tears and frowned. "What happened?"

"I don't know. Lucy, I'm sorry. I didn't think—"

"Forget it. I'll explain it to him later. Then he can torture Chad and Rachel with it." Lucy smoothed her son's hair. "Isn't that right, sweetie? You love making them miserable, don't you? Just like your daddy."

He nodded vigorously, face buried in her thigh. Cassie and I exchanged glances. Thank God *we* wouldn't ever have three-year-olds.

"Well, it was interesting," I told Lucy. "I hope I'll see you again. But not too soon."

"You mean not too soon if I have Michael with me," she said. "Don't worry—I'll either kill him or leave him home with the kids. That would probably work out to the same thing."

I laughed. The woman had possibilities after all. "Where is he, anyway?"

"Oh, he'll be back. I made him take your luggage to the car."

Yes, definite possibilities. At that very moment, there was a screech of pain from out front. We all went running, Lucy with a child still attached to her leg. Michael was sprawled on the driveway, clutching his back.

"It's that damn bag," he gasped. "The big leather one. Threw my back out."

I almost felt some sympathy for him. Cassie's beauty supplies were in that bag, so it did weigh about a ton. When I was sure he was looking, I casually picked it up by both handles and tossed it into the trunk. It just took experience—and enough IQ to lift by both grips.

Michael gave me a very nasty look, which I answered with a shrug. Not my fault.

"Go on," Lucy told us. "He'll be all right. And if he isn't...well, he has lots of life insurance."

I shouldn't have laughed, but then, Cassie shouldn't have either. In the awkward silence that followed, we jumped into the rental car, and Cassie gunned it.

With utter relief, I watched the huge house get smaller in the passenger-side mirror. Thank God that was done. We'd had the very devil of a time, but now it was over.

At least, until Christmas.

I hoped.

Not quite two hours later, we were airborne—and flying first class at that. Cassie had booked coach tickets, but somehow, they'd been upgraded at check-in. We figured Vanessa had something to do with it, which was perfectly all right just this once.

The way we saw it, she owed us.

The flight was uneventful at first. Cassie read magazines; I amused myself by editing ads with a felt-tip pen. When she saw what I was doing, she just shook her head and went back to her reading...but also slipped a sneaky hand over the armrest and started experimenting with my self-control.

The words *Mile High Club* crossed my mind. In a fierce act of will, I started blacking out a model's teeth in a toothpaste ad.

At that moment, something blocked my light from the window. The plane was still climbing; we were probably going through another cloud layer. I looked over, just to see.

Monica was outside, peering in through the airplane window. When our eyes met, she smiled wickedly, baring her fangs, and kissed the glass.

"Devvy?" Cassie asked.

Too shocked to speak, I leaned back to let her see.

"Oh, damn," she said.

Monica let go, sliding slowly down the side of the plane, leaving a red lip print on the window.

We sat for a moment in complete silence. Then Cassie lunged over me to slam the window shade down.

The flight attendant came running. "Is everything all right, Miss Wolfe? Can I bring you anything?"

Cassie pondered the question. "Tequila."

I can't drink tequila; it pretty much knocks me flat. So...

"Doubles," I added.

Well, we were going to have to face *my* family in about a month. It wouldn't hurt to get a little extra rest.

Christmas

Chapter Twelve

Wednesday After Thanksgiving

On the third day after we got back from Kansas City, I finally got around to visiting my boss and my employee in the mental hospital, where demons had driven them, with a little help from me.

All right, it was Cassie's demon who drove Jack to the hospital—literally, in a red BMW with a Jesus fish on the back. Kurt had taken a taxi. And I may have had more than a little to do with the situation. But there were demons at the bottom of everything that year, especially that December. If it hadn't been for Monica and *especially* Vanessa...

Well, it's a long story. But I guess this part of it starts at the hospital.

Clearwater Stress Center
5:53 p.m.

"This is it?" Cassie asked, incredulous.

"This is it."

"But it looks like an office park."

That it did. My guess was that it was supposed to. The development we were in was actually called a medical park, but the building ahead could have been anything. I'd probably driven by it a hundred times without a clue. Only the discreet little sign at the entrance gave it away—not just the words on the sign, but also the logo. There is no deader giveaway of rehab than bird-and-sun graphics.

"No bars on the windows," Cassie mused as we got out of the car. "What kind of loony bin is this, anyway?"

"It's not a loony bin. It's a stress center."

She snorted. "It's a loony bin if Jack and Kurt are in it. Are you sure this is a good idea?"

"No. But you don't have to go in, Cass. If you want to just wait in the car, you can."

The way she looked at my MG gave me pause. She seemed to have a personal grudge against it.

"We won't stay long," I promised, locking the door. "Then we'll do whatever you want for dinner. All right? Where do you want to go?"

She thought for a second. "Italian."

That helped. That narrowed it down to about a thousand restaurants. But she was a little edgy, and there was no reason to force the issue.

"Great," I said. "Let's go get this over with."

At the stroke of 6, a nurse appeared in the lobby to take the visitors back to the visiting area. We'd all been through the third degree—signing in, being checked against a list, surrendering our Uzis and crack pipes—and were in a fairly surly mood, so when the nurse suggested that we follow her single-file, rude words were said.

I didn't say them, partly because Cassie had clamped down on my arm as a warning. But I did smile a little.

The nurse pretended not to hear. The residents, she said, were just finishing dinner, and—

"The *what?*" Cassie asked. "The *what* are finishing dinner?"

I clamped down on her.

"We don't use the word 'patients,'" the nurse explained. "Step this way."

Cassie leaned close to murmur in my ear. "I want this hospital's account. And then I want you to change their image."

"It's not a hospital," I said. "It's a residential therapy facility."

"It's a nuthouse. Will you do it if I get the account?"

"What's in it for me?"

She whispered what she had in mind...and I walked right into a pillar. The crash, or maybe the language that followed, stopped our little group in its tracks.

"That's why I said you should follow me single-file," the nurse said pitilessly. "One of those papers you signed at the front desk was an injury waiver. Just thought you'd like to know. Now, if you'll all come this way..."

We made it to the visiting room with no further casualties. There was my pride, of course, but that had been DOA since Thanksgiving.

Cassie pulled me under a light fixture to check for damage and frowned slightly. "Honey, your nose is bleeding. Maybe you should lie down for a minute."

"That would be a cliché. Lying on a couch in a loony bin." I started to check my purse for Kleenex but then remembered they'd made me leave it at the front desk, just because they'd found a Swiss Army knife in it. Cassie had one in hers, too, but she'd batted her lashes at a male guard and gotten away with it. Sometimes, I feared her powers. "Do you have any Kleenex?"

"Not in this purse. Wait here. I'll go ask the nurse."

She took off, leaving me nothing to do but check out the room. Which reminded me of a furniture showroom, with all the brutally modern earth-tone couches and chairs. In fact, I thought I'd seen those very chairs in a Bennison's Home Store ad. It wasn't our account, but I bet I could find out whether there'd been a trade-out involved. Maybe furniture store owners went wacko, too.

Idly, I watched the double doors at the far end of the room, waiting for Jack and Kurt. A few patients had already showed up, and little reunions were going on all around. There was also some activity outside in the courtyard. Through the window, I saw a small mob of patients smoking as though their very lives depended on it. Had I looked that desperate when I was still a smoker?

Not wanting an answer to that question, I walked to the other end of the room, toward the door we'd all come in through. At that moment, it opened again. Damn. Of all people, the person coming through it was Kurt's wife. The instant she saw me, she stopped cold.

Now what? I hardly knew the woman. We'd crossed paths at company parties and unavoidable social events over the years, but I doubted we'd had a minute of real conversation. Of course, Kurt always did all the talking for both of them. But never mind that. What did I say to her now?

"Hi, Peg."

She nodded. She didn't look hostile, though—just bewildered. I tried again.

"How is he?"

"Better. Thank you."

"Good. Good news. Great to hear."

Awkward silence.

"What are you doing here?" she asked.

"I'm here to see him. Jack, too. But mostly him. I've been out of town, or I'd have—"

"Here," Cassie interrupted, holding up a wad of tissues. "Turn this way." Not waiting for me to oblige, she grabbed my jaw with her free hand and did the turning herself. "Hi, Peg. How are you?"

"How am I?" Peg still looked bewildered. "My husband's in an insane asylum. How should I be?"

Cassie let that pass, intent on blotting up the blood. I stood it for a second and then tried to shake her off, but she wasn't entertaining arguments.

"What happened to her?" Peg asked.

"She banged into one of those pillars in the hall," Cassie answered, rather absently. "I'm thinking about suing the architect for malfeasance. Dammit, Devvy, hold still."

"I'm fine," I protested. "Just a scratch. Listen, Peg, about Kurt...about what happened..."

Peg sighed. "It's not your fault. The doctor said he was already sick. I just wish I'd known it was that bad. Did *you* know it was that bad?"

Cassie tightened her grip on my jaw and leveled a meaningful look at me. I scowled back at her. How stupid did she think I was? "No, I didn't. But it's an ad agency. There's no way to tell when someone's going over the edge."

"I wish he'd gone to medical school," Peg said sadly. "I kept trying to tell him. He got good grades. He wanted to be a psychiatrist once. Did he ever tell you that?"

"Ironic," I agreed.

Peg didn't seem to catch the undertone; she even smiled a little. "I keep telling myself maybe this is a *good* thing. Maybe once he's better, he'll get motivated to do it after all. He'd make the most wonderful psy—Oh, good, here he comes now."

We all turned just as Kurt cleared the double doors. He hadn't seen us yet, which gave us some leisure to study him. Even from a distance, even for a copywriter, even for a copywriter who worked for me, he looked bad. I felt a cold stab of guilt.

"He's looking better," Peg said hopefully.

Cassie and I exchanged glances.

"Why don't you give me a minute with him alone? Then I'll bring him over. OK?"

"Of course," Cassie said.

We watched her hurry off to greet her husband. For a couple of minutes, neither of us said anything.

Finally, Cassie cleared her throat. "What if one of them asks what we had to do with this?"

"We lie," I said flatly.

She laughed. "Lead on, sweetie. I'll follow you anywhere."

The only good thing I can say about that visiting hour is that it lasted less than an hour. Peg eventually brought Kurt over, and we had a little aimless conversation with him. The aimlessness, though, was mostly due to the drugs. Whatever they had him on had flattened him right out; talking to him now was like talking to his half-bright evil twin.

Well, maybe not an identical twin. He still had the cheesy mustache, but there was less of him otherwise; he'd lost a lot of weight. He was also as pale as the underside of a trout. In my opinion, this hospital wasn't doing him any good. And maybe not even he deserved that.

On the other hand, maybe he did.

"You're looking good, Dev," Kurt remarked. "You too, Cass."

Thank you. Deviance agrees with us. "We went to Florida for a week," I said.

He nodded. "I heard. I hear that's where Lisa Hartwell went, too. Remember her, boss? The TV reporter you kissed?"

"She *didn't* kiss her," Cassie growled.

It was a long story—just a misunderstanding about something I did to scare Hartwell when she was being a nuisance in my office. Cassie still wasn't totally over it. Neither was Kurt, apparently, but for very different reasons. "What about her?"

"She was here, you know. They just discharged her a few days ago. She said she was going to Florida as soon as she got out." A tiny smile twitched on his lips. "We all hope an alligator eats her. What a bitch. Nobody could get a word in edgewise in group—not even Jack."

We tried hard to imagine.

"He's not coming down," Kurt added. "He said he doesn't want to see you ever again."

"Mutual," I said, "but impossible. We work together."

That awful I-know-something look settled on his face. It was good to see the Kurt I knew again. But not *that* good. "Not anymore, boss. He's got a new job. Want to know where?"

Cassie was starting to dismiss the subject on the grounds that nobody cared what happened to Jack when a horrible commotion started up across the room. A tall, disheveled man was clearing a path through the lounge, shoving some people out of his way and threatening all the others. It took a few seconds to recognize him.

"That can't be Jack," Cassie insisted. "He's got hair."

Kurt laughed. "Combover. When do you think we get haircuts around here?"

I didn't pay much attention to that, intent on watching Jack's every move. He was clearly not all there, and I wanted time to get between him and Cassie if he got too close. In his condition, she might hurt him.

"He's usually not like this," Peg explained, almost apologetic. "His medication doesn't really agree with him. They'll get the staff guys to take him back upstairs in a—"

"YOU!"

We looked up. Jack was standing about twenty feet away, pointing at us like some vengeful Old Testament lunatic. Everyone else in the room—including the nurse, who was on the phone calling for backup—was frozen like a still life.

Making it look as casual as possible, I stepped around Cassie. "Hello, Jack. How are you feeling?"

He bared his teeth, caps glittering in the fluorescent light. There was a wild, glassy gleam in his eyes. At which point the truth hit me: Jack was all the way out of his mind.

I turned my head slightly and tried to whisper without moving my lips. "Get to the car. Take Peg with you."

"No." For emphasis, she wrapped her arms around my waist.

"*Now*, Cass."

Stubbornly, she held on tighter.

"Idolators!" Jack roared. "Moneychangers! Fornicators!"

Not believing what she was hearing, Cassie leaned around my shoulder. "Moneychangers?"

Kurt, true to form, started laughing. Well, as long as he was feeling better. Warily, I pushed Cassie back. "What's this about, Jack?"

He waved a fist at me. "Abominators!"

"Been watching Sunday morning cable, have you?" I asked coolly.

"You'll burn in hell, Kerry!"

He was going to have to come up with something worse than that. After a few months of wall-to-wall demons, I didn't scare. "I've got lots of sunscreen."

Cassie nudged me, amused. It wasn't really funny, but it stumped Jack long enough for the orderlies to sneak up behind him.

"Think fast, Jack," I advised.

Having held off smiting me as long as he could, he raised his fist again and started forward—but the orderlies pounced. There was a short, vicious struggle. I hated myself for it, but all I could think of was a Monty Python line about the violence inherent in the system. Then a syringe flashed, and Jack went limp.

The orderlies heaved themselves up and stood guard around him, waiting for someone to bring a gurney. Satisfied that Jack was really out, I checked the rest of the room. No one had moved, or possibly even breathed, since the last time I looked.

"You said something about his new job," I prompted Kurt.

"I did, didn't I?" He sounded happy—which I knew was going to mean something bad. "Yes, he does. He has a new job."

Cassie muttered something and let go. "Spit it out, Kurt. Where?"

"It's a very good job. You'll never guess where."

"Don't make her hurt you," Cassie warned, pointing at me. Obligingly, I tried to look fierce.

"Oh, all right," Kurt said cheerfully. "He's going to the Family Foundation. Working for Howard Abner. How do you like that?"

I didn't. The orderlies managed to grab me just before I got to Jack's throat.

6:47 p.m.

"Kicked out of a mental hospital," Cassie said reproachfully as we crossed the parking lot. "Really, Devvy."

"There are worse places to be kicked out of."

"It doesn't look good, honey."

"I'm out of the caring-what-other-people-think business. Besides, so what? I lost my temper. It happens."

"I know. I didn't let them give *you* a shot, did I?"

I shoved my hands in my coat pockets and started walking faster.

"I love you anyway," she said.

"Do you, now?"

"Yes, I do. I can't seem to help it."

Annoyed, I stopped walking. She just laughed, though, and slipped a hand through the crook of my arm. "You promised me Italian, remember?"

I considered sulking a while longer, but it was almost 7, and I was getting hungry. "Where?"

"Surprise me," she suggested.

Surprise you. Frozen pizza at my place would surprise you, wouldn't it? It would just about serve you—

Then I stopped walking again.

"What now?" Cassie asked.

"My car. Look."

She looked. She said a bad word. The MG was gone, and the red Miata was back—the one Monica kept conjuring up whenever she wanted to tempt me. There was no question whose car it was: The front license plate said DEMONLVR.

To verify, I fumbled for my car keys. Sure enough, the MG keys were missing; there were only Miata keys on that part of the ring.

Cassie slammed her purse down on the hood, dug through it for something and bent down at the front bumper.

"What are you doing?" I asked.

"Taking off this stupid license plate. What's on the back?"

I walked around to check. Also DEMONLVR. "You don't want to know."

It was probably best not to tell her about the Darwin fish, either.

Chapter Thirteen

Cassie wanted to go to the most expensive Italian place in town, most likely out of spite, and I wanted to order in. We compromised by going to the most expensive Italian place in town. When had I lost control of this relationship?

"You never had it," she said when I asked.

I studied her narrowly in the candlelight. "You don't see anything wrong with that?"

"No. How about pinot grigio for a change? Or a really *good* Chianti?"

"You're saying this isn't even 50-50?"

Cassie closed the wine list impatiently. "If it were 50-50, I'd still be waiting for you to trip over a clue. Let's call it 70-30, and you're lucky I'm giving you that much."

That was outrageous. With more force than was really necessary, I slammed my menu shut.

"You know you love me," she declared.

Even more outrageous. "I can stop any time. What's with you? You were all right half an hour ago."

"I'm still all right. I'm not fighting with you. I'm just explaining the rules."

"Rules?" I could feel steam starting to leak out my ears. "There are *rules* for this?"

"There are always rules," she said, as though everyone knew that. "We should've had this conversation a long time ago. But now that you bring it up..."

Our waiter chose that moment to come back for our order. One look from me made him jump.

"When we call you," I warned.

Cassie shook her head. "Don't pay any attention to her. She was just in an insane asylum. They had to kick her out; can you believe it? We'll have a bottle—"

"Stop *now*, Cass."

She blithely developed convenient hearing. "—a bottle of your best pinot grigio. And two spinach salads. Then I'll have—"

"Don't order for me. I mean it."

"—the shrimp scampi, and she'll have the—"

We said it together: "—linguine with pesto."

She smiled at me in her most infuriating way. "Write it down," she told the waiter.

He just stood there, looking uncertain. I got the feeling that he wished he could be waiting on anyone else, anywhere else. Not that a person could blame him, the way Cassie was acting.

"Write it down," I grumbled. "And tell the kitchen to put arsenic in my salad."

He wrote it down—I couldn't see whether he got the part about the arsenic—and then fled the scene.

"Problem?" Cassie asked sweetly.

Yes, and I finally knew what. "This is about Monica, isn't it? You were fine till that car showed up."

"You mean the witchmobile?"

That was it, all right. "We've been through this, sweetheart. Over and over and *over*. I'm *done* with her. I'm with you now. Not her. *You*. Why are you so jealous, anyway? It's not like I'm some great prize."

"You can say that again."

There was a moment of hostile silence at our table.

"Well, you always *say* I have terrible taste," Cassie said.

I wasn't in the mood to be humored. "Maybe you're with me because nobody else can put up with you."

"Back at you, sweetie."

Damn. We were probably both right. Cassie was high-maintenance, no question about that, but it wasn't like I'd minded so far. And I couldn't possibly be easy to live with, but she'd been talking about just that pretty much nonstop lately. It was a terrible idea, though. I'd told her a hundred times that moving in together wouldn't work, not in—

The coin finally dropped. We'd spent our nights apart since we'd come back from Kansas City; after two weeks together full-time, I thought we both needed a break. *I'd* needed one, anyway. Just last night I'd put on my oldest, most disreputable clothes; run movies that Cassie didn't like; and had a whole tub of frosting for dinner. It had been great.

"What did you do last night?" I asked.

She hadn't expected that question. "What?"

"What did you do last night? I'm not checking up on you. I'm just curious."

"Last night?" Frowning, she ran back over it. "I took a bubble bath. I think that was the highlight. Why?"

"With the fish or with your rubber duck?"

She looked at me as though I'd finally snapped. "With the duck. I hadn't seen him in a while. Would you mind telling me what this is about?"

"If I'd been there last night, would you have taken a bubble bath?"

"Probably not. You hate them."

"So you got a break too, didn't you?"

Even in the half-dark, I could clearly see the nasty glitter in her eyes as she caught my drift. Just as she was winding up to have at me, the waiter came back with the wine. She sat back and folded her arms tight across her chest as I smiled at him. "Thank you," I said. "Perfect timing."

He didn't follow. "Pardon?"

"Never mind. Go ahead."

But he didn't—and it dawned on me that he wasn't sure which of us to pour for. I surveyed the room. It was all boy–girl couples and a few tables of business dinners, which was what it probably always was. Just Friends didn't go to dinner at places like this. At least, not in Greenville. Damn Cassie anyway.

"She ordered it," I reminded him. "Why don't we let her try it?"

Relieved to have the decision made, he sprang into action. Cassie was still waiting, ominously, so I refused to meet her eye. Instead, I scanned the room again. It was my evil luck to look up when my junior copywriter walked in with whatever she was dating these days. With a glad cry of recognition, she made straight for our table, pulling her date in her wake.

"What?" Cassie asked.

"Heather."

She scowled at me as though it were my fault.

"Public place," I pointed out.

She weighed the pleasure of making a scene against the possibility of clients in the restaurant. Business won—but she kicked me under the table to let me know it wasn't over.

There are many ways to get even. The way I chose was inviting Heather and her date to join us for dinner.

There was no conversation on the drive back to Cassie's house. Unnerved by the quiet, I grabbed the first CD that came to hand—the "Drew Carey" soundtrack—and stuck it in the player. I sang along with "Five O'Clock World" until the line about the long-haired girl who waits. Cassie gave me a look with so many sharp edges on it that I ejected the disc.

We proceeded in lethal silence for a few blocks. By the next red light, I couldn't stand it anymore. "I'd rather you yell, Cass."

"I bet you would."

Normally, I'd have followed up on that, but the stress of yet another in a string of long, weird days was catching up, and I didn't have the energy. The best thing was to drop her off, go home and get some sleep; we'd have it out sooner or later, and there was no point in doing it tonight. That decided, I waited in silence for the light to change.

Out of habit, I checked the rearview mirror to see where the car behind me was. I'd learned the hard way that a driver who gets right on your back bumper might drive into your backseat if you're a second too slow on green. Also, I half-expected to see glittering red eyes right behind me—one of Monica's favorite tricks—and was almost disappointed when I didn't.

Beside me, Cassie cleared her throat. "Green light."

I almost told her that I didn't need a co-pilot, but her tone made me think twice. Not worth getting into at this hour anyway; whatever was wrong with her, maybe a good night's sleep would cure it.

After we'd been parked in the driveway for a few minutes, I felt the need to speak. "This is it. We're here. You're home."

No answer. She just sat there as though she'd sat there for all eternity and planned to keep it up.

"You can get out any time."

Nothing.

"Cassie, sweetheart, I love you, I do, but you're making me crazy. Can we just say goodnight now so I can go home?"

"We were going to discuss rules," she said abruptly.

Fantastic. *Now* she felt like talking. But it was progress. To be a good sport, I switched off the engine.

"Then you invited them to have dinner with us."

"What could I do?" I protested. "They were standing right there."

Cassie seemed not to hear or, if she heard, to care. "That made it even worse. We were already having a bad date, and then Heather comes along on her bad date and we all have a bad date together. When you *knew* I wanted to talk to you."

"I didn't *know* any such thing. You were in a bad mood. I figured you were just taking it out on me."

"Rule No. 1," she snapped. "No 'figuring.'"

"Fine. But what—"

"Rule No. 2. No interrupting during the rules."

"Should I be writing this down?" I asked, getting impatient.

"Rule No. 3. I want you to move in with me."

She was a real piece of work. "We keep having this conversation. Why is that? I keep telling you—"

"There'll be other rules, but these should do for a start. Are you coming in?"

There were a million reasons not to, not the least of which was that she'd been hell on wheels most of the evening. But then she added one word: "Please?"

At long last, I got it. She was mad at me because she'd missed me.

Truth was, I'd missed her, too. No matter what my head said—and it was talking VERY LOUDLY about payback—my treacherous heart didn't want to be anywhere else.

Without comment, I opened the car door. Cassie got out her side. We met at the front bumper and had a little make-up hug...which got out of hand almost right away, right there in the driveway. It seemed that we really *had* missed each other.

"One more rule," she murmured.

"What?"

"The car goes."

It wasn't like I could take it back to the dealership, was it? "I'll change the license plate, dammit. Now *drop* it. Are we going to stand out here all night, or what?"

Cassie opted for what. I'd had worse sleepless nights.

Chapter Fourteen

The little red demonmobile was still in Cassie's driveway the next morning, so I drove it to work, not that I had a choice. But first thing at the office, I was calling a car dealer. Maybe this particular temptation would stop if I broke down and bought my own Miata.

Cassie, of course, thought that was a fabulous idea. She thought a Volvo would be even more fabulous, but I reminded her whose decision it was—and whose bank account.

"For now," she'd said.

Wincing at the memory of the conversation that had followed, I took one hand off the wheel to rub my aching head. She'd claimed that she was only joking, but I hadn't believed her. Still didn't. Whatever was wrong with her was getting worse, and if she made one more crack like that, I was going to lose my mind. After six years, how could she drive me this crazy in only a month?

A month. I practically rear-ended a pickup as the awful truth dawned. Damn, damn, damn. Half-watching traffic, I fumbled in my attaché for the cell phone and speed-dialed.

Cassie answered on the first ring. "Devvy?"

I almost hit the pickup again. "How did you know that?"

"Lucky guess. Wait—I've got to change lanes." A terrible squealing of tires came through, and I had to hold the phone away from my ear. "OK, I'm back. What's up?"

"That's what *I* want to know," I growled. "You've been all over my case all week. Does this have anything to do with a one-month anniversary that you think I'm going to forget?"

"What makes you say that?" she asked, all innocence.

Silence on the line for a few seconds.

"Cass?"

"Yes?"

"You know I think this sort of thing is stupid."

Her voice softened perceptibly. "I know."

"Exactly how stupid do you want to get about it? Is just the day OK, or do you want to get down to the actual hour?"

"Why?"

"Because I want to do this right," I said grimly.

Cassie laughed. "Wait a minute."

"What for?"

No answer except for more screeching-tire noises. A little annoyed, I held the phone away again and waited.

Then a black BMW pulled up on my left, honking frantically. As soon as I looked over, Cassie rolled down her passenger window.

"You! In the little car!" she shouted.

Furtively, I checked traffic. People were looking. I decided to pretend I didn't know her.

"Hey! Cutie! Sugarplum!"

I was going to kill her. "We have cell phones," I reminded her over mine. "If you have something to say to me, say it privately."

She held hers up with an evil smile, punching at it with one finger, and the connection went dead. Not amused, I switched off my own phone, threw it on the floorboard and rolled down the window.

"What?" I shouted.

"I love you!"

People were slowing down to get a better look, and most of them were laughing. I gave everyone I could a very ratty look back, making sure to watch the road once in a while.

"Poooookie! I loooooove yooooooou!"

That did it. Checking traffic first, I leaned out the window. "I love you too! And you're *fantastic* in bed!"

The shock on her face was worth the laughter in the other cars. Without even bothering to roll her window up, she hit the gas and got out of there as fast as she could—which was really fast, the way she drove.

I'd make it up to her at some point. Probably. But God, that had been fun.

The fun didn't last, of course. As soon as I got off the elevator, Heather pounced on me—literally, almost spilling my coffee.

"There's someone in your office," she reported.

What else was new? There was *always* someone in my office, usually when I didn't want to see them. "So?"

"But nobody's in there."

Frowning, I rubbed my temples again. This was already shaping up to be a bear of a day. "You can't have it both ways, Heather. Are you feeling all right?"

She tapped her foot impatiently, thinking. Then she grabbed my coat sleeve and yanked. "Come on—I'll show you."

I shook her off but let her lead the way. When we reached my office, she threw open the door and jumped back as though something might fly out.

"It's supposed to be locked," I told her. "How did you get in?"

"It was open."

I mentally penciled in a call to Rita Sanchez. The cleaning people were getting lazy about this sort of thing; she might want to look into changing contractors. In fact, I'd call her right away, before either of us got distracted by the first crisis of the day.

But Heather pulled me back before I got all the way over the threshold. "Are you *crazy?* There's something in there!"

Pointedly, I tugged my coat loose and went on in, tossing my attaché in one of the guest chairs and surveying the room. Nothing under the desk, nothing behind the chair, nothing curled up and hissing in a corner.

"It was sitting in your chair," Heather insisted from the safety of the doorway.

"'It'?"

"It was reading your mail, Dev. I saw it."

An unpleasant possibility crossed my mind. "What did you see?"

"Well, nothing. There was nothing there. Just the papers moving around. And then..."

"Then?"

"Then it started laughing." She shuddered. "It was awful. Like scratching on a blackboard or something."

What was it Cassie had said once? "Or cats in heat?"

Heather perked up considerably. "Yes! Like cats in heat scratching a blackboard. It was really—" Then it dawned on her. "Wait. You've heard it?"

No point explaining, now or ever. "A few times. Usually late at night, when I've been working too hard. Dr. Shapiro says it's stress." With a grave expression, I pretended to study her face. "You may be coming down with it, too. It's been a tough few weeks around here."

She didn't look convinced. "Well, yes, but—"

"And there was last night, too. That *Dave* person. He can't have helped."

"No," she admitted. "He didn't."

"So I think you should take the day off. Hallucinations aren't good. And we've had too much of that going around. Look at Jack and Kurt."

Heather went pale. "You don't mean...?"

I shrugged. "Hard to say. But I don't think you'd be happy in the bin. Did you know they have dinner at 5 there?"

"You're kidding."

"Nope. They do group hugs, too. Peg was trying to tell me they read Inspiring Thoughts for the Day out loud after breakfast, but that sounded too cruel, so—"

"I'm out of here," she said sharply. "I'm going to go home and lie down. I don't feel so good. Are you sure you don't need me for anything?"

"Not till tomorrow. Go home."

She bolted. The last I saw of her, she was shoving one of Walt's artists out of her way in the hall, and by the thud he made hitting the wall, she meant business.

Oh, well, she probably needed a day off anyway. I'd have to take up the slack for her if anything came up, but it beat telling the truth—let alone losing one more copywriter to the shrinks.

Resigned, I hung up my coat and settled in at my desk to check e-mail. In the very next instant, a bad Presence loomed over my shoulder.

"Cats in heat?" the Presence asked menacingly.

"I was quoting. What do you want now?"

"Want?" Monica's tone turned suspiciously sweet. "Really, Devlin." She settled on the arm of my chair, with a little smile that matched the tone. "What makes you think I want something?"

"If you're breathing, you want something."

"Then this should be familiar. How *is* the irritating blonde?"

It came out before I thought. "Irritating."

"Yes. That was my guess." A set of long, sharp talons started to play in my hair. "She's trying to close the sale. It would be more honest if she just put a ring through your nose."

"Cut that out," I demanded, pushing her hand away. "And don't try to make trouble. Everything's fine."

"Is it? I thought she loooooooved you."

"She does. It's mutual."

"You both have an interesting way of showing it."

"Why? Because we argue? Because she's a little possessive?"

Monica laughed—and I did hear something feline in it this time.

"It's just how we work this relationship," I told her. "This is how it was before. It works for us. We don't want things to get all sentimental."

"Horrors," Monica said mockingly, and reached down to rake her claws through my hair again.

This time, I threw her off so hard that she nearly went over the chair arm. "You were going to tell me what you want. Tell me, and then get out."

"You don't trust me."

I greeted that remark with the silence it deserved.

"All right, never mind," she said, a little sulkily. "I'm here to do you a favor. Do you remember my offer?"

"What offer?"

"You're headed for trouble, Devlin." She leaned forward a little too far, and I had to forcibly remind myself not to notice the cleavage. "But I can still make it all go away."

"Tell you what," I said coolly. "You just make yourself go away, and we'll have a deal."

Monica just laughed again. "That ring through the nose will be very attractive. I'm sure your family will admire it. You *are* taking her home for Christmas, aren't you? Planning to explain her?"

There was no explaining Cassie. And there was no point in having this discussion, either. Irritated, I got up and started to leave the office.

"The offer stands," Monica said. "I'll be around when you change your mind. In fact, I'll be right here. I *am* your admin now, you know."

That stopped me.

"Of course, I'm having a stress problem," she added. "I'll need to take the rest of the day off. With pay."

"Fine. Just go," I snapped.

She vanished from the chair arm and materialized in front of me—much too close. "Let me leave you with one thought, Devlin. You haven't *seen* fantastic in bed yet."

It was my turn to bolt out of the office. The artist Heather had shoved into the wall was blocking the hallway again, rubbing his head; I shoved him into the opposite wall and kept going.

Just to be safe, I spent the rest of the morning down in Video. And I made an intern check my office before I went back up.

Late that afternoon, someone knocked.

"Go away," I said, intent on a rewrite.

The intruder knocked again. Annoyed, I swiveled around toward the door. "Who is it?"

"Land Shark," a muffled voice said.

Against my will, I smiled a little. Too bad "Saturday Night Live" was no good anymore. "It's open."

The door opened, and I couldn't see who or what came in, because it was carrying an enormous bouquet of snapdragons. Surprised, I got up to help.

"Thanks," the courier said. "Should've brought this up on a dolly. Where do you want it?"

Good question. There wasn't a square inch of clear space on my desk. "The credenza, I guess. Over here. Watch out for the coffeemaker."

We managed to set the thing down without damage. Then we just stood there, staring at it.

The courier shook his head. "That's a load of flowers. What did you do?"

"I have no idea. Is there a card?"

"I'm not looking through all that," he informed me. "Have a nice day."

I waited for him to leave and then started poking through the arrangement with a letter opener. Finally, a little white envelope fell out. I opened it and read the card.

> *You're not half-bad yourself, sweetie. Dinner at 7?*
> *C*

Well, it was her version of an apology. I had a feeling that dinner could be arranged.

But we were going to have a little talk about nose jewelry, just in case she *really* had any ideas.

Chapter Fifteen

December

Several bad things happened the very first Monday of December:

- Kurt came back to work part-time.
- My mother called.
- Cassie's sister called.
- My mother called again.

Kurt was the easy part. He was still on heavy meds, so he wasn't up to being much trouble yet. I gave him bunny shots to start with—a new spot in an existing series, a couple of rewrites, a make-good for Walt's team—and pretty much left him alone after that. If he continued to be a good boy, I'd let him run another audition soon. If not...well, there'd be another Kester Mortuaries spot to write. Or I could give him Cassie's father's bank's account. That would teach *both* of them not to cross me.

But my mother was another story. She always was.

I was in a meeting when she called the first time. After that, I went straight to another meeting, so I missed the second call, too. It wasn't till lunch that I finally got the message—on Cassie's pager.

"It's for you," she said, handing it across the table.

I squinted at the tiny display. HAVE DEV CALL URGENT R SANCHEZ. What could be urgent? Jenner was still home in bed. Jack was still locked up. Kurt was under sedation. Monica hadn't been back, and neither had Vanessa. But Sanchez wasn't the type to panic, so if she said it was urgent... "Borrow your phone?"

She was already dialing. "You know, Devvy, the whole point of having a cell phone is always having it with you, so people can reach you."

"Exactly."

She laughed and gave me the phone.

"Rita? It's Dev. What's up?"

Those were the last words I got in edgewise in that call. Sanchez's voice kept rising and getting louder as she explained the situation, and by the time she read back the last message, she was almost shrieking. Then she hung up. Just like that.

I listened to the dead air in solemn contemplation for a few seconds before I hung up, too.

"She was yelling, wasn't she?" Cassie asked. "I heard it all the way over here. What happened?"

"Mom called."

Sympathetically, she reached across the table to squeeze my hand.

"Five times," I added. "The receptionists got scared after the second time and started transferring her to Sanchez."

Cassie frowned. "Is something wrong?"

"Not with Mom. Sanchez is going to need rehab, though." Unhappily, I dug in my purse for the Advil. "Go ahead and start without me when the food comes. I'll go outside to call her back. No point in both of us suffering."

"It's snowing outside, sweetie."

"Then that's the perfect place to do this. It'll be just like a Russian novel."

"You're cute when you're paranoid, you know that?"

"I'm not cute." I took one Advil, considered, and took another. "Be right back."

But Cassie locked both her feet around mine under the table. "Stay put. We're in this together."

"You don't know her."

"After everything we've already been through," she said, half-annoyed, half-amused, "I think I can cope with one little mother. How bad can she be?"

Where would I start explaining? "All right. It's your funeral." I started punching in the number. "Give me your phone bill next month, and I'll pay for this."

"Forget it. My treat."

I would have argued that "trick" was more like it, but the phone picked up at the other end. "Mom?"

Then I listened. For a long time. She gave me about a minute and a half on the indignity of not being able to reach one's own daughter at will, followed by a couple of minutes on the perfidy of said daughter, followed by a long recap of our conversation when I'd told her I wasn't coming home for Thanksgiving, and it could have gone on for hours, except that I would need more Advil. "Mom? I'm kind of busy here. Can you get to what you wanted to talk to me about?"

Across the table, Cassie winced at the volume of the reply. *In this together, are we?* Smiling very faintly, I beckoned her closer and held the phone between us.

"—Christmas, at least. You could at *least* have taken the time to call your own mother and tell her when to expect you, not to mention that your Aunt Kitty keeps asking, but if you're too *busy* to make a phone call—"

This time, I said it loud. "Mom. Stop. Breathe. *Now.*"

The silence on her end was brief but indignant. "You're just like your brothers. Insolent as the day is long, all of you. Your father will be very interested in hearing about this conversation."

"Well, when you talk to Dad, be sure to tell him I said hi," I replied, trying to sound cheerful. "Now just let me say this, OK? I haven't called you about Christmas yet because I don't know my schedule yet. We've got people out sick, and I'm having to cover for them. But I think I can get away by the 23rd, so—"

"You're management," Mom said frostily. "That's what you have employees for."

Cassie almost started laughing; not finding that funny, I pulled back enough to scowl at her. "You brought me up to work hard, remember?"

The shot didn't even slow her down. "I *also* brought you up to be part of this family. Christmas is not optional, Devlin."

"Never said it was. I'll be there. Promise."

"Don't get sarcastic with me, young lady."

"I'm not being sarcastic. I mean it. When are Connor and Ryan coming home?"

"I don't know," she said peevishly. "Their wives haven't *told* them yet. At least you don't have that excuse."

I was about to agree when Cassie moved slightly and put a small kiss on my temple. Damn, and in front of a whole restaurant full of strangers, too.

"Devlin? Are you there?"

"I'm here." Cautiously, I looked around. No one seemed to have noticed. In fact, most of the other customers were busy on their own cell phones. Sometime, I'd have to worry what that said about us. "Listen, Mom, what if I bring someone home with me this year?"

Stunned silence. "Not a man," she warned.

Cassie snorted; I had to smile myself. "No. She's not a man." Most definitely not. "You remember my friend Cassie? You met her about a year ago."

"The blonde girl? She had too much lipstick on. And that blouse! It showed *everything.* Does her mother know how she dresses?"

Now Cassie was indignant, and it was all I could do to keep her from grabbing the phone away. "Since when are you the fashion police, Mother? I've *seen* that ratty old bathrobe of yours."

"We're not discussing me," she said in offended dignity.

"Well, that's a nice change. Now listen—Cassie's spending Christmas with me this year. That part's not open for discussion. We can come visit you and have a nice Christmas, or we can stay here and have a *very* nice Christmas. Your call. What do you say?"

She didn't say anything.

"Mom?"

Still nothing. Cassie leaned close again, the better to hear.

"She can stay in my old room. I'll sleep on the sleeper sofa. It won't be a big deal. All right?"

Finally, my mother sighed. "I hope she's not one of those people who have to have turkey at Christmas. *We* always have ham. I'm not changing the menu."

"No one's asking you to. Why don't—"

"I have to go," she lied. "Call me later."

Then she hung up. Cassie and I waited to make sure she was really gone before we sat back. By her expression, Cassie was starting to rethink the holiday thing.

"She's not always like this," I said reassuringly. "Sometimes, she's worse."

Cassie smiled, but with very little enthusiasm. Fortunately, the waitress showed up with our lunches then.

"Sorry it took a while," the waitress said, "but I heard the word 'Mother' while you were on the phone, and I figured it was trouble of some kind."

She didn't know the half of it. But she made Cassie laugh, which was going to earn her a huge tip from me.

True, it set a dangerous precedent; if I was going to have to pay people to make Cassie laugh this Christmas, it was going to get expensive. But I loved her, and it was only money.

God, I hoped Mom couldn't hear that thought. The part about the money, anyway.

On the way back to the office, I bought Sanchez a make-up present.

She peered into the bag, looking doubtful. "What is it?"

"A Ping-Pong gun," I said. "You load it up with Ping-Pong balls, and then you can shoot at things. I keep one in the living room so I can shoot the TV whenever Martha Stewart comes on."

Sanchez, who was no fan of the woman's, smiled just a little. "Or Kathie Lee Gifford?"

"You need a cruise missile for that. C'mon, Sanchez, open it. You know you want to."

"Well..." Gingerly, she peeled off the bubble packaging. "I suppose it can't hurt. Mr. Jenner should be back in a couple of weeks."

"And if you practice now, you can nail him in the forehead every time you try."

"No, I mean I'll give it to him to play with. It might keep him out of trouble for a whole morning."

"Optimist," I told her. "Have a nice day."

Halfway to the door, I got a Ping-Pong ball in the back. Sanchez was smiling serenely, still pointing the gun.

"Practice," she explained. "Thank you, Dev."

"You're welcome. But you'd better not let Cassie find out you did that. She'd turn you into kibble."

"No, she won't. She owes me now."

"Owes you for what?"

"I promised to have the switchboard hang up the next time your mother calls."

Whatever the agency paid Sanchez, it wasn't enough. We *both* owed her for that.

All afternoon, the snow kept falling. Cassie was out in it, calling on clients, and even though she was a grown woman with snow tires, I couldn't help worrying. For a city in the Snow Belt, Meridian was hopeless when it came to snow removal. One winter, the mayor decided that plowing would only make the streets worse. That policy lasted one snowfall. On Election Day, only his wife voted for him, and there were rumors that she'd tried to take it back later.

Finally, after I'd checked out the window for the hundredth time, I reached for the phone. Yes, she had her cell phone; yes, she was capable of calling someone if she needed help. But what if I'd run down the battery at lunch, dealing with my mother? Or what if she'd gotten stuck in a drift and bears had broken into her car with coat hangers and eaten her before she could call AAA?

Well, all right, that last one was a long shot, but I'd feel worse if I didn't do something. Just as I touched the phone, it rang, and I answered without thinking. "Cass?"

"Close. It's Lucy."

"Lucy as in Lucy her sister?"

"Gee, she's right—you *are* smart. How are you?"

"Fine." Impatient, I stood up to look out the window again. Still snowing. "You?"

"Well, I'm married to Michael, but other than that, I can't complain."

So much for small talk. "What can I do for you? I'm sort of busy, so—"

"Too busy to talk to me? Really? Are you sure?"

I counted to thirty. This was her sister, whom I was bound by honor to love, but no law said I had to like her all the time.

"Dev?"

"Still here."

"Oh, all right, if you don't want to chitchat, your loss. I called to ask you what you're getting her for Christmas."

"Why?"

"You don't want to make a mistake, do you?"

No, as a matter of fact, I didn't. Christmas paybacks could be vicious. There'd been the year when Kurt gave Peg nothing but small kitchen appliances, and I could still make him jump just by saying the words "Salad Shooter." Not that I was fool enough to try something like that on Cassie. "I'd rather not. What do you suggest?"

"Jewelry's always nice," Lucy said, much too casually.

"She *has* jewelry. I was thinking maybe an MP3 player, or one of those—"

"Dev?"

"What?"

"Are you a complete idiot?"

"I must be; I'm still talking to you. Are you getting at what I think you're getting at?"

"What do you think I'm getting at?"

Be nice. She'll be her sister all her life. "We're not doing that, Lucy. We're not even living together. So before you start spending three months of my salary, forget it."

"I think three months is just a guideline," she mused. "You don't have to spend that much. As long as it's nice, and she likes it..."

"No."

"What you might want to do is get a loaner to put in the box. After Christmas, she can go pick out the one she really wants."

"*No.* Are we done here?"

"You love her. I can tell," Lucy said, untroubled by my tone. "You were hoping it was her on the phone just now. So if you love her—"

"Don't *you* start with that."

"Gotta run. The kids say hi. Remember: Three months is a guideline." *Click.*

I slammed the phone down and put my head in my hands. When the phone rang again thirty seconds later, I hit the speakerphone button without looking up. "Kerry."

"Is that any way to answer the phone at work?" my mother scolded.

Defeated, I slumped all the way over on the desktop, hitting it with a thud.

"Hello? Hello? What was that noise? Devlin?"

"You weren't supposed to get through," I mumbled. "They were supposed to cut you off at the switchboard."

"They did. I disguised my voice this time."

There was nothing I could say to that to make myself feel better. Silently, I waited for her to get on with it. Before she did, though, the office door swung open, and Cassie walked in.

Ahhh. That was better. I gave her what must have been a very goofy smile.

"You're lying on your desk," she observed. "Is there anything I should know?"

The speakerphone squawked a little. "Devlin? Who is that?"

I closed my eyes. "It's Cassie. She just came in. What can I do for you this time, Mom?"

"Call me later," she said quickly. *Click.*

The dial tone hummed for a while. Finally, I felt Cassie bend over me to hang up the phone.

"I was worried about you," I told her, eyes still closed. "It's snowing. Did you see any bears?"

"Bears?"

"Never mind."

"You know, we could go to the beach for Christmas," Cassie remarked, settling on my chair arm. "It's not like we have to spend *every* holiday with our families. We're grownups, after all." She reached over and started massaging the back of my neck. "What do you think?"

"You're not weaseling out of this. I had to do it. Now it's your turn."

"I'll give you one of these every night for a month," she bargained.

"Too late, Cass."

She said a bad word not quite under her breath but kept rubbing. That was much, much better. When the phone rang again, I knocked it all the way off the desk.

"It's almost 5," she said. "Let's cut out early. Want to pick up Greek? I've still got some ouzo."

"Perfect."

"You have to get up first," she added.

Reluctantly, I did. On the way to the coat rack, I heard tires squealing in the parking lot and idly looked out the window.

Cassie heard, too, and came over to see. "What in hell...?"

"Right," I said glumly, pointing.

Vanessa was doing doughnuts in the parking lot in her red BMW, with the top down, spraying snow everywhere. She looked like she was having the time of her life. I didn't know what she was up to, but then, I really didn't want to know.

"We'll sneak out the back way," Cassie declared. "And we'll take *my* car."

Chapter Sixteen

Cassie's clock radio woke us, completely against our will. She groaned and tried to pull all the covers and both pillows over her head. I could relate; I just couldn't remember what freight train had hit us. God, there were a lot of pieces missing from last night.

"'S all right," I told her. "Got it."

She gave up her futile effort with the covers and flopped back down. Unable to open my eyes all the way, I felt for the radio, found the snooze button and smacked it with genuine hatred. Then we went back to sleep.

For eight minutes.

"Give you a thousand dollars to turn it off," she mumbled.

No charge. If she felt anything like I felt, neither of us had any business waking up anyway. But we had meetings. So I shut off the alarm and scraped myself out of bed. Cassie probably would be all right by herself for a while, and if not...well, it had been her idea and her ouzo last night.

Pulling my robe off the footboard, I threw it on and staggered to the bath. Every step made my skull hurt. Why? We hadn't had *that* much ouzo. Maybe it had been the food. We might've gotten hold of bad grape leaves or toxic lamb or something.

Yeah, that was probably it.

I switched on the bathroom light and almost howled in pain as my eyeballs tried to explode. Not good. Between that and the red-hot knives in the brain, I might not live long enough to call an ambulance. Not that it mattered, because I couldn't even remember the number for 911.

Gripping the towel bar on the shower door for support, I waited till the world stopped spinning and then felt blindly for the faucets. With my remaining strength, I turned on the cold water full blast and got in the shower, robe and all. It felt great. By comparison, anyway.

It took a while to realize that someone was hammering on the shower door.

"If you're Norman Bates, forget it. I'm already dead."

Cassie wasn't in the mood for Hitchcock jokes; she slammed the door open and waited for me to turn the water off.

"Can I help you?" I asked politely.

"Phone."

"For me? Here?" Frowning, I pushed wet hair out of my eyes. "Who is it?"

"It *sounds* like your mother trying to disguise her voice. Either that or a sick rhinoceros."

A better person would have objected to that crack, but Mom had sinus problems from decades of smoking, and she *did* sound a little rhinocerosy first thing in the morning. Rhinocerosy? Rhinocerish? Rhinoceresque? Oh, to hell with it. "What does she want?"

"I don't know." Cassie grabbed a towel off the rack and shoved it at me. "You still have your robe on."

"My eyeballs were going to explode," I explained. "There wasn't time to take it off."

She clearly wanted to have words about that, but then she remembered the open line in the bedroom. *'Do* let me watch it for you while you speak to your mother. Did I mention that she's on the phone? Right *now?!?"*

Grumbling under my breath, I stripped off the robe, wrapped up in the towel and abandoned the field. The phone was in the middle of the bed, upside down; I stared at it for a while with misgivings before picking it up. "Mom?"

"You were supposed to call me back last night," she snapped.

"Good morning to you, too, Mother. Lovely to hear from you. How did you get this number?"

"A very nice girl at your office gave it to me yesterday. Vanna or Vera or someone. She said if I called early this morning, I'd find you here."

Damn Vanessa. "Did she, now?"

"Would you care to explain that?"

"No. But thanks for asking. Now, what's so important that you had to call about?"

"You sound feverish," she said suspiciously. "Are you running a fever?"

"I wouldn't be surprised. Is that all you wanted? I have to get ready for work, and—"

"I want to talk to you about Christmas."

"All right. We'll do that. But we really can't do it right this minute. What if I call you back tonight?"

"You *said* you were going to call *last* night."

A warm hand tilted my head up. Cassie was holding a glass of water and a couple of Excedrin—the kind for migraines. Wonderful timing. Covering the mouthpiece with one hand, I raised up off the bed just high enough to kiss her. "Sorry, Mom. What was that again?"

"You said you'd call last night, and you didn't. I raised you better than that, you know."

I took the first caplet before answering. "Reared. Not raised."

"It's informal conversation," she said frostily.

Good. This would derail her. Feeling a bit more hopeful, I took the second cap. "But that's what you always told us. *'Raised* is for crops. *Reared* is for children. *Kids* are young goats, not—'"

"Watch your tone; I'm your mother. And call me later. I mean it this time."

Then she hung up.

"All clear," I told Cassie.

She sighed and sat down next to me. "About Christmas, Devvy..."

"Don't even start that. You're going."

"I know, I know. You can't blame me for asking, though."

I couldn't. But it was a comfort to know that this year, I'd be going in with backup.

It would be fair to say that neither of us was at her best that morning. Even Cassie, who was fairly bulletproof that way, rescheduled her client calls and all but one meeting; she didn't think she could be nice for more than an hour. Frankly, I had doubts about even an hour. On the drive in to work, we heard those dogs barking "Jingle Bells" on the radio, and she hit the off button so hard that the whole radio nearly went through the dash.

Exactly how I felt about that one. Still, I thought I'd stay out of her line of fire, just in case she forgot she loved me. We had to do a meeting together first thing, but it would be short. And after that, we could take out our mood on everybody else for the rest of the day.

Partly appeased by that prospect, I went to my office to go over some paperwork before the client got there. No sooner had I walked in than Monica materialized on the edge of the desk.

My reflexes were too impaired for me to react in any way. Without comment, I surveyed her idea of a business suit.

She shrugged. "You should see what Vanessa's wearing."

"Vanessa isn't my problem. Are you here to work? Or just to torment me?"

"I don't know yet." Thoughtfully, she examined me. "I hate to admit it, but it might not be much fun tormenting you today. You don't look well."

"I don't know how I could be *expected* to be. First my mother; then you. And now I have to go see a man about a dog food account. *Dog food.* Do you know what's in that stuff?"

She crossed herself.

"Is that supposed to be a joke?"

"Really, Devlin. Just because I'm a demon doesn't mean I want to hear about cow parts."

"Cow lips," I said darkly. "And pig lips. And lungs and hearts and ears and—"

"There are cultures that eat dogs. Everything's relative."

I didn't want to talk about it anymore. "Go away, Monica."

Obligingly, she parked herself behind my desk and made herself at home.

"I'm serious," I growled. "You're starting to wear out your welcome. Weren't you supposed to go away after Cassie outed me?"

"I did. I got bored. I came back."

"Can you do that?"

It was a stupid question; her eyes started glittering in a particularly nasty way. "I can do anything I want. Besides, you're not as out as you think you are. All bets are still on. I can still make your life *unbelievably* interesting."

"Don't threaten me. Vanessa checkmates you, remember?"

"She's an idiot."

"Yes, but she's *our* idiot."

Monica didn't say anything to that. I took advantage of the temporary peace to start the coffeemaker. Maybe if I just stuck my tongue under the drip, the caffeine would get into my system faster.

The local line rang. And rang. And rang.

"If you're going to pretend to be my admin," I told her, "you can start by answering the phone."

Monica made a point of swiveling the chair around, turning her back on it. Muttering, I went over to pick it up. "Kerry."

"Wolfe."

Trouble of some kind, by her tone. "What's up?"

"I have demons. Do you have demons?"

I glowered at the chair back. "Yes."

"Mine wants to go to the meeting with us. Do you know what she's wearing?"

"Do I have to?"

Brief, aggravated silence. "We're coming up."

"Fine, but—"

Before I could finish the sentence, Vanessa popped in out of thin air. I dropped the receiver. She was dressed up in a Catholic-schoolgirl uniform, but wearing it in a way that it was never meant to be worn.

"I told you," Monica said sulkily, returning to her perch on the edge of the desk. "She looks like a secondhand virgin."

Vanessa tossed her head. "Oh, tut. You're just jealous because I look so cute in plaid. What do you think, Devlin? Do you like the kneesocks? Should I button the shirt just a little?"

I wasn't fool enough to answer a question like that. Fortunately, Cassie stormed in just then. She didn't seem to be armed, but I had no trouble picturing her with a really big stick—or, say, a couple of knives.

"There are no exorcists in the phone book," she said direly, glaring at the demons. "I just looked. But as soon as this meeting is over, I'm getting on the Internet. You two want to keep your broomsticks handy."

Vanessa hopped up on the edge of the desk next to Monica and leaned close to speak confidentially. "Hangover."

"I could cure that by taking her head off," Monica remarked.

That was a point. But Cassie was glaring at me now, so I had to do something about it. "Don't even think about touching her," I warned. "She's in a really bad mood."

Cassie yanked me close for private speech. *"You're* supposed to threaten her."

"I just did."

Uncertain whether that was a compliment, she loosened her grip slightly.

"C'mon, Cass, let go. Let's leave this for later. How about tomorrow? It'll be more fun when we feel better."

"I feel fine," she lied.

I checked my watch. We were going to be late if we didn't go now. Time to distract her. "I love you."

She didn't look distracted, but she didn't look like she minded either. "Are you up to something?"

"Yes," I said, and leaned in to kiss her.

But she foiled the plan by kissing back, which had the effect of distracting *me.* So I didn't see the men in the doorway until long after they'd seen us—*and* the demons perched on my desk.

Howard Abner looked as though he'd been hit on the head with one of those cartoon anvils. Jack was a professional, though; he didn't even blink.

"That's them, Howard," he said earnestly. "All of them. They're the Devil."

Chapter Seventeen

Jack said "the Devil," and everyone—*everyone*—looked at me. I didn't appreciate it. There were actual demons in the room, so how was that fair?

"No horns; no hooves. Knock it off," I demanded.

Caught, Cassie patted my shoulder in apology. Then she turned on the intruders in the doorway. "Why aren't you locked up, Jack?"

He started to answer, but Abner intervened. "Don't speak to them directly. Don't try to dialogue with Satan. Let me handle this."

I couldn't believe it. "Dialogue with?" Who taught him English? A cow? "*Dialogue* with?"

Abner ignored that. "Don't look at them directly, either."

"Oh, for crying out loud," Vanessa complained. "And I went to all this trouble to look so *cute* today."

I just managed to grab Cassie's sleeve in time. "If we're not talking and looking, Jethro, how are we going to communicate here?"

"Wait outside, Harper," Abner said importantly, reaching into his coat. Something metal flashed under the fluorescent lights. A gun? A knife?

Acting on sheer instinct, I shoved Cassie out of the way and threw myself over her. The last thing I saw before we hit the floor was Monica raising her arm, an exquisitely bored expression on her face. Then there was a flash of very bright light, followed by a weird crackling sound.

"Stay down," I warned Cassie.

She muttered something vaguely threatening and tried to push me out of her way. Intent on staying between her and whatever was going on, whether she liked it or not, I didn't even bother to check what had happened to Abner until she froze, staring over my shoulder.

I blinked a few times, certain that I couldn't be seeing what I was seeing. But it was no good.

Monica still looked bored; Vanessa was rolling her eyes.

"Wh...? Wh...?" Frustrated, I waited a few seconds for my language skills to kick in again. "What *is* that?"

"Salt," Vanessa said.

"*Salt?*"

"As in a pillar of. Trite, huh?"

"I was making a statement," Monica protested, with heat.

Vanessa snorted. "What statement? That you don't have any imagination? Turning people into pillars of salt is so thirty centuries ago."

"What else were we going to do with him? Turn him into a newt?"

Cassie's demon seriously considered the question. I was really interested in hearing the answer, but Cassie snapped out of it just then and grabbed my collar hard. "Tell me I'm dreaming, Devvy. Tell me it's the ouzo."

"It probably *is* the ouzo, but you're awake." As gently as possible, I pried her loose. "He's a pillar of salt. What do we think? Do we like it?"

She thought about it. "We don't hate it. Where's Jack?"

"Hiding behind the door," Monica said. She flicked a talon in that direction, and the door swung shut, revealing Jack pressed flat against the wall. He tried to squirm the rest of the way through it. "What would amuse you, Devlin? I could turn him into a pillar of pepper, if you like."

The symmetry of that appealed to me. The cleaning people would have an awful mess to sweep up that night, and they'd surely ask questions. But if my demon could go around turning people I didn't like into condiments, there was no reason not to have some fun.

On the other hand...

"Let them go," I told Monica.

"I don't think so. They're annoying. And they bore me."

"That's not the point. You can't keep pulling these little stunts. I'm running out of explanations."

"You've managed so far."

That wasn't the point either. It had taken all my powers to explain away the troubles before Thanksgiving. Fortunately, nobody at Channel 12 had believed Lisa Hartwell's story about seeing devils and hellfire and a pudgy copywriter turning into a possum in my office. The film had come out blank, for one thing. Also, the cameraman had been high that day and couldn't be sure what he'd seen. J/J/G's bad rep had helped, too; everyone knew the place was a madhouse, so people were just shrugging off the rumors.

Still, it hadn't looked good for Jenner, Jack and Kurt to go out on medical leave at the same time, and not everyone was really buying my stress-epidemic story. Walt, for example. He'd been giving me the fish-eye lately, and although he was dumb, it was only from the neck up; he had a certain animal instinct about things that I'd never liked.

"I'm tired of managing, Monica. Let them go. Nobody's going to believe Abner if he tells, and Jack won't say anything." I glanced at him for confirmation. "You won't, either. You're under medical care. For all you know, this is your medication talking. Right?"

He swallowed a couple of times. "I hope so. I keep seeing things. I saw Elvis the other night, did I tell you?"

"I think we'd better get him back to the hospital," Cassie said worriedly. "Can we sneak him down the service elevator?"

Vanessa sighed and snapped her fingers. Jack vanished. "He's back. Just in time for group."

"Spoilsport," Monica accused.

"Naaaah, he'll like it today. That redhead's going to tell how she lost her virginity."

Monica raised an eyebrow in question; Vanessa leaned closer to whisper.

"*No*. Really?"

"Really," Vanessa assured her. "And humans call *us* names."

Impatient, I checked my watch again. "Look, we're really late for a meeting. Would you just change Abner back now so we can go?"

"You were more fun before Blondie there got hold of you," Monica grumbled.

Cassie smirked and made a point of getting closer.

"I'll remind you who started it," I told my demon. "This is all your own doing. And by the way, thank you. Now change him back."

She folded her arms, sulking. "No."

"If you don't, Vanessa will, just to spite you."

Monica glared at her.

Vanessa shrugged. "She's right. It's my nature."

My demon made a few poisonous comments in a language I didn't understand. But she took the curse off, and Howard Abner rematerialized, clutching a crucifix. It was clear from his expression that he had no idea what had just happened.

"Go now," I advised him. "People are enjoying themselves somewhere. Somebody's got to stop them."

He stood there for a few seconds, blinking. Then he shook his head and walked away, salt pouring out of his coat pockets, leaving a trail. How would I explain that?

Easy. I would not. That decided, I got up off the floor and held out a hand to Cassie. "Let's go. We're late."

Vanessa hopped off the desk. "Right behind you. How do I look?"

"You can't go," Cassie told her.

"I don't see why not. You need all the help you can get with this account. Since you're not sleeping with clients anymore..." Delicately, she paused. "You *aren't* sleeping with clients anymore, are you?"

Cassie sputtered in outrage.

"How would it be if we had just one normal day around here?" I asked the demons. "What if Cassie and I go to work, and you two take the day off and do something fun?"

"This *is* fun," Vanessa said.

In all the excitement, I'd almost forgotten that my head was killing me. The reprieve was over now. "Fine. Just let us get this meeting over, and then you can burn the place down, for all I care. We're leaving right after this and going back to bed. Right, Cass?"

"To sleep," Cassie amended.

"Of *course* to sleep." Insulted, I threw the door open and started down the hall toward the conference room where we were meeting the dog food people. About halfway there, I heard a bad omen: barking. Even worse, it sounded like a small dog in a large mood. A Pekingese, maybe, or a toy poodle.

Sometimes, you don't even need demons to have a bad day.

For all my good intentions, I never got around to going home after the meeting. Kurt was feeling better, so he picked a fight with Heather, which wound up involving two departments and almost escalated into an international incident. I never did find out what it was about, but all I really wanted was for it to stop. So I started a rumor that Jenner was on his way in.

The rumor worked, of course. It was like a T-shirt I'd seen once: JESUS IS COMING. LOOK BUSY. But Sanchez came down later to shoot Ping-Pong balls at me for it; half the agency had run straight to her office, trying to cover themselves. Her aim, I noticed, was improving.

At least Cassie was safe. She'd left not long after the dog food crowd did, and I hoped she was tucked into bed. Only a crazy person would be at work with this kind of hangover. Besides, it was snowing again. The only sensible thing to do that night was go home and stay home.

So I went Christmas shopping.

There was no good reason to go shopping in person; I had a perfectly good Internet connection. But Christmas was different. Maybe it was the thrill of battle, or the plastic holly and Muzak, but it just wasn't Christmas until I hit the malls.

Also, I had no idea what to get Cassie, and something might suggest itself if I looked around. All I knew for sure was that I wasn't going anywhere near a jewelry store.

An hour and three jewelry stores later, I gave up and went home.

To my surprise, Cassie's BMW was in the driveway. I found her curled up on the greatroom couch under the couch throw, sound asleep, with a fire burning down in the fireplace and an empty box of Godiva chocolates on the coffee table.

Bemused, I sat on the arm of the couch by her feet and watched her. It was the strangest feeling, but it was just about the nicest thing I'd ever come home to. Living together was still a terrible, terrible idea, but...

Well, we could talk about it sometime. No time soon, but eventually. *If* this lasted, which it might not. It probably wouldn't, so there was no reason to think about any kind of future. Was there?

Cassie's eyes fluttered open just then, and I promptly forgot the question. "Hi," I said.

She smiled slightly. "Hi yourself. What time is it?"

"Almost 7."

"God. I was just going to take a nap." Annoyed with herself, she pulled off the couch throw and sat up, rubbing her eyes. "Sorry. I didn't mean to do that."

"Don't worry about it. Feel better now?"

"Lots better. Thanks."

"Didn't do anything."

We let that conversation die of its own inanity and just looked at each other. That weird feeling started tugging at me again. This was crazy. I'd known her six years. How could a few weeks of knowing her in a different way make this much difference?

"I was going to offer to make dinner," Cassie said abruptly. "Kind of to make up for last night. Interested?"

"There's not much to work with. I haven't been to the grocery lately."

"That's why I said 'I was.' All you've got in your refrigerator is Tabasco sauce and coffee."

"I have Tabasco sauce?" I asked, genuinely surprised.

She laughed and scooted down the couch to whack me. "The plan from Column B is to order in."

Actually, the plan that was forming in my mind was from a very different column, so I bent down and kissed her.

"Not that I'm complaining," she murmured, "but shouldn't you call your mother before we get sidetracked?"

"Called her from the mall on my cell. That way, I could honestly say I couldn't hear her."

Cassie had leaned in again but pulled back at that. "What were you doing at the mall?"

"Christmas shopping." I pulled her back.

This time, she waited longer to follow up. "For who?"

"Whom," I corrected.

Torn between starting an argument and continuing what we were doing, she debated which way to go. Then, without warning, she pulled me down on the couch with her. "Gotcha. Now what are you going to do?"

I had a reasonably good idea. But it could wait a couple of minutes. "What do you want for Christmas, Cass?"

She hadn't expected the question—certainly, not just then. "What does that have to do with anything?"

"I'm really not sure what to get you this year. Can't get away with a Chia Pet anymore."

"Or a Clapper," she agreed happily.

No, not a Clapper. We'd given each other deliberately silly gifts the first couple of years, but the Clapper had been the worst. Neither of us remembered now who'd given it to whom, but we'd spent the better part of an evening clapping at it, trying to get it to work. Finally, Cassie put the thing in the driveway and ceremoniously drove over it a few times.

Brushing a long strand of blonde hair back off her face, I smiled at her. "Your sister thinks I should get you jewelry. How about a great big mood ring?"

She kissed me before she answered. "What color would it be for this?"

Scarlet, probably, but that would be the wrong answer. "My favorite."

"Mine too," she said, going back for more.

Jewelry, then. I was in *so* much trouble.

Chapter Eighteen

Mid-December

Jenner finally came back to work the second week of December. Only Sanchez was really happy to see him, and only because it took a burden off her, but she was keeping the Ping-Pong gun where she could get to it in a hurry.

Everyone else was more worried about the Christmas party.

"I'm still not going," Troy said for the fifth or sixth time. Patience having failed, I gave rank-pulling a try. "You *are* going. It's not an option."

"I don't care. He fired how many people last year? Ten? Twenty?"

Heather nodded sagely. "And he was in a *good* mood last year."

I glanced at Cassie, who looked every bit as annoyed as I felt. At least when Jack was here, he ran the weekly meetings, and the rest of us were on the same side. "He's probably not going to fire anybody. I doubt he's even feeling up to it."

"Well, what if he gets better all of a sudden?" Troy countered. "Then I'm screwed. I'll wind up in a paper hat, saying, 'Do you want fries with that?'"

Kurt smiled unpleasantly. "At least you'd be working for a living, pal. We can't all be pretty and coast on our looks."

Hell's bells, couldn't we have ten minutes of peace in this place? I was only just quick enough to intercept the notebook that Heather had sailed at Kurt's head. Across the table, Cassie had a determined grip on Troy, while Chip was busy looking out the window, pretending very hard that he was somewhere else.

"You saw that. She assaulted me," Kurt told me helpfully. "Think Jenner'll fire her, too?"

Bristling, Troy pushed Cassie off and shoved his chair back. "Don't you start with her...*boy.*"

The evil grin on Kurt's face was all too familiar. "Why not? You think you might like girls this week or something?"

The silence bomb exploded, destroying the room. For a couple of seconds, no one so much as blinked. Then bodies started flying, and without really knowing how I got there, I was up on the conference table, blocking Troy, who had dived headfirst about halfway across it. Meanwhile, Heather was trying to stab Kurt with her ballpoint.

"Hey! Isn't this illegal?" he complained. "Shouldn't somebody call OSHA?"

Troy made another lunge. "I'll give you OSHA, you redneck jackass."

I didn't have two younger brothers for nothing; drawing on a lifetime of experience with physical violence, I feinted and blocked him again.

"I don't want to have to kill you, Dev," he warned. Then he tried to pull my feet out from under me. Fortunately, Cassie got to him first. She probably didn't mean to launch him as far across the room as she did, but she didn't look especially sorry about it either.

There wasn't time to thank her, because Heather was crawling onto the arm of

Kurt's chair, pummeling him with both fists. Exasperated, Cassie went around the table to help break it up. But just as I turned, Kurt called Cassie the one thing I never, ever allowed—and everything went bright red for a minute. The next thing I knew, I was in the middle of what sounded like a rather heated speech.

"—reproductively challenged. You can't get it up without a building crane. You can't *keep* it up without duct tape. Peg would be better off with an electric toothbrush. Remind me to get her one for Christmas. And *another* thing—"

Cassie practically broke a heel in her hurry to get up on the table. "That's enough, Devvy."

"That's not even a start. After what he called you—"

"Never mind. Sticks and stones."

That was a good idea, actually. "Got any?"

She bit her lip, possibly trying not to laugh. Taking advantage of her distraction, I turned to have at Kurt again. He was trying not to look like he was trying to look up her skirt, but when he saw that I'd noticed, he jumped.

"That's enough," Cassie repeated, taking a preemptive hold on me.

No, it wasn't. But there were times and there were places for certain things, and it was starting to sink in that I was standing on a conference table, losing control of a meeting.

"All right. We're done here," I grumbled. "Let me recap for you: Everyone goes to the Christmas party. No excuses. I know where you all live, and I'll hunt you down with bad dogs if I have to. Got that?"

I took the silence for assent.

"Now let's all get back to work. And I don't want any of you talking to anyone else in this room for the rest of the day. That goes triple for me. Understood?"

No one said anything.

"Now *go.*"

They shot out of the room like pinballs. I hadn't seen people move that fast around J/J/G for ages, not even that day last year when the microwave caught fire.

Cassie and I just stood there for a minute. Finally, she laughed. "Well, that was fun. You're getting better at this, you know?"

"I know." Wearily, I pinched the bridge of my nose. "I'm going to have to scare him again, Cass."

"Not today."

"No. I'll save it for the Christmas party."

Her eyes lit up. "You *are* getting better at this."

"It'll give me something to look forward to. I don't want to go either."

"No one does." She leaned closer. "Now, does that not-talking-to-you-all-day rule apply to me?"

"Depends what you want."

"I want you to move in with me. But I could settle for lunch."

"Settle for lunch," I advised.

She just smiled. I was starting to know that look a little too well.

The Friday of the party, we were in Cassie's master bath getting ready when the doorbell rang.

"Just because it rings doesn't mean you have to answer," I reminded her.

"I know. That's what peepholes are for." She handed me the earring that she hadn't finished putting in. "Hold on to this for me. I'll be right back."

Muttering, I set it down on the counter and shook the eyeliner tube again, trying to get more on the brush. Cassie thought touch liner was for amateurs, but I thought pencil was too much work, so we generally avoided putting on makeup at the same time to avoid arguments. Tonight, though, we were short on time.

"Honey?" she called from downstairs.

I finished up quickly and recapped the liner tube. "Sweetheart?"

"Could you come here for a minute? Please?"

Please? Startled, I went down to see what was wrong. She was holding a long white florist's box, looking perplexed.

"It was on the doorstep," she reported. "Nobody was there. What do you think?"

"Is it ticking?"

"No. Should I open it?"

"Only if you want to know what's inside."

She backhanded me, but she was laughing, so I didn't take it personally. With mild interest, I watched her open the box. It looked like—

"Lilies," Cassie said flatly. "Dead ones."

I didn't like the sound of that, so I took the box away from her. "Don't touch them. Did you see a card?"

She held up a small white envelope. "It was on the lid. Wait a second." Cautiously, she tore it open and pulled out the card. She looked at one side and then, puzzled, at the other. "Blank. Who do you suppose...?"

"I don't know. But let's stick together tonight. No sense taking any chances."

"Oh, come on, Devvy. It was probably supposed to be a joke."

"Did you laugh?"

Cassie sighed, conceding the point. "I just hate to go in suspicious tonight. Things are going to be tense enough already. You don't suppose Jenner's really going to fire people this year, do you?"

"Wouldn't be Christmas without a Scrooge." I started to put the florist's box down, but something inside caught my eye. Trying not to be obvious about it, I looked closer. It was a cigar butt. Jack's brand.

"What is it? Is something wrong?"

"No," I lied. "Speaking of Scrooge, you know what the best line in *A Christmas Carol* is? 'Darkness was cheap, and Scrooge liked it.'"

"You're trying to distract me."

"Nonsense. I'm just trying to have a nice literary conversation. What's *your* favorite line?"

Cassie scowled. "What's in the box that you don't want me to see?"

It was no use. Silently, I handed it back over to her.

"A cigar butt," she said. "So what?"

"It's the kind Jack smokes. I think it's supposed to be a calling card."

"I thought he was still locked up in the madhouse."

"It's not necessarily a life sentence. They might have let him out for the party. And if they did..."

"Trouble." She tilted her head in resignation. "Well, sweetie, at least you've never bored me. This has been the most interesting year of my life."

Mine too. I was still fairly sure that was a good thing.

There were two company parties at the Omni that night, but there was no mistaking one for the other. Cassie and I didn't even have to ask which ballroom was the J/J/G party; we just went directly to the loud one.

For safety's sake, we hung back in the doorway for a moment while we scoped out the room. On the surface, it all looked normal enough—normal in J/J/G terms, anyway. It could have passed for the premiere of some terminally hip independent film, if you didn't count the garish Christmas decorations. Who knew there was that much red and green tinsel in the world?

Cassie nudged me and then leaned close to shout in my ear. "Look up."

I did, expecting a piñata or a paper bell. Instead, I saw mistletoe. "Doesn't count. It's plastic."

"Too bad. You still have to kiss me."

That was true, and I was about to when Randy Harris sauntered by with a sprig of mistletoe sticking out of his fly. It put both of us right out of the mood.

"I'm going to go home after this," Cassie said, disgusted, "and unscrew my head, and wash my brain. Does he really think that's going to work?"

Yes, he probably did, and yes, it probably would; we had a pestilence of sorority girls working as interns that semester. But pointing that out would only ruin her mood. So I steered her toward the bar instead.

Unfortunately, the road to the bar ran through the last people I wanted to see together: Jenner, Jack, Kurt and Howard Abner. What was that weasel Abner doing here?

"Hi, boss," Kurt called, seeing us approaching. "Come meet the new boss."

"What new boss?"

Abner drew himself up to his full height, smoothing his vest over his paunch. I couldn't help noticing that he was still wearing the big vulgar ring. "That would be me, Miss Kerry. And I'm absolutely delighted to say this: You're fired."

Chapter Nineteen

"I'm what?"

"Fired. Here." Abner dug inside his vest and came up with a pink slip. An actual pink slip. "You have twenty-four hours to clean out your office. After that, we change the locks."

Distracted by the pink slip—and by Cassie, who had gotten all the way inside my personal space to see it for herself—I was no longer listening. It was a preprinted form with "The Family Foundation" printed at the top; someone had crossed out that heading and handwritten the agency's name, but they'd written "JJJ" instead of "J/J/G." Cousin-marrying morons. No doubt all those Klan meetings had killed off their only two brain cells.

~~THE FAMILY FOUNDATION~~	
JJJ	
DATE	*December 15*
EMPLOYEE	*Devlin Kerry*
SUPERVISOR	*Howard Abner, Jack Harper*
REASON	*Insubordination & Witchcraft*
EFFECTIVE DATE	*Immediate*

LEGAL NOTICE: *We are not responsible for the actions of former employees.*

"Witchcraft?" Cassie's voice hit a pitch that would call dogs in the next county. "Do you know what century this is, Mr. Abner?"

I recovered just in time. "Stay out of this, Cass. This is my fight, not yours."

"Don't even act like you want to go there," she snapped. "You're stuck with me. If you have a fight, I have a fight. If you're fired, I'm fired. Got that?"

"Nobody's fired. Abner's just having brain cramps. He doesn't even work here. Does he, Mr. Jenner?"

Jenner swallowed hard and tried to hide behind Kurt, who started laughing.

"I don't have to work here. Mr. Jenner made me a partner," Abner explained. "It was either that or lose his agency in court."

"What are you talking about?" Cassie asked impatiently.

He didn't even bother to acknowledge her. "Remember that little tape you made, Miss Kerry? The one you slandered me in by putting me in a dress? You didn't think I knew about that. Well, I wouldn't have, except that your friend Kurt here gave me a copy."

That was very thoughtful of my friend there. And now he was going to die. I was within two steps of Kurt when Cassie grabbed the back of my jacket and tugged me aside. "You can't kill him. Too many witnesses."

"I'm not going to kill him," I lied. "I'm just going to geld him a little."

"You can't do that, either. You don't want to touch that thing. It was up Jack's pants when he was a possum."

She had a point. Grudgingly, I let her guide me back over to Abner. "Go on," I told him coolly. "You were saying...?"

Abner rocked back and forth on his heels a few times, immensely satisfied. "I could have sued this agency. I'd have won. But I couldn't sue you personally, and you're the one who deserved to be punished. So I worked out a deal. I get a piece of this agency, and you get fired. Officially, you're fired for insubordination." Smirking, he leaned into my face. "Unofficially, you're fired for perversion."

He never saw it coming. Cassie never let go of my jacket, but she hit him so hard that his fillings must have popped out. For a long moment, he stared at her, swaying, looking vaguely surprised. Then he keeled over, landing with a splat that reminded me of the noise the turkey had made falling out of the chandelier at Thanksgiving—a disgusting sound I'd never really wanted to hear again.

"Weenie," she declared. "You want to sneak out now, Devvy?"

Yes, but I didn't think we could. Everyone in the ballroom had either seen or heard, and we were the absolute center of attention.

"What the hell's going on over there?" Walt shouted.

There wasn't time to explain. Jack was advancing on Cassie, snarling something about the wages of sin, and the world went bright red again. The next thing I knew, Jack was flat on his back next to Abner with cartoon stars flying around his head, and I was holding my right hand, which hurt like hell. But it felt good in a way, too.

"Devvy," Cassie said urgently, "we need to get out of here."

I grabbed her head, kissed the top of it and stepped over the bodies to pop Kurt in the snout as hard as I could. He dropped like a rock. Damn, this was fun. Now, where was Jenner?

Just as I saw one of his shoes disappearing under a banquet table, Chip and Troy skidded to a stop right behind me and grabbed hold.

"Hey! I'm not done!"

"We appreciate it," Troy told me, "but we're getting you out of here. *Now.* Chip? You got Cass?"

"I've got myself," she said icily. "You just get her out to the car."

Annoyed, I wrenched loose from Troy and yanked Abner's vest open. A sheaf of pink slips fell out. I managed to stuff most of them into my jacket pocket before Troy pulled me away, this time for good.

Through all that, no one in the room had moved. They seemed mesmerized by the violence, as though they were home in their underwear, watching TV.

"Excitement's over!" Chip yelled. "We're leaving!"

Still no reaction. Chip shook his head. Then he and Troy dragged me out of the ballroom, with Cassie covering our escape from the rear. We may have looked a little conspicuous going through the lobby that way, but no one challenged us, and we got to Cassie's car without incident.

Troy shoved me into the passenger seat maybe harder than necessary. "You're a real piece of work, Dev. Did you have to do that?"

I smiled thinly, dug into my jacket pocket for the pink slips and gave him the one with his name on it. As soon as he figured it out, Chip had to grab hold of him. "I take that back," he said. "I owe you one. Want me to go back in there and kill them all?"

Before I could answer, we heard a weird clicking/clopping headed in our direction. The source turned out to be Heather, who'd broken a heel but was still making good time. "Dev! Cassie! Wait up! I want to help!"

Cassie had started the car, but she started laughing at that and put the transmission back in park.

"For crying out loud," Chip complained. "What is with you guys tonight? Why do I have to be NATO?"

Silently, I riffled through the pink slips and pulled out his and Heather's. They took them, puzzled...and then the light dawned. This time, Troy and Heather had to hold Chip back.

The stripes on the roadway were starting to look like a solid line. Cassie was driving like a maniac even for her. "How fast are we going?" I finally asked.

"You don't want to know," she snapped.

Surreptitiously, I leaned over to check the gauge—and winced. She was right.

"We're not going to jail, Devvy. I don't care if we have to drive to Trinidad."

"We're not Bonnie and Clyde," I reminded her. "And we can't drive to Trinidad."

"Why not?"

I couldn't help smiling just a bit. "Caribbean Sea."

"I hate it when you get literal."

"Exactly what I always told her," Monica said from a few inches behind us.

We both spun around—not a good idea on Cassie's part, considering that she was driving. Both our demons were parked on the backseat, as far apart as they could get and still be in the same car. Even for demons, they looked crabby.

Well, tonight that made four of us. Grimly, I turned Cassie back around to make her watch the road and then leaned over the seat. "A fine time for you two to finally show up. Where were you when all that business with Abner started?"

Monica gave me one of her nastier smiles. "Are you saying you wanted my help?"

"She meant both of us," Vanessa corrected.

"You shut up. This is all your fault anyway, you halfwit."

"*My* fault?" Cassie's demon tossed her head haughtily. "Don't blame me. I didn't start this."

"You babysat the old goat while he was home in bed watching TV all day. *You* got him started on the God Channel. *You* gave Abner an opening."

Vanessa didn't like that. "I did not. I kept putting the TV on 'Brady Bunch' reruns. Can I help it if he figured out how to use the remote?"

"What's the point in making a person watch 'The Brady Bunch'?" I asked, curious. "I'm assuming it has something to do with the shortest path to damnation, or at least insanity, but—"

Monica showed me her fangs. Seeing the wild red light in her eyes, I decided it might be best to stay out of the discussion.

"I tried 'The Love Boat,' too. And 'Fantasy Island,'" Vanessa added.

"This isn't about felony television," Monica insisted. "You were supposed to keep him out of the way of people like Abner. I wasn't done making Devlin's work life miserable yet. And you hadn't even *started,* you pathetic human-loving—"

"That's not my job."

"No, but Blondie's your job. And *she's* in charge of making the *rest* of Devlin's life miserable."

Cassie, who had been listening with relative patience, stomped on the brakes. "Hey!"

Only my seat belt and a hand on the dash kept me from going through the windshield while we skidded out of traffic and slammed into a curb. It was déjà vu all over again, except that I wasn't driving this time. Fortunately, Cassie's BMW was newer and sturdier than my MG; the car rocked violently but stayed on the ground.

"She's your human," Monica said venomously, to which Vanessa flipped her hair in unconcern.

"Everybody shut up," I demanded. "Cass? Are you OK?"

A little dazed, she nodded. Not quite reassured, I leaned over to kiss her. Then I turned back on the demons. "You two are responsible for this. If she'd been hurt, I'd have taken this out on you personally. I'd have found a voodoo doctor to curse a chicken for me. Then I'd have cursed you with chicken parts. I'd have—"

"Cursed us with chicken parts?" Vanessa raised an eyebrow at Monica. "She didn't learn that from you, did she?"

Monica hissed at her.

"Quit interrupting while I'm threatening you. If you two were any use at all—"

Vanessa laughed. "That's so cute. She's threatening us. Should I turn her into something? How about...oh, I don't know...a bunny rabbit?"

"You mind your own business," Monica told her.

"She *is* my business. As long as Cassandra loves her—"

"Count on it," Cassie said fiercely.

"—the two of them are a package deal. You should know that, for Lucifer's sake. Didn't you learn anything in Malediction 101?"

Monica defended herself briskly, but I didn't pay any attention. Package deal, were we? It was an oddly appealing concept. Apparently, Cassie felt the same way; she reached over to squeeze my hand and didn't bother to let go.

We're in this together, she'd said a few weeks ago. I couldn't let her be in this getting-fired thing together, but just for this evening, it wouldn't hurt to pretend it was true.

The sudden cessation of argument in the backseat distracted me. Suspicious, I turned to see what was going on with them and almost banged heads with the demons, who were leaning forward avidly to see what was going on with us.

Vanessa smirked at my demon. "Told you. They're a twofer."

"We'll see," Monica said ominously. "Now, who takes care of this business back at the party? You or me? You started it, so—"

"Tosh. You started everything before that. *You* fix it."

Cassie and I exchanged glances. "What do you mean, 'fix'?" I asked Monica.

"I'm busy, Devlin," she growled.

"I don't care. What is she supposed to fix?"

"The firings," Monica said, aggrieved. "They weren't supposed to happen. Goldilocks here needs to turn everything back."

I was interested against my better judgment. "Can she do that? I saw Superman do it in a movie once, but he had to spin the Earth backward."

This time, Monica hissed at me. Cassie gave her an evil look and pulled me forward.

"I'm not doing it, Monica," Vanessa insisted. "And you can't make me."

"I can make you wish you had."

"You don't scare me. Anyway, you're losing your touch. You couldn't—"

She never finished. There was a little squelching sound, and then her black gown collapsed. Startled, I leaned back over the seat. Monica was smirking, and Vanessa was a toad.

"Not very original," I remarked.

My demon, in no mood for criticism, raised her hand. But just as she did, the toad sprang from the seat into her face. Cursing in a language I didn't recognize, Monica tried to swat it away, but it hopped down into her cleavage. Her eyes met mine in shock for a split-second just before her gown collapsed, too.

"What are they doing?" Cassie asked.

"Fighting. Vanessa was a toad a second ago. I think she just got even."

Then we saw something wriggling in Monica's gown, and a snake poked its head out of the neck opening. Cassie recoiled, horrified. But the toad, which had jumped to safety on the armrest, hopped up and down meaningfully a couple of times, and the snake turned into—

"What is that?" Cassie whispered.

"A hedgehog. I think." Frowning, I leaned over to get a better look. "It was a lot cuter in the Beatrix Potter books."

The hedgehog didn't appear to like that remark, but it had other things on its mind. It pulled out one of its quills and speared the toad with it, and the toad turned into a cockroach.

I'd seen enough. "Duck," I told Cassie.

"No, honey, I think that's a bug."

There wasn't time to argue. The combatants were going at it hammer and tongs now, turning each other into things at a furious pace. There might have been an actual duck in there somewhere, but it was hard to keep up with what was what, let alone who was who. Finally, one turned the other into a pigeon, which caused a violent fit of flapping and screeching.

"No birds in this car!" Cassie shrieked, hitting the window buttons. "Not on this upholstery!"

The pigeon shot out of the BMW, hotly pursued by a canary. They both did a couple of circuits around the car, flying close enough to the windshield that we saw the tiny fangs in their beaks. Then they lighted out, disappearing into the night.

When the shock had worn off, I reached over Cassie to roll up the windows. "Everything OK, sweetheart?"

She thought about it for a long time. I half-expected her not to answer. Finally, she drew a shaky breath. "Which part of 'everything' do you mean? The part where we're both fired, or the part where we have more time to spend with your family at Christmas?"

"Never mind," I said quickly.

Chapter Twenty

Three Days Before Christmas

Finally, there was nothing to do but go home.

Cassie and I had done all we could about the job thing. We had a lawyer all over it; charges were flying back and forth, and our lives would get very unpleasant soon. But the unpleasantness would keep until after the holidays. Lawyers were human, too, our lawyer explained.

An old joke occurred to me (**Q:** What do you have when you have a hundred lawyers up to their necks in sand? **A:** Not enough sand), but I was just able to resist repeating it. Chances were that he'd heard it anyway; a lawyer had told it to me in the first place.

So we had a small forced vacation, which about drove both of us crazy. By Christmas week, we were both eager for trouble. Anything to keep us busy.

Fortunately, I knew just the place to find all the trouble we wanted.

"How fast are we going?"

I glanced over at Cassie. "We're legal. Why?"

"That's not what I meant." She leaned all the way over to check the speedometer. "This car goes a lot faster than that. I bet you can get it all the way up to 55 if you really try."

"Speed limit's 55 on this road."

"Do you see anyone else doing the speed limit?"

A huge truck almost blew us off the road as it passed, making me grip the wheel for dear life. The last thing I needed today was to wreck Cassie's BMW. If the crash didn't kill me, *she* would.

"Bastard," Cassie said, glowering at the truck. "I hope you die soon."

"Your Christmas spirit needs a little work," I told her, amused.

"Don't change the subject. Can't you at least do 60?"

Of course, but I didn't want to. Every mile we traveled got us a mile closer to home, and there was no reason to hurry to get there.

"Devvy?"

"The road's a little slick. Don't want to take any chances. Especially not with you, sweetheart."

That almost got me a kiss—almost, because she caught on at the last second.

"Try lying to someone who doesn't sleep with you," she advised. "You just don't want to do this, do you?"

"It's not that I don't want to do it. It's..." No, actually, it *was* that I didn't want to do it. "Never mind."

Another monstrous truck barreled by; she threw a withering glare after it. "I can't think with all this *passing* going on. Pull over first chance you get."

"There's nothing for a few miles."

"Then that would be the first chance, wouldn't it?"

Irritably, I pulled my sunglasses down to regard the woman more closely. She smiled and then pointedly turned to look out her window.

Fine. If she wanted to be that way, fine. There was nothing much for her to see between Meridian and Hawthorne anyway but farmland, billboards and the occasional pay lake, one of which we were passing just then. CHASE'S, a big wooden sign said, right above a crudely painted fish. Fishing was none of my business, but it had always seemed to me that if the fish in that lake looked anything like the sign, people would be better off going to the grocery.

Then there was the occasional cluster of houses, not enough to constitute a town but too many to be a coincidence. They never changed, even if their occupants did. Even after all these years, I could still pick out the ones that had the lawn jockeys, the sun balls, the windmills—and the one that had all of the above *and* the concrete dwarves. Right now, in honor of the season, the dwarves would all be wearing Santa hats. It wasn't something I necessarily needed to see again.

I slowed down a little more, hoping Cassie wouldn't notice.

"What on earth is that up ahead?" she asked suddenly, tapping her side of the windshield.

"The ice tree."

"The what?"

"Ice tree. The people who live there make it every Christmas. They put this really heavy plastic over the trees and spray water on it till it freezes. It takes a couple of weeks to build up enough ice. Then they put food coloring on it." Unwillingly, I smiled. "At night, they have floodlights on it so you can see it from miles away. Want me to slow down so you can get a better look?"

Lost in stunned contemplation, Cassie didn't answer, so I slowed down anyway. It gave me an excuse to look myself. Not that I was going to admit it to her, but I kind of liked the thing.

"Wow," she finally said.

"Like it?"

She got her evasive look. I'd always hated that one. "Do you?"

"You haven't seen anything yet. Wait till we get to Hawthorne. I'll take you on a Christmas lights tour."

"You don't scare me, Devvy."

"No? Are you sure? There's a house that has a fifteen-foot inflatable snowman. They light it up at night, too—not that you could really miss a fifteen-foot inflatable snowman in somebody's front yard. The people next door—"

"Rest stop," she interrupted.

"I'm not tired. Anyway, the house next door has—"

"No, I mean there's a rest stop ahead. Pull off. I want to talk."

I considered pointing out that we *were* talking and quickly decided against it. Without comment, I pulled into the rest stop, parking as far away from other cars as possible. No point risking some idiot scratching Cassie's paint. "All right, we're pulled off. What's on your mind?"

"I want to know what's on *your* mind. You're driving like you're on your way to your own execution." Turning all the way sideways, she fixed me with her most intent blue gaze. "Is there something I need to know?"

"You'll know everything you need to know soon enough. Five minutes with my mother, and you'll think your family is the Cleavers."

"Get real—nobody wants to be the Cleavers. Besides, your mother can't be *that* bad."

I didn't even smile.

"She doesn't have a tail. She doesn't breathe fire. I've met her, remember? Sure, she was a little cranky, but—"

"You don't even know what 'cranky' is yet."

"Bet I do. I know *you*, don't I?" She reached over for my hand and discreetly pressed it to her lips for a split-second. "I think...what's wrong?"

I yanked my hand back before answering. "Don't *do* that. Not in public. Not around here."

"You're kidding. How is that a problem?"

"Being stomped to death by hilljacks would be a problem. Trust me—I'm from around here."

"Nobody noticed. I was careful." She tried to take hold of my hand again, but I stuck it in my coat pocket. "Would you just relax?"

"This might be a good time to try practicing the Just Friends thing. You promised not to touch me in public."

"Yes, but this isn't your parents' house. It's—"

"Thirty miles away. Anyone here might know them. And anyone who knows them might tell."

Cassie bit her lip slightly, looking thoughtful. Then she slid closer and put a hand on my forehead. "Don't take this personally; I'm just checking for fever."

Getting seriously annoyed, I pushed her back.

"All right, all right. Take it easy. I'll behave while we're there. But if I have to be a nun for four whole days, I'd like to get a little physical with you first."

"What about this morning? That didn't count?"

A little smirk. "Well..."

"Well nothing. We were an hour late getting started because of that." Then it hit me—I'd been so busy worrying about not wanting to get there that I'd forgotten how much trouble I'd be in for getting there late. Quickly, I checked my watch. Damn. "And now we're an hour and a half late. Mom's going to kill me."

Cassie slid closer again. "Think carefully before you answer this, honey: Are you sorry?"

"How stupid do you think I am?" I growled. "Would I say so if I were? *No,* I'm not sorry. I just don't know how I'm going to explain being late, that's all."

"Then don't." Making sure no one was close enough to see in, she put one hand way up my thigh and leaned closer. "One kiss? For the road?"

"Cassie..."

"I can't wait to see what this mother of yours is like," she said acidly. "If she's got you this paranoid from thirty miles away, she must be a real barracuda."

"My mother has nothing to do with it. I'm just not into PDAs. Now would you get off?"

She narrowed her eyes a bit. "Of course. After you kiss me."

Clearly, I wasn't going to win this one. And we weren't going to be alone for long; a battered old van was heading in our direction. "All right, dammit, I'll make you a deal. Get off me, and I'll see what I can do about sneaking into your room at night."

"You'll see?" She leaned closer and blew lightly in my ear. "You'll *see?*"

The van was getting closer—close enough for me to notice the Confederate flag license plate bolted to the front fender. And Cassie was practically on my lap, with no intention of going anywhere. If she did that blowing-in-the-ear thing one more time, I was going to be in bad trouble in front of Bubba.

"OK," I said quickly. "I'll make a *point* of it. Now for God's sake, back off before somebody sees this."

"I don't have to be a nun after all?"

"Only in front of people. Now get off. *Please.*"

Cassie glanced over her shoulder at the van, which was signaling its intent to pull into one of the parking spaces near us. Without any further argument, she backed off, rolled her window down a crack and started talking very loudly about opera—a form of gargoylism, I was sure. That would scare the creatures away, if they wanted to make an issue of whatever they might have seen.

"I love you," I told her, truly meaning it.

She didn't miss a beat, working herself up into an outrage about the subtitles at the Met, but she winked. She didn't like opera either.

The weather got worse the closer we got to Hawthorne, and I wasn't sure it was coincidental. About ten miles past the rest stop, we'd run into some snow, and by the time we hit the first city exit, the stuff was practically sheeting down. Cassie tried very hard not to look nervous, with no success, but I couldn't blame her. Only a fool or a local (same thing) would be driving around town in this weather.

Well, maybe I could distract her for a few minutes. "Guess we'll have to skip the Christmas lights tour tonight, Cass. You lucked out. But we still have to go by the Martins' house. I'll bet they have the big Rudolph on their roof again this year. What do *you* bet?"

"Maybe you should drive now and badger me later," she said in a small voice.

"I'm not badgering you. Believe me, you'd know." Not taking my eyes off the road, I reached over to stroke her hair for a second. "We're fine, sweetheart. I've driven in this town all my life. We'll be there in a few minutes. *That's* when the trouble starts."

She smiled mechanically.

"Let's go over the battle plan one more time," I suggested. "We don't tell them about the job thing yet. We don't confirm or deny our relationship. We avoid PDAs like the plague. We let *them* figure out whether there's any subtext going on. Check?"

"Check."

Squinting through the windshield, I barely made out the street sign at the stoplight ahead. But it was the right one. We'd be there after six blocks and one more turn. "One last thing."

"What?"

"Whatever my brothers tell you is a lie."

That finally did the trick. She relaxed visibly, not even flinching as we skidded a little going through the turn.

And then, too soon, the house loomed up out of the snow at the end of the cul-de-sac. There were lights on in every window, which could mean only one thing: My brothers were home. And that in turn could mean only one thing: My mother was going to be in a bad mood already, grinching about the electricity bill.

"Buckle up," I told Cassie as we pulled into the drive. "It's going to be a bumpy Christmas."

Chapter Twenty-One

Something was wrong. All the lights were on in the living room, the TV and stereo were going, and candles were burning on just about every flat surface. That was normal. But that was all. It was quiet. Too quiet.

"Hello?" I called again. "Where is everybody?"

Except for CNN and *The Messiah*, there wasn't a sound. Uneasy, I set my luggage down and opened the coat closet. Nothing.

"What are you doing?" Cassie asked, setting down her own bags.

"Looking for relatives."

"Why would they be in the closet?"

"You don't know these people. They could be anywhere." Suspicious, I poked something in the back; it was just one of Ryan's old parkas. "Give me your coat, anyway. We might as well hang ours up."

She handed hers over, and I shoehorned them both into the inadequate space that was left, most of the rest being hogged by my brothers' old coats. Why didn't they take the things home with them sometime, or at least give them to Goodwill? Of all the stupid—wait. Was that one of *my* old coats back there?

"Devvy?"

It sounded almost like a warning, but being busy digging through outerwear, I didn't answer right away. "Hmmmm?"

A wild battle cry rang out behind me, and a snowball bounced off the top of my head. I didn't even have to turn to know who the culprit was.

"Defend yourself, English pig-dog!" Connor shouted.

I scooped up the snowball and wheeled around. He and Ryan were right behind me, trying to look tough.

"So. We meet again," I said.

Ryan nodded. "We brought our armies. They're just waiting for our signal."

Not too gently, I pushed them apart to see. My sisters-in-law were standing behind them, holding big Tupperware bowls full of snowballs. "Hi, Jen. Hi, Amy."

They both wished me Merry Christmas, smiling brightly.

"This isn't a good idea right now," I remarked. "We have company. If we could be civilized here for just a split-second and introduce ourselves..."

"It's all right, Devvy," Cassie said. "We can introduce ourselves later. Your brothers want to say hello to you first."

Ryan nudged Connor. "I like her. She's not a sissy."

"And she's kind of, sort of, really, really good-looking," he agreed. "Maybe I'll marry her. Of course, that would be bigamy. Big of her, too."

Jen, long accustomed to her husband, just rolled her eyes. I shook my head and started to walk away, but Connor got a grip on my arm. "Not so fast. We haven't had the airing of grievances yet."

"Grievances, hell. You just want an excuse to show off in front of your wives. Except that you both throw like little girls." The snowball was starting to make my hand go numb; I pushed back between my brothers and dropped the snowball in Amy's bowl.

"Now, if the two of you want to put on some pathetic exhibition between yourselves—"

"Lock and load!" Connor howled. "Artillery captains! Fire!"

Snowballs started flying around the living room, mostly at me. That did it. Dodging around Ryan's left, I stole Jen's snowball bowl—she was laughing too hard to keep a grip on it—and started firing the contents back. Cassie was at my side in a flash, giving as good as we got.

"The enemy is persistent," Ryan remarked, wiping snow out of his eyes. "And the blonde one has done this before. What do you think? Should we *pitchez la vache?*"

"STOP THAT THIS MINUTE!"

Everyone froze, even Cassie, who had so little experience with the woman.

Mom waited a few seconds to be sure that her message had gotten through before she advanced on us. She was so mad that her glasses were practically steamed up from the inside, so mad that the jingle bells on her Christmas apron were tinkling a mile a minute. Connor, who towered over her, almost tripped in his hurry to get out of her way.

"Now," Mom demanded, "I want an explanation. I want to know who started this, and *why*. Connor? Ryan?"

Both of my strapping blond brothers looked at their feet.

"Devlin?"

I shrugged.

"I want to know why this happens every year. Every *year*, when you all know better. How many times do I have to tell you not to throw snowballs in the house?"

"At least one more," Ryan said solemnly.

We all looked at one another, trying our hardest not to laugh. But when I caught Amy's eye, she completely lost it, and that was that.

"Do you think this is funny?" Mom barked. "Just wait till your father gets home. He'll have something to say about this."

So she was going to try to be like that, was she? Not on my watch. Narrowing my eyes, I stepped into her path. "Just so you know, Mom, *Dad* started this whole thing. It was the Christmas Connor came home from college for the first time. Would you mind if I introduce our guest now?"

She didn't hear the last part, which was typical; it didn't involve her directly. "Your father's a grown man. He would never—"

"Dev's right," Ryan interrupted. "Dad and I snuck out of the house the night before to make the snowballs."

"'Sneaked,'" Mom corrected. "Not 'snuck.' How many times—"

Ryan sighed. "School's out, Mom. Get over it." He stepped around a big clump of snow on the rug to extend his hand to Cassie. "We haven't really met yet. I'm Ryan. You would have to be Cassie, wouldn't you? Welcome. The big dumb-looking guy is my brother Connor—"

"I didn't come here to be exonerated," Connor declared.

Without missing a beat, Ryan did a rim shot on the nearest table. "—who didn't come here to be exonerated. That's my lovely wife, Amy; his lovely wife, Jenny; and our mother, who isn't related to any of us."

It was showtime already, and Cassie hadn't been there a half hour yet. Protectively, I moved a little closer to her. "Don't pay any attention. They'll calm down after a while.

Maybe."

She smiled. There was melted snow on her eyelashes; I badly wanted to do something about that, but not in front of my family.

"You're all dripping on my rug," Mom snapped. "Go dry off this minute. All of you."

Connor started to tell her that we couldn't all, not at the same time, because there weren't enough baths to go around and a person needed privacy, for crying out loud, but she wasn't in the mood to hear other opinions. She sent him and Jen up to the master bath, Ryan and Amy up to the guest bath, and me to the half-bath downstairs. Only as an afterthought did she include Cassie. I made a mental note about that.

"And hang up the towels when you're done," Mom called after all of us. "I don't want to find towels wadded up all over the floor."

She would, though. I could have made her a list right then of all the things she'd find: water all over the bathrooms, empty beer bottles under the Christmas tree, male offspring drinking milk out of the carton when her back was turned. Not to mention all the lights on all the time, or both the TV and stereo going when no one was paying attention to either. None of it was my fault, but I would be guilty by association. That was OK, though, because it was better to be with my brothers than against them. Those two had never had a full deck between them.

Cassie waited to ask until I closed the half-bath door behind us. "Is she really mad?"

"No. She's just warming up. But so are they." Resigned, I pulled the last clean towel off the rack—apparently, my brothers had already passed through there—and handed it to her. "Go ahead. I'll use it when you're done."

A little smile flickered on her lips. "I've got a better idea."

"What?"

She looped the towel around my neck and gave the ends a tug, pulling me toward her. For quite a while, no drying off got done.

Fortunately, we'd just broken off when something tapped on the door. I opened it a few inches. Connor squeezed his face as far through the opening as he could, which was a very weird effect, which he knew. To my annoyance, Cassie started laughing.

"That's disgusting," I told him. "What do you want?"

"Police, ma'am. We got a complaint that you were having a good time in there. Will you be needing one cell or two downtown?"

I tried to slam the door on his face, but he got out in time. Cassie, being no help, was half-collapsed on the sink, still laughing.

"You only think they're funny," I grumbled.

"I do, actually. This might be fun after all."

Wisely, I didn't argue with her. She had no idea; she would find out in time.

After dinner, the first real trial of the holiday began: We played Trivial Pursuit.

Let me rephrase that: We played the Kerry Edition of Trivial Pursuit. Over the years, there'd been so many heated arguments over so many questions that we'd just started throwing disputed cards away. That left us so short of cards after a while that we started filling in with cards from other editions. Then, the horse being out of the stable and halfway to town already, we started making up our own cards. The questions about family trivia counted double.

I tried to get Cassie a dispensation for those questions, but no one would hear of it, including her. That troubled me. What *had* I told her about the family? How much was I going to regret it? It was bad enough that Connor and Jen were on our team; he was the worst one of all of us about challenging questions and starting fights. I noticed that he already had a stack of reference books handy.

"Those won't save you," I predicted. "If I weren't on your side, you'd go down in flames again, just like last year."

"I hate to remind you, Dev," Jen said, "but *you* went down the year before that. And the year before that, too."

I surveyed her coolly. "Who let you in this family, anyway?"

"Your brother." She yawned and put her head on his shoulder. "I think I'll divorce him for it in seventy or eighty years."

Was it my imagination, or did Cassie move a little closer to me on the couch? Better not have. "Shut up and roll the dice," I growled.

Mom launched into a complaint about the lack of respect we were showing one another, and at Christmas, of all times, until Dad pulled his reading glasses down on his nose and gave her a severe look.

"Thanks, Pop," Connor said, reaching for the dice.

At first, everything was fine. There were only two challenges and one incident of throwing dice at people in the first half hour, and the game was close. Then Ryan had to draw one of the family-trivia cards on Cassie's turn. *Name our ancestor who was lynched in Scotland, and why. Extra point for each reason after three.*

Visibly agitated, Mom tried to snatch the card out of his hand. "I thought you *promised* me you took that card out. Ryan, give me that. Draw another one. This—"

"George Buchanan," Cassie said calmly. "Devvy's great-great-great-great-grandfather."

Dead, shocked silence. My family looked at me accusingly. Scowling, I refused to be cowed. It was a good story, and so what if I'd told it to my best friend?

"You'll have to give me a minute on all the reasons," she continued. "There were five or six of them, weren't there?"

Touché. Proud of her against my will, I patted her on the back. My brothers and their wives, I noticed, were amused.

My mother was not. And she was not one to keep a feeling—any feeling—to herself. "This is a silly game. A silly waste of time. We could all be having a nice conversation or going for a walk, but here we sit, raking up ancient garbage and—"

"Here's a trivia question for you, Mom," Connor cut in. "In what year did you stop treating your grown children like two-year-olds?"

Exasperated, I nudged him as hard as I could. He nudged back. Then he made a buzzer noise. "Sorry, Mrs. Kerry, your time is up. The answer is: never! But we do have some lovely parting gifts for—"

Mom didn't wait to hear the rest of it. She got up and marched upstairs without a backward look. We waited in silence until we heard a door slam.

"Way to go, Swifty," I muttered. "Go apologize."

He looked to his wife uncertainly. Not liking the look he got back, he turned to Dad. Even worse. "I was only kidding. Besides, what's the big deal? It's *your* ancestor, not hers."

"Apologize to your mother," Dad told him, his tone absolutely flat.

Connor threw up his hands and started up the stairs, stomping a little harder than necessary.

"I'm really sorry," Cassie said. "I didn't know it would be a problem. But Devvy told me the story, and it's sort of a hard one to forget."

Dad waved her apology off. "You have nothing to apologize for. Martha gets a little overexcited this time of year."

And all other times of year, I thought. Carefully, making sure no one could possibly see, I rubbed the small of Cassie's back reassuringly.

"She'll slam doors for a few minutes, and then she'll go out on the balcony to smoke a couple of cigarettes. After that, she'll be fine." Dad leaned forward confidentially. "So did Devlin tell you that George Buchanan fathered thirty children out of wedlock?"

I got up and left the room.

Very late that night, I retired to the small den downstairs, where the sleeper sofa was. Cassie was reluctantly settled in my old room, which was a generic guest room now; I figured we could skip the conjugal visit that night and catch up on sleep.

But I hadn't been in bed five minutes before she sneaked in.

"You're not serious," I protested. "It's 1 in the morning."

"I don't want to do *that.* Well, I do, but I'll live tonight. I just want to sleep. Move over."

"This is kind of risky, Cass. Mom gets up early."

"So? You're being awfully proper for someone whose ancestor fathered thirty children out of wedlock."

"We don't know that for sure," I said defensively, but moved over to let her in. "Promise you'll go back upstairs early?"

She busied herself getting comfortable. "Set the alarm, and I will."

That was all I could ask, then. Reaching up to the end table, I grabbed the travel alarm, reset it and put it back. "Goodnight, sweetheart."

"You too," she murmured. "Sweet dreams."

It was very quiet for a long time.

"Devvy?"

"Cass?"

"What if we just have fifteen children out of wedlock? I think thirty would be showing off."

I pulled the pillow out from under my head, whacked her with it and replaced it without a word. Cassie just laughed.

Chapter Twenty-Two

Cassie was still there when I woke up, which was long after I'd set the travel alarm for. At first, I thought it hadn't gone off, but then I saw it lying on its face halfway across the room. Cass had an awful habit of doing that to alarm clocks.

Apprehensively, I got out of bed and slipped out of the den, taking care not to wake her. It was still early, and everything seemed quiet; I'd just make a quick reconnaissance pass before deciding what to do.

First, though, I was going to turn up the thermostat. The house was freezing.

I'd just touched the dial when a small noise startled me. Connor was sacked out in the recliner, snoring lightly. Great. Either Jen had kicked him out of bed for some trespass or he'd gotten up in the middle of the night to watch "Mystery Science Theatre" reruns, but it didn't matter; this was a problem. Cassie would complain when I woke her, loudly enough to wake *him*, and I wasn't up to explanations. Not even to lies. Not before coffee.

Troubled, I considered the situation. He seemed to be dead to the world, but you could never tell with Connor; he could doze off watching football but tell you the score if you poked him. It was one of his scarier talents.

I was on the verge of poking him just to see what would happen when a hand landed on my shoulder. The surprise was too much; a second before I realized who it was, I yelped. Cassie tried to put her other hand over my mouth, but it was too late. Connor was awake. Worse, he was in a good mood.

"Is this some strange sexual practice I should know about?" he asked.

Seriously annoyed, I threw Cassie off. "Get therapy, Connor."

"What for? I never felt better." Yawning, he ran a hand over his disheveled hair. "Morning, Cassie. You're looking lovely today. Sleep well, did you?"

She glanced at me before answering. "I did, thanks. You?"

"Oh, not so well, not so well, not so well. Jenny threw me out for snoring. She said if she has to deal with my mother all day, she needs a whole night's sleep."

"She has a point," I remarked. "Sleep, and maybe a Doberman."

Connor smiled. "Maybe an armed Doberman. But never mind that. How did *you* sleep?"

This concern about my well-being was new and unwelcome. "Fine."

"Swell to hear it. I was worried you might be...oh, I don't know...lonesome in there all by yourself. Or cold. Or *something*. Hmmmm?"

Cassie coughed significantly and announced that she was going back upstairs. I waited until she turned the corner on the stair landing to whack my brother upside his pointy head.

"What was that for?" he protested, rubbing it.

"I'll give you *something*, buster. Wait till I tell your wife you were flirting with Cassie. You may never get *something* again without a credit card."

"Flirting? That's not flirting. I'm just being friendly. Not as friendly as *you*, of course, but—hey!"

It wasn't nice to pull his chest hair, but it was his own fault for having any.

"Whatever you're up to, stop it."

"I'm not up to anything. Can't a person have a polite conversation around here?"

"No."

Unfazed, he flashed one of those big dopey grins of his. "Suit yourself. I was going to start out polite this morning and work up to charming by lunch, but if you want me to just be myself..."

"Lesser of two evils," I snapped.

"Temper," he cautioned. "It's Christmas."

Not for two more days, it wasn't, which gave me time to wreak justice on him. But before I could start wreaking, we heard the terrible scuff of Mom's slippers on the stair landing.

Connor grimaced. "You get the thermostat. I'll get the coffee. Run!"

"I don't know why you children insist on making coffee so strong," Mom said for the dozenth time. "It's wasteful."

Dourly, I poured another shot. Connor did overdo it some, but better that than the way Mom made it, which was more like essence of coffee than the thing itself.

"There's coffee cake," she added, also for the dozenth time. "Where's Carrie?"

"Cassie," I corrected. "Taking a shower, I imagine. Why?"

"I just hope there's enough hot water for everyone. All of you take so long in the shower, and—"

"Drop it, Mother."

"Well, you do."

Irritably, I looked to Connor for some help. Mom and Dad had put in an industrial-size water heater a few years ago, after Ryan got married, so that we wouldn't have an excuse to stay at the Holiday Inn when we all came home for Christmas. The only way we were going to run out of hot water now would be if Luxembourg came over for a bath.

"We do not," Connor argued. "And even if we do, at least we're clean. Isn't cleanliness next to godliness? Or is that wealthiness?"

I shrugged. "Depends on the denomination."

"Stop that," Mom ordered me.

"Stop what? I haven't said anything sacrilegious yet."

"Yet?"

Dammit. "Never mind."

Laughing, Connor tipped his chair back and started clucking.

"Forget it," I told him. "That only works on Ryan."

He clucked louder.

"You're wasting your time, Connor."

More clucking.

"I mean it."

Clucking *and* wing flapping. I sprang at him just as he was rocking his chair back again and took him to the floor with a satisfying crash.

At which moment, of *course*, Cassie and Amy walked into the kitchen. I couldn't bring myself to see what Cassie thought, but Amy was perfectly calm. In fact, she just stepped around Connor and me; pulled up a chair; and nodded to Mom, who was speechless with shock.

"I have to tell you, Mrs. Kerry," she remarked, "I have never been bored in this family."

Point to the sister-in-law. Connor and I disentangled ourselves and retreated to opposite sides of the table. Only when I was safely seated again did I risk a glance at Cassie. She had her most neutral expression on, but her eyes warmed when they met mine, and a tiny smile touched her lips. That meant she was probably going to forgive me.

Not that she had a choice. Without me, she'd be all alone with these maniacs.

"He clucked at me," I explained, a little defensively.

"Really?" My sister-in-law reached for the coffee cake. "I thought that only worked on Ryan. Want me to go get him before you lose your dignity?"

Cassie and Connor liked that. So, by her smirk, did Amy, who was getting to be too much like one of us already. If Ryan was rubbing off on her the way Connor had on his own wife, I was doomed to smart-alecky relatives all the way to the grave. Especially if they ever figured out how to reproduce.

"That's enough," Mom said abruptly. "Carrie, have some coffee cake."

I cleared my throat. "*Cassie.* Not Carrie."

"Thank God," Connor said. "Carrie Kerry would be a terrible name. Don't you think?"

No one said anything. That was very bad. You were in trouble in this family only if everyone shut up.

"I'm going to take a shower," I said, trying to make it sound like a threat. "And then Cass and I are going to go check in at the Holiday Inn."

Mom frowned. "Don't be silly. We've got plenty of room."

"It's not the room I'm worried about. It's the company." At which point I scowled at Connor. "Clucking at *me*, when you don't have the nerve to ask me outright if I'm sleeping with her."

You could've cut the quiet with a chainsaw.

"Devvy?" Cassie asked softly.

I was still glowering at my brother. "What?"

"I'll handle this. Go take your shower."

"There's nothing to handle. Just get packed. I'll be fast."

"I thought we came here to spend Christmas with your family," she said, sounding dangerously reasonable. "It would defeat the purpose if we stayed somewhere else, wouldn't it?"

For the first time, Mom looked at her with something like approval. "It would also be expensive."

"Yes, it would," Cassie agreed.

Mom nodded. "Paying for two rooms and all."

Cassie heard the slight stress she put on "two" and gave her a very charming smile. "Absolutely."

"This is *not* about money," I protested. "Or about how many rooms. It's about—"

The doorbell rang.

"I'll get it," Connor said, too quickly, and practically ran to the door. Spitefully, I clucked at him—and got such bad looks from Mom and Amy that I stopped. No one said a word until Connor came back.

"Who is it?" Mom asked.

"It's for Dev. Some hot-looking babe. Says she's from the agency."

Uneasily, I got up to see what the problem was—just as the problem strolled in. I muttered a bad word. "Vanessa."

"Razor-sharp as ever," she shot back. "Why, I'll bet you can count to twenty without even using your toes. I just came by to drop off your termination papers. I can't believe I had to come all the way to this sorry excuse for a one-horse town." A little smirk. "So where do they keep the horse?...You look awful, by the way. Is this your family?"

"She doesn't look awful," Cassie growled. "She just hasn't had a shower yet."

Wonderful. Out of all that gibberish, she chose *that* part to respond to. My mother, on the other hand, zeroed right in. "Termination papers?"

"Oh, yes. It's a long story. May I?" Without waiting to find out whether she might, Vanessa took the last vacant chair. "She was fired a couple of weeks ago. They were *both* fired, actually. Devlin's problem was something about insubordination and witchcraft, but—"

"She was fired?" Mom repeated, rounding on me with a dire expression.

I didn't need that right then. "We're appealing it. It's a misunderstanding."

"That's not the point, young lady. You were fired, and you didn't tell me?"

"How is it your business?"

"If I could finish," Vanessa said, clearly enjoying herself, "I'll tell you about the insubordination."

I broke off glaring back at Mom long enough to include her. Then I checked Connor and Amy. They looked vaguely stunned, which was fine as long as it kept them both quiet. "Just give me the papers, Vanessa. Then get out."

"What for? I might miss something."

"That's the point."

Cassie narrowed her eyes at Vanessa. "Let's have a little talk in the other room. Devvy, why don't you go get your shower now?"

"Not a chance. I'm not leaving you alone with that...that..."

"Beloved colleague?" Vanessa supplied sweetly.

I let that go. "Not to mention alone with my family. We're going to pack now and go straight to the motel, got that?"

"No," Cassie said.

"What?"

"No." Purposefully, she pushed her chair back and walked over to pat my shoulder. "I'll handle this."

"But—"

"No buts. Go shower. I'll *handle* it." When I hesitated, she gave me a little push. "Don't make me force you."

"I'd pay to see that," Connor said reverently.

Amy, somewhat recovered, kicked him hard enough to make him jump.

"Go," Cassie said again. "Now. Please?"

I couldn't very well refuse when she'd asked nicely; it would get me a lecture from Mom on top of the lecture I would already get about being fired. Besides, it would give me time to think. I did some of my best thinking in the shower; maybe lightning would strike.

Reluctantly, I turned to go upstairs. The last thing I heard was Vanessa's laughter.

I hoped she got a bad piece of coffee cake.

Some Christmas this was going to be. My relatives were already on their worst behavior, and now a demon was sitting at the kitchen table. No matter what, things were only going to get worse, and no matter what Cassie said, we were leaving as soon as I got done here.

Muttering, I took a towel and washcloth out of the linen closet and started unpacking my toiletry kit on the counter. Just as I was pulling the razor out of its travel case, something moved in the mirror behind me. Startled, I turned. Nothing was there. And for my trouble, I'd cut myself with the razor.

Great. My luck today, there'll be sharks in the tub.

I jumped again as a breeze blew past. That might have been my imagination, and so might the soft laughter that went with it, but it might also have been Vanessa's idea of a prank. The best thing to do was get a quick shower and get out.

Putting the weirdness firmly out of my mind, I hung my robe on a doorknob and turned on the tap in the bathtub. A stream of bright red liquid flowed out. It looked disturbingly like—

Blood. Quickly, I shut the tap off. A few seconds later, I turned it on again. The water ran clear.

"Humbug," I said deliberately, getting in and pulling the curtain.

It was almost the fastest shower on record. I was just rinsing my hair when the lights went out, which was inconvenient but not critical. There were candles on the counter—Hawthorne women were big on decorating bathrooms with fancy soaps and candles, which I'd learned the hard way were not for actual use—and I could always light one.

But before I could even turn off the water, I heard a match strike and saw a faint glow through the shower curtain.

"Cassie?"

No answer. Maybe she was busy lighting the candles; the room was starting to fill with flickering light.

"What happened? Did the power go out?"

Very brief silence. Then a strong wind rose out of nowhere, flapping the shower curtain and blowing out the candles.

"Vanessa?"

I half-heard that soft laughter again—immediately followed by an explosion of thunder and lightning.

There wasn't time to be scared. Whether the bathroom was haunted was pretty much irrelevant at the moment anyway; I was standing in a shower in a lightning storm, which was asking for trouble. Reaching down, I tried to shut the water off, but my hand passed through something ice cold. Alarmed, I pulled back.

In the flashes of lightning, I faintly made out the shape of a woman dressed in black, standing under the shower spray. I couldn't see her face, but her hair was blowing as though she were in a high wind—and both it and her clothes were completely dry. In the darkness between lightning bolts, I saw a pair of glowing red eyes.

Oh-oh.

Not being a fool, I tried to get out of the tub at that point. But the shower curtain wouldn't budge. That wasn't good. I was a little underdressed for an emergency, not to mention soaking wet, and the only weapon at hand was a plastic squeegee. Still, you do what you have to do with what you have. Yanking the squeegee off its hook, I held it out in front of me like a weapon.

The thing in the shower spray laughed—a weird sort of laughter, like mice on helium. Then it disappeared. But was it really gone?

Again, my peripheral vision caught movement, this time above me. I waited for the next flare of lightning.

A huge black snake was wrapped around the showerhead, its own head inches from mine, forked tongue flickering.

Well, that was just about enough shower time for one day. And it was time to get the hell out of there. Still gripping the squeegee, I gathered all my strength and tackled the immovable curtain.

A second too late, I realized that everything had suddenly gone back to normal. The storm was gone; the lights were back on; and I was hurtling through an ordinary, very movable shower curtain at a high rate of speed. Whatever I hit, it was going to hurt.

I braced for the worst as something grabbed me.

Chapter Twenty-Three

"Going somewhere?" a familiar voice asked. "Dressed like that?"

Still in shock, I tried to break free, but Cassie held on. "Easy. Take it easy. It's me. What's the matter?"

Getting words out took a few tries. "It's in the shower."

"OK," she said evenly. "Let's have a look. Let me have this first." When I refused, she tried to pry my fingers off the squeegee. "Come on—let go now."

"It's huge. *Gigantic*. It did this thing with its tongue, and—"

Still intent on disarming me, she only half-listened to that. "And you were going to squeegee it to death? Great plan, honey. Let *go.*"

With a vicious swipe, I took it out of her reach. Keeping a sharp eye on her, I put my robe on—rather awkwardly, what with having a squeegee in one hand, but on just the same. "Stand back," I warned.

"Why?"

Why? I'd show her why. *Then* she'd be sorry. Weapon at the ready, I advanced on the shower curtain and yanked it down the rod, revealing...nothing. No monster serpents, no apparitions, nothing. Just the water still running.

Sighing, Cassie leaned back against the counter. "I can't wait to hear the explanation for this."

"There was a snake in the shower," I said sulkily. "As big as Orson Welles."

"Are you sure?"

"*Yes*, I'm sure. What kind of question is that?"

"Well, honey, it's winter. There's a foot of snow on the ground. If your parents have snakes, they're probably hibernating."

"Snakes don't hibernate."

"How do you know?"

I didn't, in fact, but we were getting off the subject. "That one was wide awake."

Cassie thought it over for a second. Then she crossed the bath to give me an oppressively comforting hug. "It's all right now. Everything's fine. You've just had too much stress lately. Why don't—"

"I'm not having stress!" I shouted, pushing her away.

"—you get dressed, and we'll go for a walk. I think we could both use some fresh air. How about it?"

"Don't patronize me."

"I'm not patronizing you. I'm trying to get you to calm down and start making sense. *Give* me that." Making an unexpected move, she seized the squeegee and threw it in the clothes hamper, where it wouldn't be a distraction anymore. "Now talk to me. What happened?"

Bitterly, knowing she wouldn't believe me, I told her.

"It's probably just Monica," she said.

"Not her style."

"She has no style."

I started to argue the point but decided it would be a fool's errand. "Would it be too much trouble to tell me what you're doing in here, anyway? Aren't you supposed to be downstairs *handling* my family?"

"Oh. That." To my alarm, she looked vaguely guilty. "Well, you see, Devvy—"

"I never end up liking sentences that start that way," I muttered.

"—I was trying to tell them to go easy on you, because it's not against the law, but—"

"What's not against the law?"

"You and me. Us. Together. *You* know." *You'd better know,* her expression added. "I was trying to get them to back off, but your mother got upset, and...well..."

Worse and worse. "And then what?"

"I handled them," Vanessa said.

We both spun around. Cassie's demon was perched on the counter, filing her claws.

"What did you do?" I demanded.

"Nothing permanent."

"Meaning what?"

"Meaning," Vanessa said, affecting great weariness, "that I put them on hold for a little while. All that *talking* was giving me a headache. Does anyone in your family ever shut up, Devlin?"

Cassie tried to make it seem as though she'd been coughing. I added that to the list of things we would discuss later. "On hold?"

"They're fine. Just resting. Don't you believe me?"

By way of answer, I shoved her aside and raced down to the kitchen.

It all looked absolutely normal—Mom scowling, Connor smirking, both of them with their mouths wide open—except that everything was frozen. Tentatively, I pulled Connor's hair. Not even a blink. Amy, for her part, was sitting slumped down with one hand over her eyes.

"They were arguing," Cassie murmured.

I jumped a little, not having heard her follow me downstairs.

"Connor said you were all too old for bed checks," she continued. "But he offered to check up on *us*. Your mother said something about God not making Adam and Steve, and then Vanessa zapped them."

"They bored me," the demon said, behind us.

I didn't even bother to turn. "That's not the point, Vanessa."

"Of course it's the point. Your family is positively awful, Devlin. That explains a lot about *you*, but they're still awful. Want me to put them to sleep for you? Permanently?"

"Maybe later. Right now, I want you to unzap them and then go away so I can get dressed."

"You look all right," the demon said. "For you, anyway."

"I can't go around in a robe all day."

"Oh, I don't know about that. You're not always this uptight. And Lucifer knows *she* isn't. There was that one day at the beach..." She let her voice trail off delicately, to give us time to catch her drift.

"How do you know about that?" Cassie asked, outraged.

"I get around. It's one of the perks of the job."

I was going to perk *her* for that. But Cassie blocked me and refused to move. "You mean you see *everything* that goes on?"

"We can if we want. It's a little like being Santa." The demon smirked and then broke into song:

> *We see you when you're sleeping*
> *We know when you're awake*
> *We know if you've been bad or good*
> *So be bad, for goodness' sake...Ow!*

That last word was supposed to be "Oh!", of course, but Cassie had just pinched her.

"Just fix it," I told Vanessa.

"Oh, all right." Sulking, she started to take the spell off, but then something occurred to her. "Do you want a couple of minutes' head start?"

"What for?"

"You forgot to turn the water off upstairs. If your mother finds out, you're in big trouble."

I hated it when demons were right. Unwillingly, I turned to go back upstairs.

"By the way," Vanessa called. "About the snake."

Damn—I'd already forgotten about it. What did it say for my quality of life that I had worse problems than snakes in the shower? "What about it?"

"That was Monica's idea. I can't help you with her here. Wish I could."

Cassie blanched. "You mean there really *was* a snake?"

"An anaconda," Vanessa confirmed.

I smiled triumphantly at Cassie, who was edging closer to me.

"It might be back," the demon added. "I really don't know what Monica's up to. But don't worry—anacondas aren't poisonous. They just squeeze you to death."

There was a very long silence in the kitchen, and not just on the part of the frozen parties.

"Hurry up and get dressed," Cassie finally said. "I'll call the Holiday Inn."

As soon as we checked in, I curled up on one of the beds to review the ruin of my life: no job, two demons and a blonde girlfriend who'd just outed me to my family. She'd had the best of intentions, but we were still done for. Connor and Ryan would tree us, Mom would finish us, and the giant snake would be lucky if there were any leftovers.

"I was born in this town," I told Cassie absently. "And I'm going to die here. This Christmas."

"No, you're not."

"Yes, I am."

"No, you're not."

"Yes, I am."

"No, you're not." She quit unpacking cosmetics long enough to give me a severe look in the mirror. "Stop right there. I mean it."

I stopped. But only out loud.

"You're not going to die, Devvy. Even if you want to, I won't let you. Got that?"

The phone rang. Reluctantly, I rolled over and grabbed it. "Got it....Hello?"

"This is your mother," Mom said sternly.

Fear gripped me for a second, but then I remembered that I was a goner anyway, so what the hell. "I don't believe you. Do you have ID?"

"You're not funny, young lady."

"Wrong on both counts, Mother."

Cassie, still busy unpacking, dropped something in the sink with a terrible clatter. Mom heard. "What was that?"

"Cassie."

"She's in your room?"

For the love of God. "She's in *our* room. Was there something you wanted?"

"Aunt Kitty and Uncle Edgar are coming over for dinner."

"How nice for them. And...?"

"Don't get smart. They'll want to see you. You need to be here by 6."

"Is that an invitation or an order?"

There was silence on the line.

"Mom?" The bed shifted as Cassie sat down next to me; she gave me an inquiring look, which I answered with a shrug. "Hello?"

"This is difficult for all of us," Mom finally said. "I don't think we need to discuss the...*issue* in front of them. Do you suppose your friend could just stay at the motel?"

I slammed the phone down so hard that everything on the night table jumped.

"Devvy? What is it?"

"I'm not leaving you anywhere," I told her fiercely. "Not now, not later, not ever."

She smiled uncertainly and stroked my cheek. "Good, because I'm not going to *be* left. What brought that on?"

"My mother."

"I know." She kept stroking. "What did she say?"

It didn't matter. Suddenly, a five-alarm blaze was burning inside me, and the last thing I wanted to do was talk about my mother. With a suddenness that surprised both of us, I swept Cassie into my arms and down onto the bed.

"Something you want, lamb chop?" she asked.

There was, as a matter of fact. And I was in no mood to wait until Christmas.

Fortunately, she wasn't either.

When we finally left the room a few hours later, we were surprised by a blanket of new snow—several inches of it, topped with a thin layer of sleet. That meant digging Cassie's car out and scraping the windows, which was going to make us late.

After all the trouble I went to, teaching you how to tell time, Mom would say. *Do you know how long it took me to do that?*

I did know, as it happened; she'd mentioned it several hundred times in the course of our acquaintance. Maybe she'd be too distracted by the...*issue* to bring it up tonight, though.

"You're sure this is a good idea?" Cassie asked.

I smiled at her over the car roof. "No."

She scooped a handful of snow off the hood and threw it at me.

"Not now, sweetheart. We're going to be late."

I'd just bent back over my task when a snowball clipped my shoulder. Cassie struck a mock-defiant pose, gloved hands on hips. "Dare you," she said.

"Don't be a fool. You can't win. And you'll just get your hair all wet."

She blew me a kiss and threw another snowball.

"I love you too, Cassie. Now come on and finish scraping your side so we can get—"

A snowball exploded on my chest, scattering down my coat and inside my sweater. Swearing at the shock of the cold, I danced around a little.

"Don't make me cluck at you, honey," she said.

That meant war. In a matter of minutes, Cassie's BMW was all cleared off— we'd thrown all the snow at each other—and we were going down the parking lot, scooping ammo off other people's cars. We called a truce only when I happened to look at my watch and realized that we were already fifteen minutes late.

Back in the room, we quickly changed clothes. Then, while Cassie dried her hair, I called the house. To my relief, Dad answered.

"Hi, Dad. It's me. We're running behind. Why don't you go ahead and start without—" I broke off, realizing that I was talking to nobody; he'd put his hand over the mouthpiece and was talking to someone in the background. "Dad? You there?"

"Sorry, Devlin. Your mother's a little upset. You know how she gets. Where are you?"

"At the hotel. We'll be leaving in a couple of minutes. But go ahead and start dinner without us. OK?"

He put his hand over the mouthpiece again and relayed that information. Impatiently, I waited for him to come back. "Devlin?"

"Still here."

"Your mother wants to know if you're going to behave yourself tonight." He dropped his voice confidentially. "That's not quite how *I* would have put it, but—"

"Dad?"

"Yes?"

"Would you give Mom a message from me?"

"Of course. What message?"

I slammed the phone down again.

At the mirror, Cassie frowned and switched off the hair dryer for a second. "What now?"

"If you've got any asbestos underwear," I growled, "wear it. This is going to be a hell of a night."

Chapter Twenty-Four

The cul-de-sac was pitch dark when we got there—no lights in any of the houses and no streetlights either. That was odd. We hadn't had *that* much snow, and it wasn't even the heavy kind that knocked down power lines.

"Wonder when that happened," Cassie remarked. "I didn't notice any power outages on the way over, did you?"

"No." Warily, I studied the house. "Park away from it, Cass."

"What are you talking about?"

"The house. Something's not right. Just to be safe, let's park on the street."

She hit the brakes, making the BMW skid slightly. "Would you mind not talking like that? I'm already nervous."

"Sorry, sweetheart."

Not entirely reassured, she pulled up to the curb a few houses away—very close to the plowed-off snow, which was piled up to nearly the door handles. I had some trouble getting out but didn't mention it. Better to save my fire for a battle that mattered.

We walked toward the house in silence except for the crunch of our footsteps on the snowy street. The closer we got, the more apprehensive I got. There was just enough moonlight to show the Christmas decorations on the neighbors' houses—decorations that on this dead, dark cul-de-sac had the effect of wreaths on a tomb.

Cassie touched my coat sleeve. "Look. Full moon."

We stopped to admire it, our breath misting up around us in the frozen night. The moon was half-shrouded in haze, which meant more snow later. But it was a thing of ghostly beauty now.

"You know what they say about full moons," I said. "The inmates take over the asylums, and all the dogs go mad."

She reached into my coat pocket to squeeze my hand. "You're such a comfort, pookie."

"Just telling you what I hear."

Still holding onto my hand, she gave me a little tug to start us walking again. We passed the Hills' house, where the kids had built a crude snowman in the front yard; as we drew even with it, the head fell off, hitting the ground with a thump and rolling toward us. Startled, I kicked the thing away.

Cassie didn't say anything, but she moved a little closer.

As we reached the end of my parents' driveway, the black bulk in it resolved itself into a Cadillac parked at a weird angle. In fact, it had been driven in at a weird angle, judging by the tire tracks across the neighbors' yard. Uncle Edgar couldn't drive worth a damn. It was one of the many things Mom had against him.

Truth be told, I didn't like him either—much less Aunt Kitty. And they were both inside right now, waiting for us like spiders.

Not cheered by this train of thought, I led Cassie up the drive. We were close enough now to notice a dim, shifting glow in the windows, which had to be candlelight. I wished we'd thought to bring the flashlight from the car, but we could always go back for it. Besides, there had to be a flashlight in that barge of Uncle Edgar's. You couldn't have a car that big and not have something in it.

I'd just touched the doorknob when the doorbell caught my attention. The electricity was out, but the button was glowing. That didn't make sense. As I watched, the light began to change shape, forming into something like a human face—an old man in an old-fashioned nightcap, looking very much like...

"Stop that!" I shouted.

The face vanished and the doorbell reappeared, dark this time.

"Did I just see what I thought I just saw?" Cassie asked.

"That depends," I said cautiously. "What do you think you just saw?"

She thought about it briefly, then exhaled in frustration, sending up a huge plume of steam. "Forget it. It's too stupid."

"Then you saw it. Monica's making a little Dickens joke."

"Not a very good one." She touched the doorbell tentatively. "If we were in a movie, you know, this would be the part where the audience would tell us to run."

"But if we did, there wouldn't be a movie, would there?"

Cassie laughed. "Let's get this over with, then. I've got plans for after the show."

They were in the kitchen, drinking wine—the screw-top stuff Aunt Kitty liked, so sweet you could pour it on waffles—and they were all very civil when we walked in. But it was a chilly kind of civility, a kind I knew only too well. They'd been talking about us, and they were hacked that we'd showed up and ruined their fun.

Well, we wouldn't stay long. I didn't want to ruin *our* fun, either.

Politely, I walked Cassie over to my aunt and uncle. They blinked at her, froglike, while I introduced her. Not for the first time, I wished I had presentable relatives. By candlelight especially, their features were grotesque; they might have crawled out of drains in the middle of the night. On top of that, Uncle Edgar still wore that godawful vulgar gold chain. It was like being related to down-home Mafiosi.

"So," Aunt Kitty said. "You're Candy."

Mom shook her head. "Carrie."

"Cassie," I growled.

Cassie smiled sweetly. "Whatever's easiest for you."

"And you're a friend of my niece," Aunt Kitty said.

"A very good friend," Cassie confirmed.

Across the room, Connor snickered. Ryan and Jen both poked him hard, but I got the impression it was just for show.

Aunt Kitty frowned at him over her glasses. "What's funny?"

"Nothing," I assured her. "Connor's a jerk. You know that."

"You're all jerks," she said. "Now give me a kiss."

Cassie, expecting the worst, held her breath. But I simply did as I was told—resentfully and with only one lip, but without argument. Aunt Kitty was even worse than Mom when she wasn't happy, which was almost always.

Dad jumped in before the situation could deteriorate any further. "So now we're all here. Glad you two made it. We don't know about dinner—"

"It was almost ready when the power went out," Mom snapped.

"No one said it was your fault," he soothed her. "I'm just saying we don't know when we'll have dinner."

She refused to be soothed. "As soon as the power comes back on, *that's* when."

Everyone shifted uneasily except Aunt Kitty, who was already deep in the grape, and Uncle Edgar, who hadn't actually participated in conversation since 1971. I glanced over at Ryan; he mouthed the word "Help."

Well, what was I supposed to do? We all knew how this went. Mom didn't like her sister, who didn't like her back, but neither of them would admit it, so these little gatherings made everyone crazy. There was nothing to do but endure until Kitty got on her broomstick and left.

Correctly interpreting the unhelpful look I gave Ryan, Jen tried her luck at damage control. "I don't think we're going to starve with all this food around. Dev, Cassie, come try this cheese ball. It's fantastic."

"It's a heart attack on crackers," Aunt Kitty countered.

I gave her what may have looked like a smile. "Do let me get you some."

Cassie jabbed me.

"Killjoy," I muttered. "Come on. Let's have some anyway."

We were about halfway across the kitchen when Cassie tripped over something and grabbed my arm for balance. As she did, the lights came back on, and we all saw what she'd tripped over:

A big black anaconda.

No one moved. Not a muscle. Even Cassie, who liked snakes about as much as she liked mice, which was not at all, was riveted to the spot.

"Oh, there you are, Milton," Mom said.

Two more beats of silence—and then everyone else jumped up on furniture. It took a few extra seconds for what she'd said to register.

"M-M-M-Milton?" Amy quavered.

Mom, insultingly calm, spread braunschweiger on a cracker. "He was a science project. Got away from one of my students last year when he was a baby. He must've come home with me in my briefcase....Here, Milton. Have some braunschweiger."

Many conflicting ideas crashed in my brain, which was in serious danger of exploding. It was a real snake. My mother knew it. My mother was feeding it braunschweiger. But worst of all...

"Milton?" I demanded, as soon as my voice worked. "Milton? What evil, twisted sonuvabitch would name a snake *Milton?*"

"Watch your language," Mom said, fixing another cracker.

"And why would *you* have a runaway science project? You teach English."

She ignored me, crooning something to the snake, which was swaying expectantly on the linoleum.

Cassie's reflexes finally kicked back in. She'd jumped on the same chair as me, largely because she'd never let go of my arm, and she released her grip slightly now, but not enough to give me full use of my circulation.

"Are you all right?" I asked.

She drew a ragged breath. "I don't know anymore. It's been so long since anything was normal."

There was nothing to do but laugh. After a second, she did too. Then my brothers and their wives joined in, and even Dad cracked a smile.

"I don't see anything funny," Mom complained.

Dad was still smiling. "Never mind, Martha. Boys, get down here and help me with this snake."

They didn't move. "You said 'boys,'" Connor explained. "We're men."

"Manly men," Ryan agreed.

"Doing manly things," Connor added.

Dad's patience ran out. *"Now."*

Grumbling, they climbed down and took up battle positions. There was a long, complicated argument about tactics, but they finally agreed on herding the snake into a packing box. That led to an argument about whether a person could actually herd a snake and, if so, whether that would make them snakeboys or snakemen.

The snake settled the argument by slithering behind the refrigerator.

Mom got up and dusted her hands off briskly. "Don't worry. He'll turn up again. Let's eat."

We had chicken for dinner ("Tastes just like snake," Connor declared), and I don't think I chewed a bite. Cassie, sitting as close to me as humanly possible, bolted hers, too. She was worried about the big reptile loose on the premises; I was more worried about the smaller ones.

Aunt Kitty especially. She'd had four glasses of wine, which was three past her tolerance, and she'd been watching Cassie and me all through dinner as though we might try to steal the silverware. I tried staring back at her, but the woman was shameless.

Finally, Mom brought out the coffee and the rum cake. It was almost over. Uncle Edgar would light one of those two-bit cigars and use his dessert plate as an ashtray, which would give us two disgusting excuses to leave.

"We can go in a few minutes," I whispered to Cassie. "You OK?"

She nodded. "Just."

"Hang in there. The worst is—"

"What are you two whispering about?" Mom asked sharply. "Is there something you'd like to share with the rest of us?"

My mother, the terror of the classroom. Wishing she would learn, just once, to give it a rest, I scowled at her.

"Kids today," Aunt Kitty remarked.

Ryan cleared his throat. "We're not really kids, Aunt Kitty. I can't speak for Dev, but Connor and I are snakemen, with all the honors and privileges appurtenant thereto, and I think—"

"Don't talk back to your aunt," Uncle Edgar warned.

Connor, Ryan and I gaped at him in astonishment. That was the most the man had talked in years.

"They have terrible manners," Aunt Kitty complained to Mom. "Especially

Devlin. This is *your* fault for letting her go into advertising."

"Hey!" I objected.

"She's not in it anymore," Mom said. "They fired her a couple of weeks ago."

Aunt Kitty frowned. "Because of that girl, I bet."

The only sound in the dining room was the clatter of silver on china as everyone dropped their forks.

"No offense, Candy," she added, "but this isn't Los Angeles. Hey, do you two know Ellen?"

Cassie, finally maxed out, started laughing hysterically. But I was not amused, and I pushed my chair back with serious intent.

"Sit down," Mom ordered. "Don't pay any attention. Kitty's had too much to drink."

"She always does, Mother. She's an alcoholic."

Both Mom and Aunt Kitty froze—the latter in the act of raising a glass to her lips.

I bent down to whisper to Cassie. "Go get our coats. I'll be right out." Then, to the others, "If we're going to hang out the dirty laundry, let's empty the hamper, shall we?"

Furious, Mom started to argue back, but Dad cut her off. "She was insulted, Martha. Let her have her say."

"You always stick up for her," Mom spat.

He didn't back down. "Because you never do."

Cassie had been halfway out of the dining room and stopped to hear the rest. But Jen and Amy got up in a flash to get her out of the line of fire. "It's only safe in there for Kerrys right now," I heard Amy explain.

Wrong. It was safe for no one. Coolly, I grabbed Aunt Kitty's wineglass and poured what little was left on the centerpiece, which had a lighted candle in the middle.

Mom interrupted her argument for a second. "What are you doing?"

"Burning down the house," I explained, tipping over the candle.

The centerpiece caught fire in spectacular fashion. Cheap wine was good for that, if nothing else. I watched it burn for a second, watched them argue about how to put it out and then left the room.

On the way out, I saw the snake. It saw me, too, and its eyes glittered ruby-red.

Chapter Twenty-Five

December 24

Contrary to popular opinion, I am not a monster. The first thing I did the next morning was buy my mother a new tablecloth and centerpiece. Not being a fool either, I left them on the doorstep, rang the bell and ran.

Cassie, enjoying this outlaw moment too much, gunned the motor as soon as I jumped in and then took off in a horrible fishtailing, snow-spraying screech. It reminded me of Vanessa doing doughnuts in the J/J/G parking lot. Did she get it from Cassie, or was it the other way around?

"So much for sneaking in and sneaking out," I grumbled, yanking my sunglasses off. It had been her idea for us to wear them, even though there wasn't a hint of sun.

"We got away, didn't we?"

"We aren't away yet. We still have to go back tomorrow."

"We'll worry about that tomorrow," she said serenely. "Right now, let's just have a nice day avoiding your family, OK?"

There was no avoiding those people, not really, not in a town this size. But there was no point worrying her.

Yet.

I took her to lunch at the second-best restaurant in town, the best being booked solid, and we got in at this one only because I knew the owner. True, we didn't like each other; she'd been a cheerleader in high school. But she'd also been one of Mom's students and was still afraid of her, so we got a very good table.

"This is kind of a cute place," Cassie remarked. "What would you call it? Country French?"

More like Alimony French; I'd heard that Debra got a bundle in the second divorce. "Something like that."

"I might redo the kitchen like this. Would you like to have breakfast every morning with calico chickens?"

"No."

She shrugged. "Well, we could lose the chickens."

"Don't let me stop you. It's your house."

"I was talking about your condo."

I looked up from the menu in surprise. "What would I want chickens in my kitchen for?"

"They'd be cute. They'd be decorative. Your place is so...*earth-tone*. A little color would cheer it up."

"I don't want it cheered up. Especially not in the morning."

She made a show of studying her fingernails. For an awful moment, I thought she was going to start filing them. "Fine. Then I'll redo my kitchen and your bedroom."

I was rapidly losing track of this conversation. "You want to redo my bedroom?"

"No—I *want* you to move in with me. But if you're going to keep being stubborn, I think you should let me redecorate something."

"Why is that fair?"

"I don't know that it is," she admitted. "But it would be a nice Christmas present from you to me."

Unnerved, I considered the implications. I'd already gotten her a nice Christmas present. Several of them, actually; Visa would probably send a thank-you note with my next statement. But this wasn't about Christmas. It wasn't about interior decoration, either. It was about—

"Ah. There you are."

We both jumped a little. Vanessa was pulling up a chair, looking very much at home. She was, in fact, wearing the same dress that the owner of the restaurant had on.

"Can anyone see you?" I whispered.

The demon flipped her hair. "You're kidding, right? I didn't get this cute just so nobody could see me."

All right; whatever. If Debra came out to check on us later, I'd let *her* deal with it.

"Go away," Cassie told her. "Devvy and I are talking."

"And you're losing," Vanessa replied, getting comfy. "Didn't you ever learn anything about redirection? You don't just *tell* them what you want; you weasel around it. If they don't think it's their idea—"

"I'm not a them," I growled.

"—they won't do it. You know how they are."

"I'm not a guy!"

"No one said you were, pumpkin," Vanessa purred. "Now, what's good here? I could go for eels or snails or something."

We both stared at her, disgusted.

"What's the problem? This is a French joint, isn't it?"

"This is Hawthorne," I explained.

A dark Presence loomed over my shoulder. *"I'll* give her eels."

Damn. *Damn.* Without even looking at her, I reached over and pulled out the last empty chair.

Monica took it with exaggerated grace. "I can give her sautéed rat, if I really want to. But it's Christmas. I'll be nice." She shot a bad look at Cassie, who gave it right back. "Hello, Cassandra. You're looking lifelike."

"So are you," she said insincerely. "The implants are holding up really well, don't you think, Devvy?"

I didn't think. If all went well, I would never have to think again. In grim silence, I studied the menu.

"For the record," Cassie continued, addressing the demons, "this is a private lunch. You two weren't invited. So you should go now. We really wouldn't want to have to ask the owner to throw you out."

Monica laughed scornfully. "Did you meet her?"

"No. Why?"

"She's a Junior Leaguer. She wouldn't do anything that might break a nail. Including sex. Ask her ex-husbands."

She hadn't bothered to lower her voice, of course, and a few titters broke out among our fellow diners. Mortified, I made a don't-mind-her-she's-crazy gesture to the area at large and then turned on my demon. "Keep it down. This is a public place."

"Would keeping it down make it any less true?" She raised her voice slightly. "Would you rather I discuss *your* sex life?"

Cassie and I answered together: *"NO!!"*

"Humans," she sniffed. "You act like sex is a life-and-death secret, but you all do it. Or want to. Even your parents, Devlin. Did you know that?"

Yes, I knew that technically. Connor, Ryan and I had worked it out years ago: Mom and Dad had Done It three times. But it wasn't something a person liked to think about.

At all. *Ever.*

Seeing my expression, Monica smiled evilly. "Do you know what a prude is? A prude is someone who's ashamed of having been born naked in bed with a woman."

The titters turned to open laughter. Even Cassie started to smile. To her credit, she caught herself and reached over to pat my knee reassuringly.

I wasn't reassured. "What do you want, Monica? Aren't you supposed to be slithering around my parents' house?"

Cassie still had her hand on my knee, and her grip tightened at that. "What?"

"That wasn't a runaway snake last night. Or in the shower. That was *her.*"

"It might have been," Monica said airily. "It might not have been. There really *is* a Milton. There might be two snakes around at any given time, just for fun. But your mother's a head case. You know that, too, don't you?"

Our waitress showed up at that moment, and I could have kissed her for it. Cassie would have ripped my lips off, though. So I settled for smiling.

"Do you have sautéed rat?" I asked.

The girl blinked, uncertain. "Sautéed what?"

"Never mind. We'll start with a bottle of your best champagne. And one of *them* gets the bill." I gestured between Monica and Vanessa. "I don't care which one. Whichever annoys you more."

"But they haven't—"

"They will," I assured her. "Don't worry; I'll make up for it in your tip."

The demons just sat there demurely, looking as harmless as Easter eggs. *Brother,* I thought.

We made it all the way to dessert before the trouble started. I suppose that was some kind of record, considering the personnel. But trashing the restaurant, on Christmas Eve day...

Well, it didn't look good.

Monica started it. Debra had flounced out to see how I was doing, not that she cared, and we'd both been excruciatingly polite. She'd even pretended not to notice that Vanessa had the same dress on. (In perfect truth, it looked better on Vanessa.) She was just leaving when Monica decided to have some fun.

"You knew Devlin in high school, did you?" she asked Debra, all deceptive innocence.

The woman faked a big fat smile. "Not *well,* but yes, I did."

"Not well? Does that mean you didn't sleep with her?"

Cassie almost snorted coffee. I looked around for a trap door in the floor.

"Of *course* not," Debra said, offended. "I had boyfriends."

"So did your boyfriends," Vanessa piped up.

Monica scowled at her. "Keep out of this. I'm working here."

"Oh, working, hell; you're just trying to guilt Devlin out. *Again.*" Cassie's demon tossed her head. "So she wanted to sleep with that little bitchkitty in high school. So what? She's got better taste now."

Everyone looked at me—everyone at my table and at every other table within earshot. The people at the next table actually moved their chairs closer. I tried to look outraged, but it was too hard to be outraged and guilty at the same time.

"You *didn't,*" Cassie informed me. "You *told* me—"

"Of course I didn't!"

"*I'll* say," Debra barked. "Just so you know, Devlin Kerry, I'd sooner sleep with a goat."

A *goat?* I shoved my chair back. *Now* I was outraged.

"What kind of goat?" Vanessa asked, interested.

Debra and I were both standing now, glaring at each other. We ignored the question.

"Don't flatter yourself," I told Debra. "*I'd* sleep with a cow first."

"No cow is that hard up," she shot back.

The room found that cute. Cassie did not. She jumped to her feet and to my side, menacing the woman with her worst expression.

But Vanessa just looked petulant. "What kind of cow? I need details."

"I think you should leave," Debra said icily. "And take your...friends with you. What cathouse did you find them in, anyway?"

Cassie slapped her face so hard that one of her earrings flew off. *Attagirl.* I didn't get a chance to congratulate her, though; Debra was trying to slap her back, and I was having a devil of a time keeping between them.

"You get your hands off," Debra snarled at me. "You're not going to cop a feel this way."

Was she crazy? Even if I'd wanted to, even if Cassie wouldn't have killed me for it, I wouldn't have done it in front of an audience. The whole restaurant was paying rapt attention now; even the staff had stopped work to goggle at the spectacle. A couple of the cooks were standing in the kitchen doorway, wiping their hands. I recognized one of them, and vice versa; he waved at me. Great. Our mothers were in a few clubs together, which meant this would be the talk of the town for months.

Then everything went completely to hell. Before I could stop her, Debra dodged around me, grabbed Monica's dessert and smashed it into Cassie's face.

That would really irritate Cassie; she didn't like meringue. Without thinking about the consequences, I straight-armed Debra into the table behind her. It collapsed with a crash as I turned to help Cassie.

The next thing I knew, the very air was alive with flying things—food, tableware, even wine bottles whizzing in all directions. It wasn't even us; the other patrons had snapped. Cassie and I watched, appalled, as they brawled like beasts. What *was* it with us that this sort of thing kept happening when we were around?

Check that—I knew exactly what it was with us. We had demons. The demons in question were still sitting at our table, looking bored now. Good. I'd meant it about giving them the check.

"Let's get out of here," I told Cassie.

"Right behind you, sweetie."

At the door, she told me to hold up while she dug in her purse for her sunglasses. Reluctantly, I put mine on, too.

"They already know who we are," I reminded her.

"That's not the point. The point is looking dignified." Frowning slightly, she pulled her sunglasses down to study me. "You have mashed potatoes in your hair."

With all the dignity possible under the circumstances, I opened the door and let her out.

Back at the hotel an hour later, showered and wrapped up in robes, we were lounging on one of the beds, watching an *It's a Wonderful Life* marathon on cable. It was the first peaceful moment we'd had all day.

So of course the phone rang.

Cassie muttered something about red-hot axes but snuggled closer. I reached over to answer. "Hello?"

"Hi, Dev. It's Jen. What's up?"

She didn't really want to know. "Nothing. We're watching *It's a Wonderful Life*. What's up with you?"

"Nothing."

The conversation stopped at that point. What now?

"Jimmy Stewart just called Lionel Barrymore a scurvy spider," I reported. "Lionel Barrymore doesn't seem to be impressed. So he's—"

"Your mom says thanks for the tablecloth and the centerpiece."

"Does she, now? Hang on." I put my hand over the receiver and turned to Cassie. "Mom says thanks for the stuff. Not herself personally, but through Jen. What do you think?"

"I think your mother is a scurvy spider," she said.

I kissed the top of her head and got back on the phone. "Tell her she's welcome. What does she really want?"

Jen started laughing. "I hate this family; you're all so *smart*. She wants to know if you're going to church tonight."

I told her to wait again.

"What kind of service is it?" Cassie asked.

"Candlelight service. Nothing religious; we're Methodists."

She sighed. "I guess it can't hurt. Can it?"

"Probably not," I told her. "What else could happen?"

Chapter Twenty-Six

Christmas Eve

We were in trouble from the minute we walked into church that night. There were many things wrong with the situation, but the wrongest was that the place was full of people who'd known me when I was little. Nice people. Well-meaning people. People who wouldn't know a clue if it dropped out of the sky on their heads. Before we'd made it past the first gauntlet of welcome-home hugs and kisses in the narthex, Cassie was having big trouble not rolling on the carpet laughing.

"It's not funny," I muttered.

She gave me her sweetest smile. "Of course it is."

"Don't let them fool you. They only look friendly. If they knew *anything*, they'd stone me."

"Not while I'm around, honey."

Abruptly, I pulled her off to one side—as much privacy as I could manage in that crowd. "Don't call me 'honey.' Not here."

"What's wrong? Don't you love me anymore?" Wicked blue lights started dancing in her eyes. "Does this mean I have to fall asleep empty and unfulfilled tonight?"

I grabbed her coat lapel viciously. Then, politely, I started shoving churchgoers out of the way so I could drag her outside. Cassie was laughing so hard that she didn't resist. Only when we got to the very back of the parking lot did I feel it was safe enough to talk.

"This is the last place on earth you can do that," I snapped. "I grew up going to this church. I learned everything I know about hellfire and damnation here. If you don't cut it out, God's going to smite me."

She turned serious, finally. "I don't much like your God, Devvy."

"I don't either. But you know what the Jesuits say about getting a kid before he's seven. These people got hold of me when I was born."

"And what did they teach you? That love is evil?"

I said it without thinking: "No. Just sex."

There was long, long silence in the parking lot. Then Cassie pulled me closer to the streetlight and studied my expression. Uncomfortable under the scrutiny, and freezing to death now that we were standing out in the open, I shifted from foot to foot a few times.

"Well, that explains the witch," she finally said.

Did it? Monica herself had suggested as much all those months ago when she'd told me what she was. But...

Never mind. There wasn't time for theology now; we were due in church.

"It's not that simple, Cass."

"You were little. It had to be simple." She sighed in exasperation, her breath white on the calm air. "So does this mean you think *I'm* evil?"

"No. You're just high-maintenance."

Surprised by that answer, she laughed.

"Very, very high-maintenance," I added.

"You can stop any time."

"But I wouldn't have you any other way." Before she could say anything to that, I kissed her. "I love you, no matter *how* evil you are."

"You too, pookie."

"Now will you behave yourself in there? For me?"

She pretended to consider. "For you?"

"You will if you love me."

"That is *so* not fair," she grumbled.

"I know. Believe me, I know." I kissed her again. "Ready?"

She shook her head but took my arm, and we headed back. Light snow was starting to fall, dusting the windshields of the parked cars; it made the brightly lighted church look more inviting. We passed the floodlighted Hawthorne United Methodist Church sign, built close to the ground per the zoning ordinances in that part of town, and as we did, Debra and her current family crossed our path like so many black cats.

Bad luck, all right. I'd meant to go back to the restaurant later to pay for lunch and/or damages, but Cassie had other ideas about how to spend the afternoon. So I'd never—

"Why, Devlin Kerry," Debra said with simulated pleasure. "I haven't seen *you* for a couple of years at least. How are you?"

A couple of years? I frowned. "Fine. You? Listen, about your restaurant..."

Her smile grew larger and phonier. "Oh, you've heard about it? Yes, I'm really enjoying it. It's doing really well. Do stop in while you're in town, won't you? I'll make sure you get free dessert."

Cassie and I glanced at each other warily. We'd *had* dessert at her restaurant just a few hours ago, and neither of *us* was likely to forget it as long as we lived.

"Maybe we will," I told Debra.

Her charity work complete, Debra turned sharply to go inside. She hadn't bothered to introduce her family to me or herself to Cassie, but somehow I felt no loss.

Cassie stared after her. "That was strange. Is she loony?"

"Probably." Privately, I suspected Vanessa was up to something, but it wasn't the time to discuss her. "C'mon. It's cold out here."

All the good pews in the back were full, so we had to sit way up front. That meant going down the center aisle in front of everyone, which meant more being recognized and more getting hugged. I hated it. We'd had a hard time even getting past the greeters, and although Cassie was trying hard not to laugh, she was having a fabulous time. I'd almost had to clock her when Mrs. Rose, who was passing out the candles, started talking about how well behaved I'd been in her Sunday school class.

"Selective memory," I insisted when we finally got away. "My friends and I used to throw spit wads in church."

She just smiled.

"How come *you* didn't have to go through this at Thanksgiving?"

"I'm not stupid, Devvy. I wasn't about to introduce you to any more people than I had to."

Smart. She was smart, all right. I was doomed with this one.

We passed another pew, and I felt the temperature drop sharply, as it does in the most haunted part of the house. Mom and Aunt Kitty were sitting there along with Dad, Connor and Jen, looking particularly unappeasable.

"Evening. What happened to Ryan and Amy?" I asked.

"They'll be along," Mom said curtly. Her glance swept up and down us both, clearly disapproving of our nice wool trousers.

"We didn't pack prom dresses," I explained. "Besides, it's 15 degrees out. Too cold for pantyhose."

She didn't respond except to cross her pantyhosed legs ostentatiously. Well, if she wanted to catch pneumonia, that was her business.

"You can sit here," Aunt Kitty said grudgingly. "There's probably room if we all move down."

With maximum effort, I smiled. "Wouldn't think of putting you to any trouble." Then I pulled Cassie down the aisle to an empty pew, Mom and Aunt Kitty glaring holes in the back of my head all the way.

"What do we do with these things?" Cassie asked, gesturing with her candle.

"This." I stuck mine into one of the holes in the pew back in front of us. They were, I dimly remembered, for the little cups of grape juice Methodists got at communion, but they were just candleholders to me now. She did the same. No sooner had we finished getting settled than Ryan and Amy shoved in.

"You're late," I said, feeling virtuous.

Ryan shrugged. "We were watching a movie. You going to move down and let us in, or what?"

"Depends. What movie?"

"*Santa Claus Conquers the Martians.*"

"Move," I told Cassie.

We scooted down to give them room. Ryan climbed over both of us to sit on my right, and Amy sat on Cassie's left.

"It's probably not safe to let them sit together," Amy told her, "but it'll probably be more fun in the long run."

Cassie laughed. "I've known Devvy for six years. It's really hard to scare me."

"Happy to try," Ryan offered.

I was about to have back at him when the choir started filing in. I knew most of the members in one way or another—a friend's father, a local pharmacist, my junior high geography teacher—and was careful to smile. But the friend's father saw Ryan and me sitting together, and a dark look crossed his face.

"I bet he's remembering the Jesus Christmas," Ryan whispered in the sudden hush.

That almost caused me to lose it. A few Christmas Eves ago, for reasons known only to them, Connor and Ryan had started telling me Jesus jokes during the candlelight service, and they got so intolerable that I had to laugh out loud a few times.

Of course, sitting next to either of my brothers at this service was never a good idea. If "We Three Kings" was on the program, which it usually was, they always sang the version about the rubber cigar. Then we'd all start doing commentary on the sermon, not always sotto voce, and at least one of us would have to leave the sanctuary to laugh.

This year, though, Cassie was with me. I wasn't going to subject her to showtime with the Kerry kids in the middle of church. Even though she might never have to come back to this town, I would, and I wasn't going to have people thinking badly of her for something that wasn't her fault. Let them think whatever they wanted about me, but not—

Something small, hard and wet hit me in the back of the head. Scowling, I turned around. Connor tried to look innocent, pretending to be fascinated by the poinsettia arrangement on the altar, but I wasn't fooled for a second. If he was going to start throwing spit wads, I was eventually going to revert and start throwing them back.

Closing my eyes, I repented most of my life to date. Somehow, I hadn't realized that bringing Cassie to this church would mean giving her a tour of my childhood—the moral equivalent of touring a swamp in a glass-bottom boat. By seventh grade, my friends and I were sneaking out during the sermons to steal Cokes out of the Coke machine in the basement. We'd started filling out the guest books with fake names. We'd even called the church office a few times to ask if their refrigerator was running. And on top of all that, I had these *brothers* to deal with. No wonder I had a demon.

Cassie nudged me. "What's wrong?"

Another spit wad whizzed through my hair; I got a hand up just in time to catch it. For answer, I showed it to her.

Where was Mom while he was being such a brat, anyway? I turned around again. She was deep in conversation with Aunt Kitty; they appeared to be gossiping about someone in the choir. Oh, well, she probably didn't even know why Connor was doing it, so it would be no fun making her mad about it. The reason was that when we were kids, we'd gone to Gatlinburg on vacation several times, and our favorite thing to do there was ride the chairlift up Crockett Mountain. It wasn't that we liked the ride so much; it was that at one point, the line went over a motel swimming pool, fairly low. Connor and I liked to spit on whoever was in the pool.

I repented that, too, as yet another spit wad hit me. *Verily, it is more blessed to give than to receive.*

"He's been practicing," Ryan observed. "Just proves he has no life. Let's make a bunch of wads and ambush him after church."

Amy leaned around Cassie to give him a stern look.

"Oh, c'mon, babe," he protested. "This is about honor."

She shook her head but sat back. It was just as well; the choir was about to sing. I glanced over them with little curiosity, more or less counting heads. One head in particular caught my attention.

I blinked, but it was no use; it was Vanessa, trying to look angelic in a choir robe. *That* was no use, too.

Alarmed, I leaned over to whisper to Cassie. "Third row, second from left."

"I saw," she whispered back. "Fourth row, far right."

Fourth row, far right, fourth row, far... Oh, hell.

Monica waited till our eyes met. Then she smiled just enough to show her fangs.

"Where do you want to be buried?" I asked Cassie.

Chapter Twenty-Seven

There is a French Christmas carol about the Devil. I'd always thought that concept was a little peculiar. But now there were demons in the choir on Christmas Eve, so why not?

Cassie was taking it fairly well, I thought; she looked as though she'd bitten into an apple and found half a spider but decided it was better than half a rat. "We'll get out of this," she whispered.

"In how many pieces?"

She didn't answer. Right—that was my guess, too.

All around us, oblivious to the impending doom, the congregation waited for the choir to get on with it. At the same time, the choir waited for the choir director. He was a real fossil, the oldest man on earth after Strom Thurmond, and you could see his hearing aids from the back row. Technically, a deaf choir director probably wasn't a good idea. But if I remembered this choir right, deafness might be an asset.

The director finally nodded to the organist. She hit the keyboard—and a flock of bats shot out of the pipes along with the chord.

Everything went straight downhill from there. No sooner had the bats left (yes, through the belfry) than an altar cloth caught fire. And no sooner was the fire out than one of the decorative angels fell on an old lady, totaling both her hat and her good will to man. By the time Rev. Pritchard restarted the service for the third time, he was sweating visibly.

I glanced at Cassie, who had been speechless since the bats and hadn't let go of my arm either. "It's usually not like this," I assured her.

She let out a long-held breath. "It's *never* like this at Episcopalian services."

"So you're not having fun?"

"I didn't say that."

No, but she would. Resigned, I checked over my shoulder to see how my family was holding up. Ryan and Amy had moved back to sit with the rest of them after the fire, thinking it might be safer there. They were wrong, but at least the demons were gone; they'd disappeared during the confusion with the bats.

Meanwhile, the choir was at it again. It was impossible to tell what the song was or what key it was supposed to be in, but with these people, there never *was* any telling.

"Just out of curiosity," Cassie asked, "what are they singing?"

I checked the program, which listed some obscure number from the Methodist hymnal. "No one ever knows. It's not really singing. It's performance art."

She snorted.

"No, seriously. It's like folk art that way. Did I ever tell you about the folk art show I went to once? There was a painting with a big rooster on it, and the caption was 'JIM BOB, THE MIND-READING CHICKEN. HE KNOWS WHAT YOU ARE THINKING.'"

Cassie lost it, laughing out loud. The choir was making such a ruckus, I figured no one could hear her or blame me. But seconds later, a wadded-up program hit me in the back of the head.

I refused to acknowledge it. Besides, Rev. Pritchard was staring right at me, not in a nice way.

"Judgmental creepazoid, isn't he?" Vanessa asked, materializing on Cassie's left.

We both flinched a bit. She wasn't wearing the choir robe anymore and was dressed conservatively, for her, but she still looked spectacularly out of place.

"Relax. This crowd can't see demons. Not enough imagination." The demon yawned. "This is boring. What if I set something on fire?"

"Again?" I asked sharply.

"Oh, tosh. That was Monica. Don't worry—she's not here right now. She said something about going downstairs to steal Cokes out of the Coke machine."

Cassie, puzzled, waited for me to explain. But I folded my arms and stared at the altar in grim silence.

"So what about this Jim Bob?" Vanessa asked. "Is he a real chicken or just something you smoked?"

"Something I smoked? C'mon, I haven't touched that stuff for—"

"In the church parking lot," she prompted.

Oh. *That* time. Well, it *had* been that many years, hadn't it?

Vanessa nudged Cassie. "She was kind of bad when she finally started rebelling. Kind of wussy bad, though. Not the real thing, or we wouldn't be here tonight."

"What's that supposed to mean?" Cassie asked, impatient.

"Quiet," I warned. "We're in church."

Both my beloved and her demon glared at me.

"Well, we are."

They continued to glare until Vanessa leaned in to whisper to her. I didn't want to know. So I concentrated on the music, or whatever that noise was, until something settled in on my right.

Monica didn't say a word. She just handed me a stolen Coke.

Nothing blew up, caught fire or collapsed for the next half hour or so, which let us sink into the torpor common to these occasions. Even the demons were quiet. Connor had thrown another spit wad, but Monica had deflected it, and it might not have been her fault that it hit the minister. The wad had stuck to his forehead, where you couldn't miss it if you were far enough up front; it was distracting but not distracting enough to mention.

Otherwise, the only thing that kept most of us conscious by that time was having to stand up and sing every so often. Vanessa, I noticed, sang like a squeaky gate.

Finally, Rev. Pritchard got up to deliver the sermon. What with all the delays early on, it was getting late—almost midnight, by my watch—and children were getting restless. A few pews over, there was increasingly loud conversation about needing to get home and go to sleep *now* so Santa would come.

With perverse pleasure, I listened to that for a while and then checked the program to see what the sermon was about; it was easier than actually paying attention. I found the title, frowned and checked again. It still read:

THE SERMON
Dr. Pritchard
"Yes, Virginia, There Is a Baby Jesus."

Cassie leaned on my shoulder. "Something wrong?"

I pointed at the offending text. She closed her eyes briefly and then slipped a hand into my jacket pocket for comfort. After a second, I joined her.

"That breaks one commandment or another," Monica remarked.

It probably broke several, but it still wasn't as bad as being a demon. So I ignored her. Cassie squeezed my hand in approval.

Monica narrowed her eyes to glittering red slits but said nothing. Relieved, I sat back again, lacing my fingers with Cassie's and half-listening to whatever the minister was saying. This wasn't so bad. Nobody could see anything. Who would know?

Then I happened to glance at the choir. They were all looking at us reproachfully. So, when I checked the pulpit, was Rev. Pritchard.

Well, sue me. Mary Beth Miller had gone all the way with her boyfriend in the balcony when we were in high school, and nobody said anything to *her.*

Vanessa, looking very much as though she'd just read my mind, leaned past Cassie to smirk at Monica. My demon scowled at her and then faced the altar again.

A half-second later, the lights went out.

"Goddammit," someone groaned.

Most of the house laughed in sympathy. We weren't in any danger this time, we already had candlelight, and we were getting used to the curse on this service. But Rev. Pritchard was not in a forgiving temper. "I see that we're still having problems," he announced. "I apologize again. Whoever is responsible, we will find them, and we will punish them. Now, if you'll just bear with us a few more minutes, we're almost done here, and then—"

He never finished the sentence, because then the bats came back. And that finally did it. The congregation snapped. People stampeded for the back of the sanctuary, which started to look like one of those tragic nightclub accidents. One little old lady was smacking people with her purse to clear an escape path; another was flailing them with a cane.

"Please," Rev. Pritchard said helplessly into the microphone, which was still working. "Please don't hit each other. It's Christmas Eve."

A bat swooped into his robes at that point, which finally broke him. The last anyone saw of the right rev that night was the soles of his shoes, following him through a stained-glass window. *That* was going to come out of the collection plate every week for a couple of years.

"That was fun," Vanessa told Monica. "It didn't work, but it was fun."

My demon huffed and puffed a bit. "What do you mean it didn't work? I trashed the service, didn't I?"

Vanessa nodded in our direction. "They're still holding hands."

What with one thing and another, I'd lost track of that fact. But yes, we were. There being no point in concealment now, I pulled both our hands out of my pocket.

"You might be a little more than you look like," Monica told Cassie, very grudgingly. "Either that or insane. Any normal woman would've dropped Devlin ages ago. Or at least when the bats came."

I bristled a little, but Cassie spoke first. "I *am* normal, and I'm not afraid of bats anymore. Not after that mother of hers."

Monica did her best not to laugh, but her lips twitched suspiciously.

"Come on, girlfriend," Vanessa told her. "The night's still young. Let's go debauch a priest or something. What do you say?"

She thought for a second. "All right. But I get the wishbone."

Cassie and I watched in shocked silence as she vanished in a pillar of flame.

"She's just teasing you about the wishbone," Vanessa said. Then she frowned a little. "I think. I'd better go see. Merry Christmas."

With that, she herself went up in flame, and it was just us. Well, us and the bats.

"What do you want to do now?" I asked.

"What do you usually do now?"

"*Usually*, I go home now and watch really bad movies with my brothers. But you're more fun than my brothers. A lot prettier, too."

Cassie smiled. "Thanks, sweetie, but I don't think they want to be pretty."

"No danger of that. So what now? Do you want to go back to the hotel? Drive around and look at Christmas lights? What?"

"I'm probably crazy," she said, "but let's go to the house for a little while."

"You're probably crazy," I agreed.

"Just for a few minutes. It's Christmas Eve. OK?"

"What if the snake's there?"

"Let it eat braunschweiger," she declared.

I couldn't help it; I had to kiss her for that. Let God strike me dead.

But I checked first to make sure we were really alone.

We drove around for a while before we went to the house. By that time, everyone had gone to bed except Connor and Ryan—which had been my plan, of course.

"So," Connor said as we settled in. "What was *your* favorite part? The bats? Or Mrs. Zender hitting her son-in-law with her cane?"

I shrugged. "Doesn't count. She's wanted to do that for years."

"He deserves it. His eyes are too close together."

The rest of us waited for an explanation.

"That's what Mom says, anyway. She says you can't trust a man whose eyes are too close together."

Ryan cocked his head in interest. "She does? I thought she said you can't trust a man who has tiny lips."

An image of Cassie's brother-in-law floated into my mind. Michael had tiny ones, all right.

"Well, you know what they say," Connor said happily. "Tiny lips, tiny shoes."

Cassie frowned. "That's not what they say."

"I know. I'm just being polite. They *really* say—"

"Stop being polite," I growled. "We have company."

Ryan coughed significantly. "I don't know about that, Dev."

"What do you mean, you don't know? None of us has many manners, but—"

"I mean," he said, "I don't know that she's really company. She might be sort of *family*. Wouldn't you say?"

Connor almost choked on his beer. "Not now, you ass."

"Well, when? It's not like—"

"I'm having a brandy," I announced in a tone that stopped all conversation. "Cass? What can I get you?"

She said brandy would be perfect.

"Nobody says *one word* till I get back," I ordered.

They promised. But I heard whispering anyway.

We stayed through about half of some Godzilla movie and too much of the brandy. Connor and Ryan made some bad "Same bat-time, same bat-channel" jokes, and then we left to get a few hours' sleep. By fiat, Christmas started whenever Mom woke up, which was always too early.

Cassie was already yawning by the time we got back to the motel. There was something in my coat pocket that I'd been thinking about giving her that night, but it was late, we were both tired, and it could wait. Besides, my family was civilized; we opened presents Christmas morning, not Christmas Eve.

So I got into bed and flipped on the TV while I waited for her to come out of the bath. There was nothing on except *It's a Wonderful Life*—I was starting to suspect that it was the only thing on the air anywhere—but it was only for a few minutes.

I was almost asleep when Cassie came back, wearing her robe. Instead of getting into bed, she sat on the edge, smiling.

"What?" I asked.

"I have something for you."

"You do? Now?"

"Yes."

Damn. Well, all right; I could give her that present tonight. It would take a couple of minutes. Then we could finally get some sleep. "Don't go anywhere."

She didn't. I climbed out of bed and fished the package out of my coat pocket.

"Who first?" I asked.

"I think probably you."

Her smile when she said that was interesting—something I couldn't quite place. But I was tired, and I could analyze it tomorrow. "OK, then. Here." I handed her the present and got back into bed.

God, I hoped her sister had been right about this. If she wasn't, I was going to kill her. I was going to get on a plane first thing in the morning, take a taxi from the Kansas City airport and kill her as dead as—

"Oh, my God," Cassie said.

I looked over, uncertain. She was staring into the box as though she didn't recognize what was in it. "It's a ring," I said helpfully.

She didn't respond. She didn't even move. Was that good or bad?

"It's not *that* kind of ring," I added. "We're not doing that. And it's not like we've even been doing *this* that long. But Lucy said you might like...and I thought...and...well..." Suddenly, I felt about sixteen years old, without the first or faintest clue. I hadn't liked that feeling then; I *really* didn't like it now. "C'mon, Cass, say something."

She spoke so softly that I could barely hear her. "It's beautiful."

"You sure? Because you can exchange it if you don't like it or if it doesn't fit or—"

"I like it."

"It's a real sapphire." I was uncomfortably aware of my heart hammering. Had I really been that nervous? This was Cassie, not somebody I hadn't already been to Hell and back with. "I know you've already got too many bracelets, and I thought about earrings instead, but the setting in this ring is interesting, and...well, I just thought you might like it."

"I do."

Silence.

"So are you going to try it on?"

She looked at me for the first time since she'd opened the box. No, I didn't recognize that expression, not at all. But it changed my mind about going to sleep.

The ring fit. As for what she gave me...well, it wasn't in a package, exactly. And it turned out to be the best Christmas Eve of my life.

Chapter Twenty-Eight

Christmas Day

The condemned arrived promptly at 10. It was too bad I'd quit smoking, because the cigarette and blindfold were starting to sound like good ideas.

"Cheer up," Cassie demanded as we walked up the drive. "It's Christmas."

"Exactly."

"Cranky. Why are you cranky after last night?"

"That was then. This is now."

She sighed. "We really have to work on the romance thing, honey."

I knew from hard experience to ignore remarks like that. Besides, if she wanted romance, she could go buy a cheesy paperback at the drugstore.

"Devvy?"

"Light of my life?"

"You're not fooling anyone, you know. You're sappier than I am."

I stopped walking. "Excuse me?"

"Oh, don't worry—I won't tell. But you *are.*"

There she went, leaping to conclusions again. Just because I'd given her jewelry didn't make me sappy. Maybe she meant the poetry later. But that didn't prove anything either. A person ought to be able to get *some* use out of all those years of English lit.

"Are we going to go in and get this over with?" I asked in injured dignity. "Or are we going to stand out here and make false accusations all morning?"

Cassie just laughed and pulled me the rest of the way up the driveway.

We walked into a tableau out of Madame Tussaud's. They were all sitting around the living room like waxworks, not talking, not doing anything. For my family, that was beyond weird, and I didn't like it.

"Hello," I said experimentally.

Mom turned her head slightly and frowned. "Oh. It's you."

Who was she expecting? Reindeer? "Yes, it is. Good morning. Merry Christmas."

I couldn't quite hear her response, but it didn't sound festive. Oh, well, she'd probably just gotten up on the wrong side of the moat. So I tried again. "Where's Dad?"

"Out looking for you," she snapped.

God, give me patience this instant. "Well, he won't find us unless he's looking here. Why would he be doing that anyway?"

"You should have been here an hour ago. He thought something happened to you."

Cassie shook her head slightly in warning; I pretended not to notice. "Nobody said anything about a schedule. I told Connor and Ryan we'd be here by 10. And we were. Why didn't he just call the hotel?"

"He was worried."

Impatient, I speed-read the situation. My brothers weren't talking. Dad was out driving. Yup, Mom was on her horse. It was going to be one of those Christmases.

"Coffee," I said to no one in particular and went to the kitchen.

By the time Dad got back, everyone was more or less done sulking. It had taken several threats and a few blunt reminders that we had company, but I'd finally gotten them talking again. On Planet Kerry, this passed for progress.

So we sat down to open presents. Ryan played Santa, which he'd done every year since he was six, and we were teddibly, teddibly polite about it all. We took turns; we didn't rip the paper off like savages; we didn't even count packages first. That last part was for Cassie's benefit, though, because Connor, Ryan and I *always* counted first. One year, we'd also measured and weighed. But Mom had thrown a fit, so we rarely did that anymore, and only in private.

"Don't shake this one," Ryan told Connor as he handed him another package. "It's from Dev. It's probably ticking."

Cassie smiled at him. "Not that one. But be careful you don't cover the air holes. They get really mad when they can't breathe."

Very funny. My brothers actually thought so, however, so I let her get away with it. Anyway, it was just another of the toys that we always gave one another: laser guns, guns that launched little helicopters, little containers of goo and eyeballs. This one was a Magic 8 Ball. Connor had broken the one he got last year when it didn't give him the answer he wanted.

Cassie looked on, bemused. Mom had been decent enough to get her a couple of small things so that she'd have something to unwrap, but they were along the lines of berets, which she didn't wear. Neither of her daughters-in-law did either, but they got them every year anyway.

Never mind, though—Cass and I were going to have a private Christmas when we got home. I didn't know what might be in all those packages from her parents, but I knew for a fact that there were no berets in the ones from me.

"I love it," Connor said, displaying the 8 Ball for general admiration. "It's stunning. Just stunning. What is it? Does it come with directions?"

"Wise guy," I muttered.

He winked and sailed a small package across the room at me. Then he tossed an identical one to Cassie.

"Hey!" Ryan huffed. *"I'm* Santa around here."

"These aren't from Santa. They're from Jen and me."

Skeptical, I opened mine. Cassie watched a little apprehensively; the last thing from Connor and Jen had been one of those singing fish. Ryan had liked it, but then, Ryan was weird.

"What is this?" I asked Connor, staring at the plastic egg.

"Open it and see."

I pressed the latch, and the top popped up. Inside was a miniature ocean with plastic whales. "I see. But I still don't—"

"You have to open it all the way," Jen directed.

So I did. The little egg shuddered, and the scene came to life in my hand, the tiny whales swimming and the tiny waves churning. Totally against my will, I was enchanted.

Relieved, Cassie opened hers. She got a pond with little ducks, which was almost— but not quite—as cool as mine.

"I love this," she told them. "Thank you. I'm going to take it to client meetings and play with it when I get bored. Which will be *all* the time."

She started her toy again, and as she did, Mom leaned forward, suddenly alert.

"Something wrong?" I asked her.

"I don't remember seeing Carrie wearing a ring yesterday."

Cassie looked up from her ducks with a quizzical expression.

"Cassie," I corrected wearily. "And she has lots of jewelry, Mom. She can't wear all of it every day."

It wasn't a lie, exactly. I wasn't even sure why I'd told it. But it was none of my mother's business where the ring had come from, and if she pressed the issue, Cassie could simply lie and say—

"It was a Christmas present from Devvy," Cassie said.

Hell and damnation. I mentally subtracted one of the packages under her tree back home.

Everyone else, of course, was all ears about this news. Amy jumped up to have a closer look, and only then did I realize which finger Cassie was wearing the ring on. It didn't mean anything; it wasn't a diamond; we weren't doing that. But did she have to wear it on that finger, in front of my mother? Mom took the etiquette books so seriously that she probably didn't wear white underwear after Labor Day, and she wasn't going to care that people wore rings everywhere nowadays. Including some places I didn't even want to think about.

"Let me see that," Mom said brusquely, moving Amy aside.

Cassie patiently let Mom study the ring from all angles. "It's beautiful, isn't it?"

"It looks expensive," she said. "I thought you didn't have a job anymore, Devlin."

I scowled at her. "We're appealing. We'll be back to work any day now. And how is it your affair anyway?"

"You shouldn't be giving such expensive gifts to a girlfriend. People will talk."

Of course they would. Talk was the only thing most people of my acquaintance were good for. But it was none of their business either. "Well, she *is* my girlfriend."

"That's not funny."

Cassie started to excuse herself, but I spiked her in place with a look. "You're right, Mom; it's not. Which part are you having the trouble with? 'Girl'? Or 'friend'?"

"You know very well what I mean, young lady. It's—"

"Immoral?" Connor supplied.

Jen backhanded him hard in the stomach. Fortunately for him, he was getting a little paunchy, so it couldn't have hurt much.

Mom frowned—not at the violence, but at the interruption. "Indecent."

"Indecent," I repeated. "I see. It's indecent. Cass?"

"Devvy?"

"Will you answer a question? For my mother's edification?"

"Shoot."

"Are you wearing underwear right now?"

Ryan spat coffee several feet across the living room. For her part, Cassie was speechless.

"It's a serious question," I assured her. "My mother has really specific ideas about decency. When I was little, she said it wasn't decent to go around without underwear, even if it *was* August."

Cassie relaxed visibly. "That's interesting. *My* mother said it wasn't decent to say the word 'underpants' in front of company. So I don't know if we should even be having this conversation."

I didn't try to hide the goofy smile. God, I adored her.

"But since you ask," she added sweetly, "yes, I am. My very best underpants, because it's Christmas."

My brothers and sisters-in-law collapsed in snorting, hiccupping laughter. Dad looked as though he wanted to laugh too but didn't want to pay the price his wife would charge him for it.

Satisfied, I turned back to Mom. "Does that clarify your thinking?"

"You get this from your father's side of the family," she said darkly.

Dad cleared his throat. "Now, Martha..."

"Stay out of this, Patrick."

For a moment, we all thought he was going to stand up to her. It happened as often as once or twice a year. But the moment passed, and before anyone could stop him, Dad had grabbed his coat, hat and keys again.

No one spoke until the sound of the Oldsmobile's motor faded in the distance. And when she did, she said exactly the wrong thing.

"I hope you're happy now," Mom growled. "You've ruined Christmas."

Was that all it took nowadays? Exasperated, I turned to my brothers for help—and got none, which I would remember. "Me? This is *your* fault, Mother."

She gave me a severe classroom stare over the rims of her glasses. "I don't mean just you. I mean both of you. You and...Carrie."

Jen and Amy knew a small-craft warning when they saw it; they jumped up and ran for their lives.

"Go there," I warned her coldly, "and it will be the last place you go on this earth."

Mom pulled her glasses down even farther. "It takes two to tango, Devlin."

I don't remember much about the next few minutes. Cassie told me later that it was the most methodical rampage she ever saw—supposedly I tore off the Christmas lights first, batting ornaments in all directions, and then shook the tree to knock off the rest of the decorations before I started swinging it around the living room like a mace. There was some property damage, but she said I was careful not to hit the TV. She said I was less careful not to hit Connor, who barely dived off the loveseat in time.

The next thing I do remember was standing in a snowdrift up to my knees, staring at a battered Douglas fir in the street, where I'd apparently thrown it. A few strings of tinsel left on it fluttered in the breeze.

I was bending over the tree, carefully taking off the last of the tinsel, when Cassie put a warm hand on my shoulder.

"I brought your coat," she said. "Want to get out of here for a while?"

"You're not mad at me?"

As soon as the question was out, I regretted having asked it. But her smile was worth my having sounded so stupid. "No, sweetie. I'm not mad. I'm proud of you."

"Proud?"

"Mmmhmm." She held up my coat, indicating that she would help me put it on. "Very proud."

I thought about that while she smoothed my coat front. "But I really *did* ruin Christmas just now."

"You think so? Well, I don't know about that. I think you just gave your mother a great Christmas present."

Not following, I blinked at her.

"She gets to tell all her friends about it," she explained. "She'll be the martyr of Hawthorne for a whole year."

Damn. Cassie was right. "I love you," I told her, meaning every syllable.

"I love you too, honey. Here. I saved your whales."

I stuck the toy in my pocket and kissed her with feeling, right there in the street, in broad daylight.

"Devvy?" she murmured after a while.

"Hmmm?"

"I really *am* wearing my best underpants."

She was crazy. She was absolutely perfect. "C'mon, wild thing. Let's vote each other off this stupid island."

Chapter Twenty-Nine

Christmas dinner was Hunan chicken at Happy Lucky Dragon, which might not have been the worst name for a Chinese restaurant but couldn't have been far from it. Under normal circumstances, I avoided restaurants with weird names, but nothing else was open. This time, Cassie and I were lucky dragons; the food wasn't bad, and the service was outstanding.

Granted, it should have been; we were the only customers. But the waiter didn't *have* to keep checking on us every few minutes. I watched him with suspicion, trying to decide what he was more interested in: Cassie, or her duck toy. She'd been playing with it all through dinner. Then she'd borrowed mine. By the fortune cookies, I was starting to worry.

"Are you ever going to give it back?" I asked, watching her watch the whales.

She didn't even look up. "No."

"So you admit it. You only like me for my stuff."

Still no response. But a stockinged foot slipped up my trouser leg under the table.

"Then I get to open all the fortune cookies," I said. "And I get to keep the fortune I like best."

Cassie finally put down the toy. She made unnecessarily sarcastic kissing noises at me, reached for a cookie and cracked it open. A look of evil triumph lit up her face. "Read it and weep, Devvy."

Scowling, I leaned across the table. The fortune said YOU WILL ALWAYS GET WHAT YOU WANT THROUGH YOUR GRACE AND CHARM.

"Read it out loud," she requested. "I want to hear you say it. Don't forget to add 'in bed' at the end."

"Oh, all right, just *keep* the whales," I grumbled.

Cassie laughed. In the next instant, the waiter was back at her elbow, refilling her teacup from the pot that had been sitting right in front of her all along.

"With all due respect to the little blonde lotus flower," I told him, "her arm's not in a sling. She can probably manage a teapot."

The foot that was still up my trouser leg gave me a kick. But its owner was smirking, and the waiter seemed not to understand anyway. He nodded at me, beamed at her, and left us again. Cassie's smirk got a little bigger.

"You love when this happens," I accused. "You do it on purpose."

"Do what, pookie?"

I *hated* that word. But the more I objected, the more she used it, so I was trying to let it roll off. "Collect waiters."

"It's a hobby," she said, amused. "I never had the patience for needlepoint."

"You're getting an attitude on you, Wolfe."

"Can't help it. Look who I'm with."

Trumped. Again. I threw down my napkin in surrender. "I could take the ring back."

"You could get your heart carved out," she replied.

I considered the next few moves. No good. Best to take the high road and concede. "Then I'm glad you like it that much. If we're still speaking next Christmas,

I'll get you earrings to go with it. Are you done playing games with me now?"

"Maybe. Maybe not. Why?"

"Because you really ought to call your parents."

Stricken, she checked her watch. "Oh, no—it's *afternoon*. They're going to kill me!"

"They'll have to go through me first." Easy to say; they were several hundred miles away at the moment. Which was the only reason I said it. I could probably handle Mrs. Wolfe in an emergency, but all bets were off with the rest of that crowd. "Do you want to go back to the room and call?"

She was already rummaging through her purse. "That'll make it even later. I'll just call them on my cell....Dammit, where *is* that thing?"

In the spirit of Christmas, I declined to point out that this was what happened when you bought a Barbie-size phone and kept it in a big purse. While she was occupied, I took back my whales. Then I frowned at the waiter, who was making another pass. "She's having a crisis. Tea can't help her now. But if you have a flashlight, or maybe industrial salvage equipment..."

Victorious, Cassie emerged from her purse. "Ha! It was in the little pocket."

"Just the check, then," I told the waiter.

I followed him to the cash register, to pay and to give Cassie some privacy for her call home. Not coincidentally, this meant I wouldn't be on hand if one of her family wanted to say hello. But she didn't have to know that.

After paying the check, I wandered around the lobby, admired the big Buddha, peered into the fish tanks, wandered some more. Then I consulted my watch again. She'd been on the phone for fifteen minutes. How could a person have *that* much to say to relatives?

The waiter, ever attentive, came along when I headed back toward the dining room to check on her. So I pulled him aside. If this didn't stop now, we were going to have an incident.

"Quite a looker, isn't she?" I asked casually. "My friend in there, I mean. Very beautiful. Wouldn't you say?"

He smiled, nodding agreement. Encouraged, I put a friendly arm around his shoulders and went on.

"She has a thousand engagement rings in her old room at home. She kept them all. Every last one of them. And she keeps her old boyfriends' heads in jars in the basement." I pretended that he'd just asked a question. "What kind? Ball jars, I think. She had to shrink the heads first, of course. Ball didn't make jars that big."

The waiter's smile didn't waver, but it was starting to look a bit forced.

"Her parents are dragons, you know. I've seen them myself. The father has spikes on his tail ten feet high. And the mother breathes green fire when—"

"Devvy!"

Yikes. Where had she come from?

The waiter, who apparently knew more English than he let on, took off like a shot. And just when I *didn't* want to be alone with Cassie. She didn't look upset, exactly, but...

"Feel free to start explaining any time," she said.

I tried to look innocent. "Writing practice?"

"You already get lots of practice."

Not enough, if I was going to keep getting into situations like this. "It's not what you think. The boy was lusting after you. I know *you* don't know this, based on your past, but lust is a deadly sin. I was trying to scare him for the good of his soul."

"How? By telling him my parents are dragons?" Her eyes narrowed dangerously. "What did I miss that you told him about *me?*"

"Nothing."

"Why don't I believe you?"

"Because you're really, really smart. Have I told you today that you're beautiful, too?"

"Nice try. But it won't work, Devvy."

"You don't sound 100 percent sure," I said, encouraged. "What about amnesty on this one, on account of Christmas?"

"One condition."

That was easy. "What condition?"

"We go back to your parents' house for a few minutes."

"Are you *crazy?*"

"There's a 50-50 chance. *You* are. It might be contagious."

I was not amused. "I just trashed the living room with a Christmas tree, Cassie. I'm not going to be very popular."

"No, but it'll help mend fences if you apologize. You don't have to mean it. You just have to pretend."

"Why should I apologize? My brothers acted like frat boys around you. My mother kept calling you the wrong *name*. And don't even start me on that hellcat sister of hers. If she were any more impossible, she'd be co-hosting with Regis. If you think for one second that we're going back so they can insult you again—"

"They're your family, Devvy."

"I know. That's the problem."

"That's not what I mean. I mean, you have to see them at least once a year, whether you want to or not. And I really don't want to go through this again next year. So—"

"*You're* not going through it next year. I'm not throwing you into that snake pit again."

She got her determined look. "You didn't throw me; I jumped. And if I feel like jumping again, I will."

"But—"

"And if you won't go back, *I* will. By myself."

"That's not fair," I argued. "You know I won't let you go in there alone."

"Never said it *was* fair."

I glared at her for a couple of minutes, trying to break her resolve. She refused to break. Finally, I threw up my hands. "All right. Five minutes. In and out. Deal?"

"Deal. Thank you. You can win the next one."

"The next *two,*" I countered. "And you buy dinner tonight."

Uncle Edgar's big black Caddy was parked half on the lawn and half in the street this time. The sight of it did nothing to improve my mood.

"Aunt Kitty's here," I told Cassie.

She patted my shoulder. "She can't live forever."

"I'm not up to taking the long view right now. I just want to get through the next few minutes without tearing someone's face off."

"Why would you want to do that?" she asked in an insultingly reasonable tone.

"I don't know," I said irritably. "It was the first thing that came to mind. But it would probably *hurt*. And a person would be in trouble without a *face*, right?"

"All right, all right, calm down. I was just asking."

"I *am* calm!"

Cassie bit her lip to keep from laughing and tried to look sympathetic.

"I know what you're thinking," I growled. "I don't even have to ask Jim Bob the psychic chicken. For your information, I don't need Prozac."

"Devvy, honey, precious, I really wasn't thinking that."

I wasn't convinced. "You weren't?"

"Of course not."

Her expression said *I was thinking Lithium instead*, but she didn't actually say it, so what could I do? Nothing. I just went on into the house, determined to get it over with fast, no longer determined not to take faces.

I could hear them in the dining room. They were still talking about it—had been, in all probability, since we'd left. It sounded as though they didn't approve, but it would be unfair to judge on so little listening in. So I just walked into their midst without a word.

It took a few seconds for anyone to notice. Amy was first; she let out a little scream and threw her napkin in the air. As the others realized what was going on, a whole constellation of reactions went around the table. My favorite was Aunt Kitty's. She'd frozen with the wineglass not all the way to her lips, so wine was trickling out of the glass and down her cleavage. That would do it for *that* dress.

"I came to say goodbye," I told them. "I'm not sure yet whether I came to say I'm sorry, too."

"You have your nerve, showing up here like nothing happened," Mom snapped.

Cassie moved a couple of steps back, out of the direct line of fire, but she put a comforting hand on the small of my back.

"I do have nerve," I admitted. "It comes on one of the chromosomes in this family. My guess is that it would be from *your* side, Mom, but if Dad wants to make a case for his..."

Connor snickered, and Ryan looked a little less hostile. But Dad frowned. "This isn't a good time, Devlin. Your mother's a little upset. Maybe you should come back tomorrow."

"There won't be a tomorrow. We're going back to Greenville tonight."

"Why?" Ryan chirped. "Are there innocent Christmas trees *there* you have to murder?"

Amy and Jen, flanking him at the table, elbowed him hard on each side. Very nice. That would take him out of play for a while.

"We're going back tonight," I repeated, "so I wanted to come by and thank you for the hospitality. Such as it was."

Mom looked daggers at me in absolute silence. But Aunt Kitty was muttering. To be annoying, I cupped a hand to my ear. "Excuse me, auntie dearest? Didn't catch that."

"I said, 'Good riddance,' that's what I said," she barked. "Tearing up your mother's house like an animal. And sleeping with that...that..."

Only Cassie's sudden grip on my sweater kept me from de-facing her then and there. "Woman. That *woman*. I'm aware of her gender. What's your problem with her, anyway? It was *her* idea to come over here and apologize. Not mine. And you were about to call her something I'd have to hurt you for, weren't you?"

She just stared at us, at a loss for words for once.

"My Aunt Kitty is a nut case," I told Cassie. "You already knew that, but sometimes it's nice to have these things confirmed. Do you know what she and Uncle Edgar do every Christmas Eve?"

Mom said my name in a menacing way. I ignored her.

"They open their presents on Christmas Eve. That's barbaric all by itself. But do you know what they do right after they open presents?"

"This is awesome," Connor told Jen cheerfully.

I ignored him too. "Right after they open presents, they take their tree down. *On Christmas Eve.* And you know what the worst part is?" For dramatic effect, I paused. No one interrupted. "The worst part is, it's not even a real tree. It's one of those *aluminum* things. You can't put tinsel on an aluminum tree, now, can you? No. That would be stupid. But guess what? *They do it anyway.* And you know what *else?*"

Amy was starting to recover her wits a bit. She looked around the room nervously before she spoke. "Um, Dev, I really don't think—"

"Then don't think. In this family, you'll live longer." Perplexed by the interruption, I turned to Cassie. "Where was I?"

"You were about to tell me what else," she said, enjoying the spectacle. "Aluminum tree, tinsel..."

"Oh. Right. I forgot the revolving spotlight. It turns the tree different colors. If you half-close your eyes, you think you're in a disco in Hell." Evilly, I smiled at Aunt Kitty. "Go on, Cass. Ask me what's on top of the tree."

Cassie released her grip and slipped her hand inside the back of my sweater. "What's on top of the tree?"

"An angel kitten."

She burst into startled laughter.

"God, I'd forgotten about that," Connor said thoughtfully. "The angel kitten. That's a bad one, all right."

I glanced at Aunt Kitty, who was too poleaxed by now to respond, and then at Mom, who was ditto. But Uncle Edgar might have been on the moon, for all the attention he was paying. I suspected that he secretly agreed with me.

"So let's not get into an etiquette smackdown," I said. "I shouldn't have wrecked the living room with the tree. But *you* shouldn't have driven me crazy. Agreed?"

There was complete silence for at least a minute—a very long time for silence, especially among people who never shut up.

Then Dad pushed his chair back, crossed the room and extended his hand to Cassie. "It was a pleasure meeting you," he told her sincerely. "I hope we'll see you again."

Cassie shot a bewildered glance at me. "Thank you. I hope so too."

He nodded. They shook and let go. When they did, Dad put his hand on my shoulder. "Devlin, take care of yourself. Come see us again soon."

Aw, dammit, this was going to ruin my exit. Reluctantly, I gave him a hug. "Merry Christmas, Dad."

It wasn't his fault he married into a family of monsters, after all. But next Christmas, I was going to buy him a spine.

There was one last thing I wanted to do in Hawthorne: make snow angels in the park. It was a tradition. And it wouldn't hurt to do *one* traditional thing.

The park was full of kids trying out their new Christmas sleds, so we skirted the hills and went to a flat area by the merry-go-round.

"I haven't done this in years," she mused.

"You'll love it. It's just like you remember."

"I hope not. I got snow in some really bad places the last time."

After a second's debate, I decided that I didn't need to know. "C'mon. Over here."

We jumped as far as we could into a patch of snow that didn't have footprints on it. Then we dropped back into it and made the angels.

"They look great," she said, inspecting them. "People are going to think *real* angels—" Then something caught her eye. "Devvy?"

"Angel?"

To my annoyance, she didn't hear that. "What did you do when you made yours?"

"The same thing everyone does. Why?"

She pointed. I leaned farther forward. There in the snow where I'd made my angel were the clear, unmistakable outlines of horns and a long pointed tail.

"Monica!" I shouted.

When the demon didn't show after a few seconds, Cassie slipped her arm around me. "I guess you're just a devil. But you're *my* devil."

"Very funny," I said, trying not to look flattered.

Chapter Thirty

December 26

One more Christmas was over. That much more blood was under the bridge now, and I was tired. It had been a very long couple of months. Maybe I could rest now, just for a while.

That was the plan. But Leonard Nimoy foiled it the first morning back. And then a fish finished me off.

"This is your fault for giving them that tape," I informed Cassie while we threw some clothes on. *"Your* fault for buying it in the first place."

"It is not. Besides, I thought you liked 'Star Trek.'"

On the front porch, "If I Had a Hammer" got even louder. Gritting my teeth, I willed myself not to hear it. "This isn't 'Star Trek.' This is *Golden Throats.* And this isn't the first time they've done this to me."

She stopped misbuttoning her sweater long enough to give me a very crabby look. "Well, now they're doing it to *me,* too. Satisfied?"

"No."

We regarded each other in hostile silence. It was nothing personal; we knew we still liked each other. But it was very, very early in the morning to be awake, let alone to be awake while Mr. Spock was singing. And that part *was* her fault.

"I'll go let them in," I said. "If they don't have a fantastic reason for being here, *you* clean up the mess. You'll need a big mop."

"Sweet-talker," she groused.

Perversely, that made me feel better. I went downstairs, rummaged in the toolbox, and threw the front door open, ready for anything. Or at least for Heather, Chip and Troy.

"Turn it off," I told Troy.

He turned off the boom box.

"Give me the tape."

Uncertain, he looked to the others for advice. Heather shrugged. He ejected the tape and handed it over.

"Now you *do* have a hammer," I told them, bringing it out from behind my back.

They backed off, which was the first smart thing they'd done that day. Carefully, I positioned the cassette on the porch railing.

I was still whacking it when Cassie came out. She watched for a second and then borrowed the hammer. Little chips of plastic flew in all directions as she reduced what was left to scrap. We would never have to hear Kirk or Spock sing again.

The woman had her points.

After truce was arranged, we all went in to have coffee. Cassie tactfully put the hammer away, and we sat around the kitchen table like civilized people.

"If it's not a secret," I said, "you might tell me why you're here. At this hour, the day after Christmas."

"We're on our way to work," Chip answered.

"Work? We were all fired a few weeks ago."

"Well, that's just it, Dev. We're kind of un-fired now."

Cassie rolled her eyes but didn't comment.

"Un-fired?"

Heather took over. "It's Howard Abner. Jenner hates him. Ever since he found out that Abner won't let him have girlfriends—"

"Won't *let* him?"

"Doesn't want him to, I mean. He says it sets a bad example."

"For who?" I frowned, debating whether it should be "whom" instead, but finally decided I didn't care. "It's an ad agency, not church camp."

"Just let me tell it, will you?"

I gave up and let her. She always took twice as long as necessary to tell a story, but if you kept interrupting her, she took even longer to get to the point. The point in this case was that Jenner feared marital fidelity more than he feared lawsuits. Consequently, he was maneuvering to get rid of Abner, and his first move was to reinstate all of Abner's firees.

"'All,' as in *all?*" Cassie asked.

Heather nodded. "You two especially. He's been after us every day to find out when you're coming back. I bet he'll reinstate you with big raises, if—"

"We don't want to be reinstated," I said.

They all stared at me in disbelief.

"Sorry—I shouldn't speak for Cass. *I* don't want to be reinstated. At least, not without a lot more information this time. She can do what she wants."

"Not without you," she protested.

I motioned to her to save it for private discussion. "Is that why you're here, then? Jenner sent you to tell us the good news?"

"In a nutshell," Heather admitted. "He really wants you two back. But that isn't—"

"Tell him not to kill the fatted calf just yet," I said. "Now you'd better go. You don't want to be late for work."

"OK, OK, we're going. But we've got a Christmas present for you first."

"It's for both of you," Chip added. "From all of us."

Cassie took the package from him, thanked him and tore the paper off. For quite a while, she just stared at whatever it was.

"Something wrong?" I asked.

Too moved to speak, she handed it across the table. And then I understood. It was one of those singing-fish-on-a-plaque things, just like the one Connor gave Ryan for Christmas, except that...

"It has a Santa hat on," I said numbly.

"Oh, come on, this is really cool," Troy said. "It sings 'Jingle Bells.' Push the red button."

Cassie pushed her chair back so fast that it tipped over. "We will later. Thanks, guys. It was really sweet of you. *Really."*

She went on to usher them out, leaving me alone with the fish. It was a while before I could look at it again. It *seemed* harmless. Stupid, but harmless.

I poked it a few times. Plastic. Nothing scary. I inspected the little hat. I pried open the mouth, to see what was in there. Furtively, I checked to see whether it was anatomically correct—not that I would know one way or the other. Finally, and only for research purposes, I pressed the button to make it sing.

Cassie came back to find me literally rolling on the floor laughing. It took her a few minutes to get me to give up the fish and a few more to get me back upstairs, tucked into bed.

December 28

"She's been in there how long?"

"Two days," Cassie said, sounding weary. "Give or take an hour or two."

Already bored with eavesdropping on the conversation in the hall, I went back to flipping channels. When the knock came, I ignored it.

"Dev? It's Rita Sanchez. Can I come in?"

No. It was nice of her to stop by, and now she could go. Yawning, I switched over to the Cartoon Network.

The bedroom door opened anyway. Sanchez walked in, Cassie right behind her.

"You look awful," Sanchez declared.

I shrugged. "I'm on strike."

"That's not what I hear." She took a seat on the bed—not too close, just in case I hadn't showered lately. *"I* hear you think you've cracked up. Have you?"

"I went to pieces over a singing fish."

"That doesn't prove anything."

"It's a *fish,* Sanchez. It sings Christmas carols. How much more evidence do you need?"

Under her breath, she said something Spanish. I hated when she did that; she was from Illinois.

"I'm going along with her for now," Cassie explained. "If she wants a little time off from reality, I guess she should have it. She really doesn't ask much." She reached over to pat my cheek. "Do you, bunny?"

Impassively, I turned up the volume on a Marvin the Martian cartoon.

Cassie shook her head. "Two days, Rita. *I* may be crazy by tomorrow."

Well, why not? There was plenty of room in this bed for her, too. And I'd showered and changed the sheets every day, so it wasn't like she'd have to be insane in squalor. No law said crazy people had to be slobs.

"Can you just tell me why?" she'd asked at the start.

"Stress."

"But Christmas is over."

"It's not just Christmas. It's everything. Nothing makes sense anymore. Every time I turn around, my office is on fire, or people are turning into possums, or I'm in trouble with God or Jack or

Jenner or Channel 12. On top of that, you and I are trying to figure out this relationship thing, and—"
    "Problem with that?"
    "No. But it's still new. That's more stress. And when you add in my family...or yours..."
    "Oh, come on, Devvy. It hasn't been that bad."
    "Michael," I said flatly.
    She considered. "All right. Michael's bad. But—"
    "Buster."
    "He's just a dog."
    "Just a dog? He almost had a close personal relationship with me."
    She considered again. "OK, you can have that one, too. But that was a month ago. You were fine up till—"
    "My mother."
    Deep, thoughtful silence brooded over the bedroom. Then Cassie bent down to kiss my forehead.
    "I'll get you some more pillows, sweetie," she said.

Back in the present, Sanchez studied the situation. Engrossed in the cartoon, I paid her no mind.

"Mr. Jenner wants you to come back to work," she finally said. "Both of you. He sent an offer along with me. It's in writing. What more do you want? An engraved invitation?"

"No, but I could do with a frappucino. You want to pop over to Starbucks for me?"

Cassie smoothed my hair down. "You're not going to get anywhere with her today, Rita. Maybe if you just leave the offer, I can get her to read it later. OK?"

"Maybe if I just shoot her with Ping-Pong balls," Sanchez grumbled, going into her purse.

Still focused on the cartoon, I reached over to the night table and pulled my own Ping-Pong gun out of the drawer.

"You're kidding," she insisted.

Not kidding, I shot her.

Sanchez gave up and put her weapon away. "You could be in trouble here, Cassie. She might really *be* loco. Let me see this fish that started this mess."

"I hid it. If I'm lucky, she'll never find it again."

"I could find it if I wanted," I told her.

"No, you couldn't, Devvy. I hid it where you'll never even think to look."

"Kitchen, huh?" Sanchez asked.

They had a nice laugh at my expense. In response, I turned the volume up some more.

"Oh, all right, I'm going." She gathered up her purse and then handed an envelope to Cassie. "It's all in here. Make sure she reads it, would you? He's going to bother me about it all afternoon."

"Suppose I walk you out," Cassie said.

She was up to something. She always was, though. Unconcerned, I fluffed my pillow and settled back again, intent on staying there another two days.

A second later, Monica tapped me on the shoulder, and I shot straight up in the air, scattering pillows everywhere.

"Don't *do* that!" I yelled. "I *hate* that! What are you doing here?"

"Visiting the sick. Move over."

Not having any better ideas, I moved over.

"Isn't this cozy?" she asked. "Just like old times. Have you missed me?"

"You never give me a *chance* to miss you. You never go away."

The demon was unperturbed. "The better to keep an eye on you."

"Ha! She's just nosy," Vanessa said.

I jumped again. No matter how long I was around demons, I could never get used to the way they came and went, and there was no way to prepare for what happened when they did. Right now, for example, I was in bed with two demons through no fault of my own, and if Cassie walked in...

Which, of course, she did.

After interminable silence, she crawled up on the bed and wedged herself in between Monica and me. Thoughtfully, Vanessa handed her a pillow to use as a backrest. No one said a word.

Chapter Thirty-One

Late that afternoon, we left the demons watching the shopping channel and went out for pizza. Cassie was careful to cloak her triumph in finally getting me out of bed, but I knew she was enjoying it anyway.

"So? What do you think?" she asked.

"I think I need a bigger house if they're going to keep hanging around."

"That's not what I meant. I meant about what Vanessa said. But now that you bring up houses—"

I cut her off at the pass. "Vanessa's loony."

"Still mad about the shirt, honey?"

Of course I was still mad. Vanessa had given me a late Christmas present—a T-shirt that said CLEOPATRA, QUEEN OF DENIAL—and I didn't see why Cassie thought it was so all-fired funny.

"Guess you are," she observed. "Never mind, then—we'll talk about her later. What do you think about going back to work?"

"I don't know. Jenner's sold us out twice already. And I don't think I can work for Jack if he's got religion; he was bad enough without it. What do *you* want to do?"

"Seriously?"

I gave her a severe look. "Of course seriously."

"I want to start our own agency."

"We've had this talk before. You didn't really mean it. So—"

"I'm not going back there without you. Get that all the way out of your mind."

"Why?"

Cassie exhaled in frustration and pulled the BMW over to the curb—not recklessly, for once. She put on her flashers. Then she turned all the way sideways in her seat and waited. And waited. And waited.

"What?" I finally asked.

"What do you think? I'm not going anywhere without you. Especially not back into that hellhole." An involuntary smile tugged at her lips. "Who would scare clients for me when they need scaring?"

"Forget the clients. There are worse problems in-house."

Now she was smiling openly. "You're the worst problem. Remember the day Chip had to peel you off that creep from Meridian Motors?"

It was probably bad that I couldn't place him offhand. Then it came to me: He'd wanted to use his teenage stepdaughter in the ad as a hood ornament, in a bikini, so I'd flattened him. Fortunately, he didn't press charges. "I'm not big on incest."

"Or the time you told Walt to kiss his boys goodbye? In front of a client?"

"If we're going to dredge up the past, Cass, I could tell a few stories on you."

"We could tell stories on each other forever. That was half the fun. We *did* have fun, didn't we?"

Past tense.

"Yeah, we did," I finally said, wondering why it hurt. "Come on. Let's get a *big* pizza."

The sun was starting down by the time we drove back to my condo. It wasn't quite dark enough for headlights to help yet but too dark to do without them. Cassie squinted at the street ahead. "This is the worst time of day to drive," she complained. "I can hardly see."

As a passenger, I didn't find that statement reassuring. But being her passenger was never reassuring, so I saw no reason to panic. "Do your best. We're almost there."

We traveled another block or so, and then I noticed the smoke just over the treeline. She noticed too. "That's strange," she said. "It looks like somebody's burning something."

"Better not be. We've got all those open-burning ordinances."

Before she could say anything to that, we heard sirens. They were very high-pitched, higher than ambulance or police sirens, which meant—

"Fire," she said, pulling over.

For no reason, my blood went cold.

"It must be close," she added. "Look."

Now we could see an orange glow through the trees. It was close, all right. And the bad feeling was getting stronger.

I stood it another few seconds. Then I jumped out of the car and started running toward the trouble.

"Devvy! Where are you going?" Cassie yelled.

Home. I knew it for a fact now: My condo was on fire.

We sat on the curb, watching the firefighters finish the job. As fires went, it probably hadn't been much, but no fire is small when it's yours. I'd written off my living room furniture an hour ago, when they'd started hosing it down through the hole in the roof. Now it was starting to dawn on me that what hadn't burned had drowned and was every bit as lost.

"It'll be OK, Dev," Heather said again. "You're insured. You can get all new stuff. We'll go shopping for *days.*"

I gave her a tiny smile. She'd come over as soon as Cassie had called her and then started calling people herself on her cell phone. Half the agency was here now, and I thought I would be touched by their concern later, after the shock wore off.

Someone handed me another coffee. I thanked him and tried to warm my hands on the cup. The fire people had given Cassie and me blankets, but even with the blanket and my coat, I couldn't seem to get warm. Not even Cassie helped, and she'd been as close as decently possible the whole time.

Chip parked himself on the curb next to us. "I'm not that kind of person, Dev, but I wish I could beat somebody up for this."

"She usually does her own beating-up," Cassie said—a little absently, watching a fireman carry a smoldering couch cushion out of the condo.

Where did I get this rep, anyway? I'd never really damaged anyone—except Kurt and maybe the Meridian Motors guy—and never anyone who didn't have it coming. "Thanks anyway, Chip. I appreciate the thought."

"Still wish I could. This sucks."

"Yeah. It does."

Cassie put her arms around me again and squeezed a little. There was nothing really to say beyond that.

Then I saw the top of a familiar head moving toward us. "Cass? Chip? Over there. Who does that look like to you?"

"Jenner," he said. "But it can't be. Can it?"

No, but it was. We just sat there, astonished, as he wormed his way through the crowd. Even more astonishing, Wife No. 5 was tagging along behind. They were both dressed to the teeth, as though they were on their way to some nightmarish society event, and I couldn't imagine what they were doing here.

As soon as they got within view, Jenner made straight for us. "Derry? Are you all right?"

As opposed to what? But I kept it to myself; he seemed to be genuinely concerned. "I'm fine. Thanks, Mr. Jenner. What brings you here?"

"Your house is on fire, isn't it?"

"Yes," I said thoughtfully. "It has been for a couple of hours now."

"Well, there you are. I don't like fires. They're bad for business."

Cassie pretended to be coughing. Under the blanket, she gave me a little nudge.

"I don't think insurance companies like them much either," I agreed. "But that still doesn't explain why you're here."

He wagged his finger at me. "I can't have an employee homeless. That would look bad."

"But I'm not an employee anymore. You fired me at the Christmas party."

"Yes. Well..." He shifted from foot to foot for a second, trying to think how to put it. "That was Howard Abner. Howard Abner was a mistake, Derry. A bad, bad mistake. I want you to come back. You and Miss Wolfe. It's not the same without the two of you."

"Yeah. It's a lot quieter," Heather chipped in.

I turned to glare at her. She'd sneaked up behind us, the better to hear every single word.

"You read my offer, didn't you?" Jenner asked. "You're both getting raises, you know."

His wife, suddenly petulant, tugged on his coat sleeve.

"Oh, for heaven's sake, Effie, you don't need another fur. And it's my money." He turned to Cassie. "*You* want to come back, don't you, Miss Wolfe?"

"Yes, I do," she admitted. "I may be partly insane. But I'm not coming back without Devvy. And she's not coming back if Jack—"

Jenner didn't have to hear the rest of that sentence. "Forget Harper. He's gone. The miserable son of a bitch found God. I can't have that. What do you say, Derry?"

"This probably isn't the time or place," I told him. "My house is on fire. Could we talk about this later?"

"No," Jenner said.

"No?"

"Yes. I said no." He dug in his coat pocket and produced a key ring. "This is for the house at the country club. We don't need it for clients right now, and you need a place to stay. The catch is, you have to be an employee to stay there. So if that would help you make up your mind..."

"She's not homeless," Cassie protested. "She'll move in with me."

"Is that what you want, Derry? Or is that what *she* wants?" A little glint appeared in his eyes under the streetlight. Unwillingly, I had to admire his deviousness. "It's a nice house. It'll give you a nice place of your own"—he put a slight extra stress on "own"—"to stay till you find a new one. So what do you say?"

Without any cooperation from my brain, my lips said yes. I may have been the most surprised person there. But a few seconds' reflection didn't change the answer.

As for Cassie, she didn't quite know what to think yet; she'd won one battle, lost another and wasn't sure which counted more. "We'll talk about this later," she whispered.

"Of course we will," I assured her. "Let me finish this." I took the key ring from Jenner. "Thanks. Which key?"

"The square one. You can move in tonight. And now that you're both employees again, you'll come to the New Year's Eve party. Abner's going to be there." That little glint appeared again. "I won't be responsible for anything you might decide to do to him, Derry. Understood?"

Ahhhh. It was good to be back. "Understood, sir."

"All right, then. We're off to a dinner party. Good luck with your fire."

We waited until they were out of earshot again to breathe.

"I'll be damned," Heather remarked.

A faint possibility was tickling at me. But better not to discuss it yet. "We already are," I said.

Cassie was uncharacteristically quiet on the drive to her house. She'd talked me into waiting till morning to move in at the country club—not that she'd had to do much talking-into, because we were both dead tired.

"Well," she finally said, "at least we get to do lots and lots of shopping now. I always *did* want to do something about your wardrobe."

"And you can just keep wanting."

She laughed. "We'll see. I still wish we knew what happened, though."

"They'll find out. It's probably electrical. The wiring in that place was never much good."

She glanced over—maybe a little too long for safety, for someone who was driving. "Do you really believe that?"

"I don't have many choices, Cass. I can believe it was an electrical short. I can believe it was spontaneous combustion. Or I can believe that demons did it. Which explanation do *you* want to give my landlord?"

"I think it was them. They were there. They probably got into a fight over the remote and started throwing fireballs around."

"Tosh," Vanessa said from the backseat.

The BMW skidded a few hundred feet before Cassie recovered. I kept both hands braced on the dash, just in case. "What do you mean, 'tosh'? She's got a point," I snapped. "It probably *was* you."

"Of course it was me. But I didn't have to throw fireballs. Really, Devlin. Did you read too many comic books when you were little?"

Cassie, who had pulled the car over the second Vanessa confessed, slammed it into park. *"You* burned her house down?"

Monica appeared at the other end of the backseat, looking bored. "She had a theory."

"A theory?" Cassie asked dangerously.

"She thought it would finally get Devlin to move in with you." She smirked at Vanessa. "Wrong *again.*"

"It's not over till it's over, Broadzilla," Vanessa shot back.

That started hissing and hair-pulling between them. Not in the mood for it, I reached over to honk the horn—and held it down until they quit. "I don't know about you," I told Cassie, "but *I* think we got Teenage Mutant Ninja Demons instead of the real thing. There was nothing about hair-pulling in *The Exorcist.*"

She studied me critically for a second. "You're being awfully calm about this. Vanessa just said she burned down your condo, and you're making jokes?"

"What should I do instead? Call the police? Sue her? Bite her?"

"Empty threat. You wouldn't even bite *me,"* Monica sulked.

Cassie murdered her with a look, which she chose to ignore.

"She's a demon, Cass," I continued. "I can't do much about her. If she wants to burn my place down every day of the week, she can. The only option I know of is going back to men—"

"Only if you want to die," she warned.

"—so I'm going to have to live with this till I figure something else out. And so are you."

"She *is* being calm," Vanessa fretted. "I don't like it."

Monica frowned. "Neither do I. She should have blamed you. And then Cassandra."

"Me?" Cassie asked, infuriated.

"You're the one who's been bothering her about moving in together. She might have thought you put Vanessa up to this."

"She wouldn't ever have thought *anything* if you'd kept your big mouth shut," Vanessa snapped at her.

"Don't blame *me,* you toad. Any competent demon would know how to do this. You should have burned *Cassandra's* house down."

Vanessa, who had started to argue back, suddenly fell silent.

"Then moving in together would have been *Devlin's* idea," Monica added. "She's a sucker that way. But giving her no choice—"

"What would she do with choice?" Vanessa replied hotly. "If *you'd* given her a choice, she'd still be lusting in her heart after actresses. They were all prettier than you, by the way."

Cassie winced and reached for the door handle, to save time in case we had to run for it.

"This isn't about me," Monica insisted. "This is about you. You should never have gotten above junior apprentice tempter, with *your* powers of logic."

Vanessa sneered at her. "Oh, go kiss a Baptist."

This time, *I* reached for the door handle.

"Go kiss one yourself. You burned down the wrong house, girlie."

Vanessa's eyes blazed bright red. "Well, I can fix that, can't I?"

"No!" I shouted, trying to dive over the backseat and kill her, in complete disregard for what I'd said minutes before. But Vanessa had already aimed her index finger, and just before I grabbed her, she fired.

Cassie jumped as though she'd been stuck with a pin. For a second, nothing happened.

Then we saw the orange glow in the distance.

Chapter Thirty-Two

Cassie's house didn't burn down that night after all. Her demon was a nimrod; Vanessa missed and burned down a neighbor's storage shed instead. (By general consensus, it was no great loss; it had been one of those little-red-barn-in-a-kit jobs, with a white plastic picket fence and plastic cows grazing around it.) But the situation led to some hard talk between us.

In fact, we stayed up all night talking about it. Well, arguing.

"You'd move in with me if you loved me," she finally said, exasperated.

That made two of us. "If *you* loved *me,* you wouldn't keep saying, 'If you loved me....'"

"Oh, yes, I would. Because it drives you crazy."

Blindsided by the admission, I glared at her. "Why do you have to drive me crazy?"

"Because it's such a short *trip!*"

Silence.

"I didn't mean that quite like it sounded," she said, looking a little sheepish.

"Yes, you did."

"No, I didn't. Really. What I meant to say...what I *meant* was..."

More silence.

"Fine," I said sharply, getting up. "I'll be at the guest house, if you ever decide what you *meant.*"

Surprised, she grabbed my sleeve. "You can't go now. It's 3 in the morning."

"It'll be 3 in the morning there, too. But at least it'll be *quiet.*" Frowning, I searched the dresser again. "Where are the keys?"

"I'll tell you if you answer one question."

"What question?"

"Why won't you move in with me?"

Annoyed, I started to repeat all the reasons I'd given her, over and over, for weeks. (1) We were both used to living alone. (2) We hadn't been together *that* way very long. (3) We had no idea whether this kind of relationship could last. And (4) I didn't want to wake up in a peach-and-white bedroom every morning. But none of those reasons was the whole truth. The whole truth was—

"I don't want to."

Cassie looked stunned.

"It's not that I don't love you. I do. But I also love that we're both independent."

She gave me her very worst bad look. "I'm not asking to put a leash on you."

"Too kinky."

She didn't even smile.

"All right, let me put it another way. I don't think we'd last very long if we moved in together. You know what women say when their husbands retire? 'I married you for better or worse, not for lunch.' You're not with me for lunch, Cass."

"That's not for you to decide."

"Maybe not. But how do you know it would be any different with us?"

"Because I love you." She glowered at me. "Well, *sometimes* I love you. When you're not being impossible."

"Forget that for a second. I *know* you. You're not good at the long-term thing. And I don't have a clue about relationships anymore. What if we moved in together and then decided we hate each other?"

"We already do," she snapped. "What's your point?"

Wearily, I rubbed the bridge of my nose. This could go for on for a few more hours—or the rest of our lives. "Tell you what. I'll make you a deal. Interested?"

"Depends," she said suspiciously. "What deal?"

"Let's try it this way. We keep our own places for now. I'll rent another condo or something, and we leave things the way they are. Then—"

"That doesn't sound like a deal to me."

"I'm not done yet. Then, if we're still together after a year, we'll talk about moving in. OK?"

She thought it over. "That's your best offer?"

"It's the best you're getting in the middle of an argument. What do you say?"

Cassie thought a little more. "All right, fine. But we make the year retroactive to Halloween."

"What? Why would we want to do that?"

"That *was* when all this started. I would say it's our anniversary, but you hate that."

"I hate it," I agreed.

"Anyway, I gave; now you have to give. One year from Halloween. Deal?"

That was two months less than I'd bargained for, and I wasn't sure I wanted to give them up. So I told her to give me a minute and then started to pace. How many things had I already done that I didn't want to do?

- I'd admitted to our relationship in public.
- I'd admitted to it on TV.
- I'd admitted to it in front of her parents and—much worse—my mother.
- I'd gone home with her for Thanksgiving.
- I'd taken her home for Christmas.
- I'd bought her a ring. Well, not *that* kind of ring, but...

"Am I taking you out New Year's Eve?" I asked.

She smiled. "Stupid question."

That was that, then. I was finished. Not just because I'd done those things, but also because, given the choice, I'd have done them all over again.

"Deal," I finally said, and spat in my hand. "Shake."

Cassie looked disgusted, but she reciprocated, and we shook on it.

Wouldn't want to get sentimental, after all.

Chapter Thirty-Three

New Year's Eve

By the time we got to Jenner's house, the casualties were already stacking up. There was nothing strange about that, considering the guest list, but 10:30 *was* a bit early in the evening to ride the pink elephant.

Cassie stepped cautiously around a victim, trying not to catch her heels on his fake-suede jacket. "Do you think he's dead?"

"Only if the fashion police shot him," I said, half-seriously.

She laughed and reached over the body to hang her coat up. "I'm going to work the room for a while. You *will* dance with me later."

"We'll see."

"You will," she repeated, leaning over to give me a quick kiss before she left.

We'd see.

I'd never liked New Year's Eve, even when I'd had dates. The only really good New Year's Eves were the ones I'd spent at home watching old movies in my pajamas. Cassie, however, loved dressing up and going out, which meant no *Casablanca*, no *Citizen Kane* and no pajamas. Most of my clothes had perished in the fire, except for what I'd kept at her place, so she'd taken me shopping. Which was why I was wearing black leather tonight. Was she crazy?

Rhetorical question.

Dourly, I gave the crazy woman another once-over. She was holding court in a herd of overheated males, reveling in the attention, which was understandable given what she had on. Or, more precisely, didn't. It was less a dress than an innuendo—the black halter was cut too low; the long black skirt was slit too high—and it could only lead to trouble.

Speaking of which...

"So Dev," Walt said, "where'd you two get the Bride of Satan getups?"

I gave him a thin smile and no satisfaction.

"Oh, c'mon, I'm kidding. I like 'em. No kidding." He threw down a shot of Scotch—not his first. "You gonna dance with her? Can I watch?"

"Weren't you married a minute ago?" I asked, unamused.

"Married doesn't mean dead."

"It will if your wife ever hears about this conversation."

He was a good enough sport to laugh, but not very hard. "You take all the fun out of working with gay babes, you know?"

"We're not g—" Oh, hell. "Never mind."

He was about to punish me for that mistake when Heather raced over, breathing hard. "I got here as fast as I could," she told me, glowering at Walt. "Has he been stupid yet?"

"Baby love, you hurt me," he complained. "I was just making nice polite conversation about how I want to see Dev and Cass do the horizontal mambo tonight, but if that's what you call *stupid*—Ow! Ow! Damn!"

Heather, who had just stamped on one of his wingtips with a very sharp heel, rolled her eyes as he hopped off.

One down, but way too many to go. And Kurt wasn't even here yet.

We met up again a while later in a more-or-less private end of the room. Cassie looked amused. "I've had some interesting comments on the clothes," she said.

I didn't doubt it. "Have you, now?"

"And a lot of questions about our living arrangements."

"What kind of questions?"

"Interesting ones." She smiled, daring me to take the bait.

"Cassie..."

"All right, all right. I'm not telling anyone much. I'm just saying you're staying at the guest house until you figure out what to do."

Watching her narrowly, I shook my head. "That's not what *I* heard. I heard you said we're going to buy a house together."

"Gossip," she said dismissively.

"Gossip that started somewhere, with somebody."

She frowned. "Well, not with me. Who would start that kind of rumor anyway?"

"Guess," Monica said.

We spun around. Monica had Vanessa by the ear, clearly having dragged her along, and Vanessa didn't look happy about it.

"Let go!" she told Monica. "That hurts!"

My demon was unsympathetic. "Don't be a baby. It's your own fault for wearing all those earrings."

Vanessa wrenched free and retreated a few steps, rubbing her ear. It probably *did* hurt; she had enough jewelry on that ear to make her list slightly to starboard. But the excess went with her dress, which might have been something Bob Mackie designed for Barbie.

"Why are you both here?" I asked. "Don't tell me there are no parties in Hell tonight. I've always thought New Year's Eve was invented in Hell, as far as that—"

"Save it," Monica snapped. "You have bigger problems. Little Miss Disinformation here has been making people think you two are picking out silver patterns."

"What for? We both have our own silverware."

"Literal," she muttered. "Great Satan, I never *saw* anyone so literal. You do it to spite me, don't you?" Before I could answer, she waved me off. "Never mind. Living together is a terrible idea, Devlin. Don't let anyone tell you otherwise."

"I don't remember asking *you*," Cassie told her hotly.

The look Monica gave her was enough to start a small fire, so I got in the middle. "We're not moving in together. Not for a year at least—"

Cassie cleared her throat significantly. "Ten months."

"—and maybe never. I don't see what it has to do with you anyway. What's it to you where I live?"

Monica scowled. "Vanessa."

"What about her?"

"I'm not sharing a house with *that.*"

Cassie and I exchanged puzzled glances.

"Think," Monica insisted. "If the two of you live together, the four of us live together. And I am *not* living with her."

"Same to you but more of it," Vanessa huffed.

Pretending to have given it some thought, Cassie offered a solution. "We could build doghouses for you. Devvy could walk you once in a while so you don't get fat. Would that work?"

Monica studied her with distaste. "I can't imagine what you see in her, Devlin. She's always going to be like this."

"Good." I almost meant it, too. "Now, is that all you wanted? Because if it is, we're done here."

"We're done," Vanessa said. "Except for one little thing."

She was Cassie's demon, so I let Cassie handle it. "Make it really little," she told Vanessa.

"You're wrong about the ten months, girlfriend. You'll get hooked up sooner than that. I give it six months. Maybe less. You never know."

"Over my dead body," Monica warned.

Vanessa smiled sweetly. "It could be arranged." Then she threw up a hand, and Monica vanished in a little puff of black smoke.

"Did you really kill her?" Cassie asked hopefully.

"Naaaah. Just sent her to visit Devlin's crazy aunt. With any luck, they'll kill each other." The demon regarded me critically. "So what's with the leather? You planning on making love or war tonight?"

Who knew? "The night is young," I said darkly, and stalked off.

Everything started downhill shortly thereafter, when Kurt finally showed. I was listening to Troy and some of the guys from Video lie about their manhood at the time, so I didn't notice him right away. The commotion was another matter.

"What the hell...?" J.B. asked, jerking his head toward the door. People were stampeding both toward and away from whatever had just come in, which we couldn't see from our angle.

Instantly, I scanned the room for Cassie. She was safely removed from whatever was going on, but she could see it from where she was standing—and she didn't look happy.

"Hold this," I said, handing my drink to one of the editors, even though I knew he'd only finish it. Then I headed for Cassie on a path that would put me between her and the trouble. The idea was to protect the trouble.

Meanwhile, the screaming, shouting and laughing around the doorway never stopped. What was wrong with these people?

"Kurt," Sanchez explained when I grabbed her.

"What about him?"

She just dissolved into a fit of giggles, which was no help at all. Annoyed, I pushed aside the last few obstacles, and then I saw all.

I do mean all. Or at least most of it. Kurt was dressed up like Baby New Year, wearing nothing but a sash and a diaper. And he hadn't been particular about how he'd fastened the diaper.

"Criminey," I growled. "Kurt, this had better be a medication accident."

He lit up as though he were glad to see me. "Boss! What's wrong? You don't like the outfit?"

"No. Where's Peg?"

"She stayed home. Said she didn't want to be seen in public with me."

Go figure. "You'd better go home and change. You can't leave your wife home on New Year's Eve."

"It's OK. She went to her mother's. I think they're running Harrison Ford movies or something." Absently, he scratched himself. "What's that guy got that I don't, anyway?"

Fortunately, Cassie turned up before I had to answer. "Hello, Kurt. Don't scratch diaper rash. You'll only make it worse."

He didn't respond, mainly because all the blood had just rushed from his brain to his eyeballs. Lust was a disturbing look on a grown man in a diaper, and I decided I didn't like it.

"Stop it," I ordered.

Cassie smirked at me a little; I pretended not to notice. Kurt certainly didn't.

"Kurt!"

He jumped, causing the diaper to slip and a few girls to shriek. But he didn't notice those things either. "Whoa," he said, still riveted on Cassie.

"I'll take that as a compliment," she told him.

"Oh, *yeah*. Damn, Cass, that dress is something. Really something. You're a piece of work when you want to be, you know that?"

She smirked at me again. I was starting to hate this evening. "Drop it, Kurt," I told him.

"Awfully touchy for someone in leather," he said, unfazed. "And by the way, I kind of like *your* outfit, too, boss. Have I told you how glad I am that you're coming back?"

Unsure which comment to jump on, I waited to hear what he had to say next.

"It hasn't been any fun without you. I thought it would be, but it's not. Abner's a bastard. He's like Jack used to be when he couldn't get laid, only worse, 'cause Abner *never* gets laid. It's against his religion or something." Hitching up his diaper, he looked around furtively. "You haven't seen him yet, have you?"

"Abner? No. But I'm not looking for him. Why would he be here anyway? Parties are evil, right?"

He leered at Cassie again, this time including me at the very end. "With any luck, they are. You two going to dance?"

"If we do," I said wearily, "I'm selling tickets. Now, what's the problem with Abner?"

"Well—"

He never got any further. A large, Baptist-shaped shadow fell over us, and we didn't even have to look to know.

"Mr. Wheeler," Abner intoned.

Kurt tried to squirm behind me. "Hello, Mr. Abner. Sir."

"Does Mr. Jenner know about..." He gestured at the diaper. "That?"

"I haven't seen him yet, sir. But it's a funny thing, you know? At the Halloween party, *he* was dressed up like a c—"

I cut Kurt off with a well-placed grip on the windpipe. Abner was not impressed.

"I'm going to go find him," he declared. "We'll discuss the new dress code. I'll make sure it includes a clause specifically about diapers. Excuse me."

Cassie and I stood back so that no part of him would touch us as he passed. But before he cleared us, something occurred to him, and he backtracked. "Aren't you two supposed to be fired?"

"Not anymore," I said.

Abner's brow contracted. He essentially had only one. "I'll talk to him about that, too."

Cassie stuck out her foot to trip him; I barely managed to pull her back in time. Then I happened to glance after Abner's retreating bulk.

Vanessa was following him, looking as happy as I'd ever seen her. I hoped no one else noticed the bright-red blaze in her eyes.

All the usual suspects were on the scene now, and the closer it got to midnight, the more nervous I got. Demons in one corner, Baptists in another, Kurt in a diaper and advertising people with access to alcohol. *And* Cassie. Something had to happen.

Something worse than just the music, anyway. Jenner had a Wurlitzer that I'd always coveted—one of those huge jukeboxes with neon and bubble tubes and enough chrome for a T-Bird—but his music collection was too retro. We'd been listening to the Beach Boys, Jan and Dean, and that crowd all night, and most of us were getting restless. Didn't Jenner have anything harder? Or at least a little more current?

On the other hand, maybe I wouldn't have to dance with Cassie after all if this kept up. She'd started leaving the room every time someone played "Wipeout," which seemed to be every few minutes.

Bored myself, I wandered over to the jukebox to see what else was in there. Chip joined me. "Find anything good?"

"Depends what you call good." I checked again; one title caught my eye. "How are you for car songs?"

"Car songs?"

After a brief mental debate, I punched the numbers. "You heard me. I always thought the Go-Go's wrote 'Skidmarks on My Heart' to get even for this whole genre. Want to dance?"

He did. "Little Deuce Coupe" wasn't bad as car songs went, and we weren't going to do much better, so we had a little fun.

OK, maybe more than a little. So Cassie got even by dancing with Randy

Harris. Then with Walt. And after that with Kurt. That last one wasn't pretty, to the point that I might have made a trip too many to the bar.

Then, without warning, it was almost midnight, and Cassie was back to oppress me. "One dance. With *me* this time. No excuses. Ready?"

"There's nothing good on the jukebox," I protested.

"Don't worry about that. Vanessa's got it covered."

I tried another tack. "I think I broke my leg a few minutes ago."

"No problem," she said calmly. "I'll lead."

"Dancing's against my religion?"

Cassie shook her head. "Give up, Devvy. You're outnumbered."

"Counting who? Demons?"

"Not them. *Them.*" She indicated everyone in particular; they were all watching with great interest. "It'll kill them if we don't."

"Problem with that?"

She ignored the question and pulled me out to the dance floor. I tried limping, but it didn't work.

Cassie closed in and searched the room for Vanessa. The demon was standing by the jukebox, trying to look casual; when she caught Cassie's signal, she kicked the machine. "Louie Louie" cut off, and to my dismay, "Hot Stuff" cut on.

To her credit, Cassie was dismayed too. "That's not what I asked for. I *asked* for Sade."

She turned to glare at Vanessa, who pretended not to understand what the matter was. Meanwhile, the crowd was getting impatient.

"We're not seeing any dancing!" someone yelled.

A second voice added, "Or anything else!"

That caused general merriment at our expense and more encouragement from the peanut gallery. Even Cassie was starting to look like she was having second thoughts. I was about to suggest that we run for it when I saw Howard Abner standing a few feet away, grim as a stone idol.

And that single instant pushed me over the line. Enough was enough was enough. Political Correctness and censure are two sides of a very thin coin, and thanks to Cassie's parents, my parents, my brothers, our co-workers, the Family Foundation and 90 percent of the population, I'd finally had all of both that I needed—enough for a lifetime, probably. It was time to start the payback. And Abner was as good a place to start as any.

So I pulled Cassie in and locked eyes with her. "If they want a show," I told her, "I say we give them one. Want to make this a slow dance?"

She smiled, closing the rest of the distance between us. "Very slow."

We never heard the thud.

"Did you have a good time tonight after all?" Cassie asked, kicking her shoes off.

"Mostly." I kept searching through the CDs; it was here somewhere. "The best part was Abner."

I'd liked that part, all right. True, I hadn't meant for him to have a heart attack, not even a mild one like that. But when the paramedics came and opened his shirt, and found the tattoo on his chest...

Well, Kurt had said it best: God save the Queen.

It was Vanessa's doing, of course. Even at my most suspicious, I knew Abner wasn't gay. But it had been very fine just the same to see him with a heart-and-snake tattoo with MITCH in the middle. And if the paramedics—and everyone else at the party—had seen it, who was I to say it wasn't real?

Ah, there it was. I opened the jewel case and stuck the disc in the player just as Cassie leaned into me.

"The *best* part?" she asked menacingly, her breath warm in my ear.

"Second best," I corrected.

She didn't back off. In fact, she got closer. "I had all kinds of offers tonight, you know. I could have gone home with anyone. Did I tell you Walt offered me a kidney?"

"You don't need any more kidneys." I pressed Play, cued the disc to "A Common Disaster" and then turned toward her. "Last dance?"

"I thought you'd never ask."

There are worse ways to wind up New Year's Eve. We took one last spin in Cassie's peach-and-white bedroom while Cowboy Junkies told our future.

We weren't out of the woods yet. We were still going to have trouble—maybe even disaster—and it might never get any easier. But when they're playing your song on the jukebox in Hell, you might as well dance.

The Last Word

Cassie again. Everything Devvy said is true, but the way she puts things sometimes is just her opinion. Take the parts about my family. I know what she's going to say about them from now on: She's going to get all sarcastic and say who needs demons after this. But I thought Thanksgiving went pretty well overall. She got off light compared with some of the guys I've brought home. Daddy used to give them dirty looks while he was carving the turkey, and we all knew what he was thinking.

OK, that wouldn't work on Devvy, but he could still have done something stupid—especially after they caught us on the couch. I think she still feels bad about that. But like I told her, my parents have had sex themselves at least twice, so what's the big deal?

Then there are the parts about *her* family, which are a little bit biased too. I think she went *way* too easy on them. Don't get me wrong; I liked her dad and her brothers and her sisters-in-law. But her mom and her aunt and uncle ought to be locked up in a maximum-security zoo somewhere. I can't *say* that, because she's related to them and I love her, but I can think it all I want.

Anyway, even though there were a few bad moments, I loved spending the holidays with Devvy. I told her that, and she asked me whether I'd learned anything at all from the experience.

Well, let me see.

- She's good with kids.
- She's not so good with dogs.
- Daddy doesn't hate her. Much.
- I think we should spend next Christmas with *my* family.
- I think it's time for us to move in together.

I wonder whether I should tell her *before* I tell her where we're spending next Christmas?

About the Author

K. Simpson was once described as a "surprisingly affable Devil-worshipper," none of which is true. She spends most days working, drinking coffee and listening to VERY LOUD MUSIC.

Although she likes Halloween best, Simpson has no problem with Thanksgiving and Christmas. She got a baby brother one Christmas Eve and decided to keep him, even though she asked for a horse. She hates fruitcake, eggnog and Christmas decorations before Thanksgiving, but loves the Macy's parade, *A Christmas Story* and the Grinch. Under oath, she'd admit to liking her relatives, too.

No one has ever thrown food in the Simpson family except a small nephew and niece, who are on probation.

Now Available from Fortitude Press

THE AVERAGE OF DEVIANCE
BY K. SIMPSON

After *Several Devils*, Devlin Kerry and Cassandra Wolfe aren't just friends anymore, but they'd rather not advertise. Trouble is, they're already in advertising, where secrets are practically illegal. Word is out ... so to speak.

Worse, Dev has a demon. Cassie says it's her own fault for being celibate for years ("You can't go around not sleeping with people and *not* expect to get into trouble"). They thought they'd exorcised the demon, but Monica is back. And this time, she plans to stick around.

This sequel picks up where *Several Devils* left off, as the staff of J/J/G Advertising tries to get back to normal the morning after a wild Halloween night. But every day is Halloween at J/J/G, the way these people behave, and everyone there is a devil of some kind. The last thing Dev and Cassie need is an actual demon — a chance for mischief that Monica can't resist. Thanks to her, they have trouble coming from all directions: co-workers, clients, TV reporters, the family-values crowd and even a possum.

Worst of all, a new co-worker may not be what she seems. Dev and Cassie are about to learn the true meaning of "hell to pay."

ISBN: 0971815011

Also by K. Simpson

SEVERAL DEVILS
Published: August 2001
ISBN: 0967768799

Even though she's in advertising, Devlin Kerry doesn't believe in Hell; she thinks that would be redundant. But a demon named Monica believes in her. Between her demon and her best friend, Dev's in for a devil of a time.

Now Available from Fortitude Press

THE BLUEST EYES IN TEXAS
BY LINDA CRIST

Kennedy Nocona is an out, liberal, driven attorney, living in Austin, the heart of the Texas hill country. Once a player in the legal community, she now finds herself in the position of re-evaluating her life - a position brought on by a personal tragedy for which she blames herself. Seeking redemption for her tormented past, she loses herself in her work, strict discipline of mind and body, and the teachings of Native American roots she once shunned.

Dallasite Carson Garret is a young paralegal overcoming the loss of her parents and coming to terms with her own sexual orientation. After settling her parents' estate and examining her failed past relationships, she is desperately ready to move forward. Bored with her state of affairs, she longs for excitement and romance to make her feel alive again.

A chance encounter finds them inexplicably drawn to one another, and after a weekend together, they quickly find themselves in a long distance romance that leaves them both wanting more. Circumstances at Carson's job develop into a series of mysteries and blackmail attempts that leaves her with more excitement than she ever bargained for. Confused, afraid, and alone, she turns to Kennedy, the one person she knows can help her. As they work together to solve a puzzle, they confront growing feelings that neither woman can deny, complicated by outside forces that threaten to crush them both.

ISBN: 0971815003

Now Available from Fortitude Press

CASTAWAY
BY BLAYNE COOPER & RYAN DALY

Where "Survivor" meets "Gilligan's Island" in "The Twilight Zone." Sixteen men and women are stranded on a tropical island–with an intrusive camera crew and a psychotic producer, where they fight for survival, TV ratings, and a million dollar prize. The winner is anyone who loves thrill-a-minute misadventures, gut-busting laughs, and 'broad'-minded women.

The premise may be familiar, though the contestants are anything but, when a desperate network owner is hell-bent on blockbuster ratings and casts the show accordingly. Shannon, a budding novelist and former network employee, falls deeply in lust with tall, dark, paranoid Ryan, a Kentucky survivalist who is determined to win. "The course of true love never did run smooth," Shakespeare said. Even he couldn't have imagined the road bumps Shannon and Ryan will encounter en route to love and hot monkey sex.

The women are not only star-crossed, but insect infested and sand crab bitten. In this irreverent spoof, which focuses on an industry where nothing is as it seems, and no one can be trusted, Shannon and Ryan pull out all the stops to 'get the girl' – and win the prize. Join them as they discover the best thing about 'Paradise' is each other.

ISBN: 0971815089

Now Available from Fortitude Press

ENGRAVINGS OF WRAITH
BY KIERA DELLACROIX

Bailey Cameron is a woman with secrets. The reclusive owner of a successful corporation, she is also hostage to a covert life she neither wanted nor asked for. One that refuses to become a part of her past.

Blackmailed into a return to her deadly role as the Wraith, a frightening entity in the world that lives in the shadows, Bailey decides to break free. She settles in for a brutal game of chess with her former employers, prepared for every eventuality but one -- Piper Tate, her new assistant, who decides that the dark, mysterious Bailey is someone she wants to know better. A lot better.

The stakes continue to rise, as Piper discovers in Bailey a gentle, innocent heart. A heart that beats within the body of a killer who can't be tamed and who is prepared to do whatever it takes to preserve the new world Piper has introduced her to.

ISBN: 0971815054

Now Available from Fortitude Press

First
by Kimberly Pritekel

Emily Thomas is a successful New York attorney who enjoys a happy homelife with her beautiful partner. Beth Sayers was the childhood best friend with whom she shared big dreams as they grew up in Pueblo, Colorado. Inseparable by age nine, together they learned about life, each other, themselves, and most importantly love.

When Emily hears of Beth's death at the age of 34, after more than a decade of estrangement, she must piece together her tumultuous past and come to terms with the defining relationship in her life. Why had her friendship with Beth deteriorated and what part of herself had she lost with it?

First is Emily's journey back to Colorado, back to her childhood, and back to face the ghost of a woman who had captured her heart and never really let it go.

ISBN: 0971815070

LORIMAL'S CHALICE
BY JANE FLETCHER

The quest for the stolen chalice is a sham - her family's way to banish Tevi from the island without causing a scandal. She soon discovers that the outside world is a dangerous and confusing place. Bandits and monsters are the least of her problems. Someone is prying into a long hidden secret and Tevi is about to get caught up in the deadly consequences.

Jemeryl has her future planned out. A future that will, hopefully, involve the minimum contact with ordinary folk who do not understand sorcerers. Her ambition lies with the Coven and the study of magic. Her goal is to rise up the Coven hierarchy and someday become ruler of the Protectorate. It is all very straightforward - until she meets Tevi.

The fate of the greatest civilisation the world has known is at stake. Tevi and Jemeryl will have to risk their lives in the race to uncover the traitor and retrieve the chalice. If this is not enough, they will both have to re-evaluate their assumptions about society and their places in it, and then figure out exactly what they want from life and each other.

ISBN: 0971815062

Now Distributed by Fortitude Press

AT FIRST BLUSH
A JANE DOE PRESS ANTHOLOGY

Twenty-two stories of first glances, first blushes, first loves and first times – of all kinds. Representing a variety of voices, the stories reflect a diversity of experiences. All profits from this anthology will be donated to charity.

The table of contents from this wonderful collection of stories:

ISBN: 0971154996

Now Distributed by Fortitude Press

CONSPIRACY OF SWORDS
BY R.S. CORLISS

FBI Agent Alexia Reis is an out-lesbian determined to make it in the bureau. As a junior agent she spent time in the research department, as well as the serial crimes unit where she and her partner, David Wu, were recognized for their work. After breaking several major cases, the two are moved to the hate crimes unit, which is Alex's true area of expertise.

Following the murders of several prominent activists and politicians, Alex and David become part of a task force charged with solving the killings. Together, they are sent to protect a newly declared candidate for the U.S. Senate. For the first time in her career, Alex is named the agent-in-charge, and when the candidate is assassinated, she can't help but take it personally.

During the investigation the agents run into ex-CIA assassin Teren Mylos, who is convinced her partner's death is somehow connected to the FBI case. While wary of each other, Alex and Teren agree to share information in an attempt to find answers to the deepening mystery.

The case takes them to Europe and back, searching for pieces to the unfolding puzzle. As they dodge killers and turncoats, they come face to face with Nazis old and new, stumble upon a hoard of looted gold, and uncover a conspiracy that stretches over forty years and two continents.

And, somewhere along the line, they discover each other as well.

ISBN: 0971154902

To Order:

Title	Quantity	Cost per Unit	Total Cost
At First Blush		$21.99	$
The Average of Deviance		$12.99	$
The Bluest Eyes in Texas		$15.99	$
Castaway		$13.99	
Conspiracy of Swords		$19.99	$
Engravings of Wraith		$18.99	
exChanges		$13.75	$
First		$13.99	
Hell for the Holidays		$13.99	
I Found My Heart in San Francisco		$18.99	$
The Life in Her Eyes		$13.99	$
Lorimal's Chalice		$18.99	
Warlord Metal		$13.99	$
Shipping and Handling	First Book	$4.50	$
	Each Add'l Book	$2.00	$
Texas Residents Add 8.25% Sales Tax			$
Total			$

To order by credit card, please visit our Web site at: www.fortitudepress.com.

To order by check or money order, please mail the above form to:

Fortitude Press, Inc.
PO Box 92694
Austin, TX 78709-2694